Raven or Crow

Joshua Amses

Fomite
Burlington, Vermont

ISBN-13: 978-1-937677-38-1

Library of Congress Control Number: 2013932824

Fomite
58 Peru Street
Burlington, VT 05401
www.fomitepress.com

Cover Image - Lisa Uhlig http://lisauhlig.carbonmade.com/
Author Photo - Katharine McDermott

For my family

"But truth, *mon cheri*, is a colossal bore."

-Camus, *The Fall*

1.

I'm sorting the recycling in my parent's basement when I realize the weather may be a problem. As I emerge from the cellar and stand in the yard with an oily satchel of trash in either hand, the possibility of a thunderstorm hangs in baleful yellow warmth above the lake. Or what I can see of the water, which, far from glimmering through the trees at the property line, is instead reflecting the bruised cloudbank above. It is late morning, 11AM (or thereabouts), but I don't wear a watch. I judge the hour by the position of the sun, an hour which has only now become important.

I load three black trash bags into the trunk of my Volvo station wagon, and the car begins to stink in the somewhat uncharacteristic humidity of Vermont (during early summer). Eleanor's clothes are primly folded on the passenger seat. A patterned (I cannot identify it), vaguely yellow skirt, a burgundy tank top, pale yellow underwear (generous, practical, and ugly), and a pair of red sandals. She may have chosen these items to match, but I'm no good at judging such things.

The stench from the back of the car, and the inclement weather (sitting like some physical expression of evil against the cheerless horizon) direct me to leave. But I start the vehicle absently, my attention focused on the outfit sitting beside me, which I examine as if it conceals a snake. Even divorced from Eleanor, the clothing is a proximate threat, like a reptile's freshly shed skin. She is absent, yet nearby. I shift the car into reverse, and nearly back over the wellhead in the side yard on my way to the driveway, at whose mouth I realize I've forgotten something.

Though cats live a short life in the countryside (compared with dogs, for instance), my parents are fond of them. Over ten years ago, they acquired a pair of male kittens, Ignatz and Bormann (the former black, the latter striped), from a neighbor. Of these two, only Ignatz remains. Bormann was likely devoured by a fisher cat (a member of the mustelid family, like a weasel) or eaten by a coyote, but these are my father's theories. The simple truth is that one morning, only Ignatz returned to the house, prowling from beneath its foundation in much the same way as he does now as I unlatch the front door. Since the disappearance of his brother, Ignatz has soured with age, adopting a peculiar, learned weariness, like a county judge who has lost a daughter to polio. He is twelve. I am twenty-one.

He slips in behind me when I enter the house, sifting the tired valise of my memory for some tragic instance that would explain my current situation within the context of my age, but I discover nothing new about myself. There are only facts. My name is Marlowe. I am twenty-one, recall, six feet tall, one hundred and ninety pounds. I have brown hair that needs a trim, weak hazel eyes that require glasses, and 'beautiful skin,' according to someone I once knew. I used to be pleasant looking, and I suppose I still am, but as I pass a mirror in the mudroom, my reflection is somewhat swollen, my features underfed, and my torso bloated from inactivity. I appear neglected.

I remove several towels and one bathrobe from the hallway closet, and place these in a voluminous cerulean bag from IKEA, and with Ignatz padding gloomily in my wake, and return to the front door, where, on the threshold, he kneads the welcome mat while I hold the portal open like a servant.

"Decide," I say.

Ignatz continues to make invisible bread on the floor of the mudroom while I consider the weight of the bag, as though testing the gravity of a particular ethical problem. Ignatz pauses in his work and appears to be weighing his choices as well, dipping his cautious black head out the door. His whiskers twitch.

"You vex me."

I nudge him outside with my foot, and take ten steps toward the car before detouring in the direction of the woods. I turn jaggedly, so jaggedly that I nearly trample the cat (who has remained faithful to my itinerary so far), as I step into the somnolent shade of the forest surrounding the driveway. My destination is a tree house set fifty yards inside the treeline, and built on a severe slope terminating at a slough beside the dirt road leading to the lake.

It is a low-roofed, rotten structure that came with the property, the sort of thing built for a neglected child (during a moment of regret). I didn't come here much when I was young. But since moving back home, I've become fond of it. When the afternoon grows long, and peepers (tiny frogs that make a pleasant noise) begin to chirp in the swamp below the outpost, and birds (a robin, hermit thrush, a raven or crow) perch on the glassless sill through which there is a scant (but existent) view of the lake, I come here to sit in a folding chair beneath the palsied roof and watch cars pass on the lower road. This is my hobby.

My parents have either forgotten the tree house exists or cannot be bothered to inspect it. In either case, there is no reason to conceal anything. As we enter, Ignatz brushes against several bottles lining the floor along one wall. An overfull ashtray occupies a camp chair's right-hand armrest. There is a distinct odor of ammonia issuing from the structure's southeastern quadrant. I ignore whatever this scene might indicate, and search among the bottles, holding each up to an arm of sun falling through the verdure overhead in order to determine that it does in fact contain liquor. In one, a stale finger of amber whiskey remains, which I use to fortify myself for the trip to the dump. An incredulous Ignatz looks on.

"Judge not," I warn, settling the now empty bottle among its cadre, which, when divorced from need, or the calm which precedes the satiety of need, sits like some rank of incrimination against the supporting wall. I'm not intemperate, but this evidence would certainly suggest otherwise. Before leaving the tree house, I briefly consider burying the liquor bottles it in the woods. But there is a chance that a heavy rain, like that now establishing itself above the lake will unearth the sepulcher and that my father, during one of his transcendentalist rambles through the surrounding woodland, may happen across it.

I like to compartmentalize my habits. Everything makes sense when settled in the proper context. Explaining this to him, or my mother, or anyone, except perhaps Ignatz, would bear little fruit. But Eleanor understood, didn't she? Yes. I think she did. That's why she agreed to walk deep into the forest beside the lake earlier this morning. I took her clothes and whispered, "run." She ran. And I left her there.

At the dump, Wallace, the caretaker, verbally assaults me. Or I suspect he does. It's a suspicion that has been growing for some time. But it's impossible to confirm, since he refuses to remove the cigar from his mouth when speaking, though rheum has entirely soaked the brown paper, and a string of mucous dangles from the tip in place of an ember. This accessory (the cigar) is framed by an areole of jaundiced beard resembling a singed bird's nest. And despite the heat hovering at a balmy (and somewhat humid) seventy degrees, he wears a dark beaver Ushanka with the flaps tied in an elegant bow atop his head.

"Three bags," I mumble, pointing (one, two, three) to the black plastic sacks knotted within the car. I'm speaking to him downwind, with my head cocked in order that he not smell my whiskey breath.

"Wuddafuka. Nahnollders," he hisses, a patter of saliva dropping from his chin onto a worn, Carhartt jerkin.

"Nine dollars?" I venture, though I should be able to translate by now. It's been nearly two months since I returned home, and several weeks since I began bringing my parent's garbage to the dump.

"Hreeaggs. Nahnollders," he confirms.

I open the passenger door to retrieve money from the console, and he spots the clothing folded on the passenger seat.

"Wuddafukat? Fukawiddadressup?"

I shake my head, blocking the view with my body, and handing him nine dollars.

"No, sir. Holding onto it. For a friend."

He shakes his head, dropping spittle on the money as he counts it.

"Ahn. Oo. Hee. Aht. Oodayuhfagat."

I thank him somewhat bitterly, resolving to disvolunteer for this particular errand in the future. I imagine myself socially capable, and I find that each interaction with Wallace greatly disturbs this image. It's fortunate that Irma is working at the general store in East Calais, where I stop for coffee and fuel after fleeing the dump. Her shopworn presence allows me to recapture a measure of what seemed lost after dickering with Wallace over my family's trash.

Irma and I have a history of common circumstance. We attended elementary, middle, and high school together, and for some of this time (the middle portion largely), I wanted her. She seemed beautiful before I became a licensed driver. But, on a Friday evening sunk in the murk of an intractably sober school dance held in the cafeteria, the odor of warm milk and sweaty, low-grade meat not yet faded from the drop-ceiling above our heads, the decoration limited to a length of disheveled crepe strung between painted cinderblock walls, and the lighting provided by several security lamps with colored paper taped over them, I did, in this moribund scene, ask her to dance with me — and she accepted. I wish the memory were more vivid, but I remember only two things about her, close to me then, swaying to a song we did not choose. Her hands, which she did not so much drape as plant upon my shoulders, were so moist that, afterward, when I retreated to a restroom to regroup, I noticed paw stains to both the right and left of my collar. There was also her odor which, years later, I realized was the scent of unwashed clothing. And though I couldn't identify this at the time, it was here that my interest in Irma began to wane, eventually disappearing completely, long before a forest service employee got her pregnant and left. But she never makes me pay for coffee. She cuts me deals on beer. And she often smiles.

"Your dad was in here this morning, Marlowe," she says, as I walk through the door. "He said if I saw you to tell you to take the recycling."

"Indeed," I say. "Thank you, Irma."

"Gas on which pump?"

"The one nearest the door."

Being either half or a quarter Abenaki (the percentage is unimportant as long as it exits), Irma is perhaps the most exotic person among the herd of Italianate and Scotch/Irish children with whom I attended school. Though early motherhood has left her looking rather tired, her hair and eyes are still morbidly black. Her skin remains the delicate pink of a healthy sunburn. In eighth grade, she had the largest breasts of any girl in our class, which imbued her with a steady, capable aspect. When I imagined her naked then, she was usually outdoors, with her leg up on a stump, her moist palms balanced on impossibly perfect hips, and (shame on me) an eagle feather angled in her hair.

"Beer?" she asks, gesturing toward the cooler as though I might have forgotten its location. I shake my head, selecting instead a red and black checked deerstalker cap dangling from a rack above the register.

"No. Thanks. This will do fine," I say, placing it on the counter. "How much, please?"

"Nine bucks. Try it on."

The same price as the garbage. What odd symmetry.

"No. No, it's a gift," I lie. "I'm sure it will fit."

She shrugs, stuffing the hat in bag, but pauses.

"There's a fire. Tonight. We'll be at the lake. Out by your house."

The pause continues.

"I should…come?" I supply.

"Sure. Bring…what's her name?"

"Eleanor?"

"Bring her."

"Well thank you, Irma," I say, struggling not to appear unusual. "That sounds nice. Unfortunately, I can't just tonight. I have to…pick something up…"

I check the space on my wrist where a watch should be.

"Yes, in fact, I need to get going so I can be on time to go get it. Thanks for…everything. Next time?"

Another shrug. Is this is meant to suggest something aside from ambivalence?

"Whenever, Marlowe. I'll be here."

Outside, the jaundiced horizon has become a dark, cumulonimbus archipelago. The sky appears to move closer with each second I spend trying to judge its distance from me. Wind rolls through the small lot, genuflecting a stand of roadside trees. A loose shutter slaps against the side of a dilapidated house across the road. A low roar, like a growl rising from the interior of a cavern, issues from the darkest patch of horizon. I was right about the weather. It will be a problem.

I return to the house to get a few things, which I am now wearing. A pair of elderly Sorrels, beaten, shit-colored dungarees, and a red and black-checkered woolen logging smock which complements the new hat perched like a vandalized mallard atop my skull. As I leave the car in a meadow and walk down an access road leading to the south shore, I am (sartorially) a hunter.

The light retreats with each step heavy-soled step as I enter the forest beside the lake. It would be ominous had I not grown to adulthood gamboling through it (my parent's home is a ten-minute walk). I sweat in my costume. Blood boils in my pelvis. The current in my body mingles with that arriving on the static tail of the storm, thickening the air, and filing my purpose to an extreme point, as though I now wander through the exact proportion of my desire in order to fulfill it.

I cross a brook amicably babbling from an inlet, the pellucid water sitting green below grey clouds and black hills two hundred yards through the trees, while the opposing shore rises in a steep hill like the humped back of a breaching whale. At the top, I scuttle down the side of a defile cut in the ridgeline. This is where we parted. I sit on a flat rock in the damp gut of the ravine, and, for a moment, I can smell her. The sweat on her back, beneath her arms, between her legs, and I smell myself. My body beneath the wool and duck is slick with perspiration. The boots could be lined with coals. I feel like I'm on fire. But I will not remove the hat to wipe my brow. A hunter must maintain focus. Discomfort is a trade.

I wait nearly forty minutes before the first roll of thunder, at which point I begin to worry. The sun is nearly eclipsed, but I judge it to be the hour arranged for Eleanor to suggestively rustle the brush beside the ravine, yet the hilltop is bare, and dormant. The sound of the storm has caused all species of woodland creature to repair to burrow or nest, leaving only a dense cohort of pine and a few stray boulders as company. A gust of criminal wind nearly tears the hat from my head. I can no longer smell her. But somewhere in these woods, my quarry is nude and exposed, wearing nothing but my wristwatch, and I need to find her.

Rain begins dropping through the tree cover. Droplets smack the ground like marbles tossed from a celestial balcony, scattering needles and dead leaves with each impact. The hill is a rough peninsula, the ground sloping to water on three sides. She would stay away from the there (too many day-trippers in boats, or frolicking on ribbons of private beach on the opposite shore). The only direction to go is deeper, into the trees.

As I follow the projected trail of my game, the flora thickens. The rain has soaked through my clothing, which seems to add the weight of an unnaturally large child to my entire body. I consider calling her name. But over the concussion of the thunder and tympanic roll of the rain, I would be lucky to hear myself. My vision is no good, and for this, I have been prescribed glasses, which work wonderfully to correct the problem. However, in rain, they become easily fogged and the sodden wool of my shirt only spreads the water like petroleum jelly across the lens, softly focusing my surroundings until the trees, ground, and sky are a single amorphous smear. It is nearly a relief when they are knocked from my face by a rogue branch.

Bad choreography often arrives in triplicate. When I drop to the ground to search for my spectacles, I find them immediately with my left knee. The frames snap, and the lenses are ground mightily into the dirt. As I shift to recover them, I place my hand in a gopher hole, which swallows my arm to the shoulder. My jaw clunks the ground, and my teeth snap shut on portion of my cheek. I taste blood.

A hunter should not cry. And I may not be crying. It is impossible to tell in the rain. But even if a hunter weeps, he should never panic (though in this situation, even Hemingway might excuse me). I jerk upward, twisting my arm from the hole, choking on a wash of blood and vomiting some of it onto my chin. My new hat falls over my eyes, blinding me further, but I continue stumbling deeper into the forest, screaming now, screaming as loud as I can over the thunder and the rain. The only illumination arrives from an occasional eruption of lightening in the cloudbank overhead. And in the darkness, I scream. But what am I screaming? What else? Her name.

2.

When I reach the car, I get into the driver's seat and start the vehicle. Blood drips from my mouth onto the steering wheel and the wipers beat a frenetic tempo on the windscreen. Her clothes remain, folded neatly on the seat beside me. I stuff them mechanically into the glove compartment, and use one of my mother's towels on my face. I get out, and strip off my clothes in the rain, flinging each item away from me as though it is the impetus behind whatever has gone so drastically wrong, which (in a way) it may be. Thus divested, I sit nude in the driver's seat once again, trying to decide whether anything in my suddenly narrow index of life choices ('the tired valise') has adequately prepared me for a situation like this.

It is too embarrassing to call the police. Even if Eleanor is dead, surely she would prefer to be remembered as someone who got lost in the woods, rather than someone doing something else. In the woods. With me. No. I won't call them. By the time I finish explaining the reasons and agreements behind everything, she will likely be either dead or found. Police would just make a mess of the whole mess. And they would not be able to change the one fact of the immediate situation, the single solitary problem paralyzing me: Eleanor is gone.

The drive home is eventful due to the fact that without my glasses, I am legally blind. I creep along the dirt road toward my parent's house at the pace of a glacier, my face pressed as close as possible to the glass. Despite the rain, I keep the window down, perennially ejecting a spume of blood through it like a rickshaw wallah chewing paan. Before reaching home, I stop beside the slough below the tree house, and throw the elderly Sorrels, shit-colored dungarees, the red and black checked shirt, new hat, and myself into the muck. I can't see where I step, and the earth at the roadside is loose from the rain. I emerge from the mire filthy and naked, my nudity bathed in a jacket of off-grey mud and pond scum, as though I, like some haruspex, had sifted the afterbirth of my own impenetrable mistake.

My mother is reading a book in the living room when I walk through the door wearing her bathrobe. Being a parent, she asks the most important question first.

"Marlowe, where are your glasses?"

I blink too many times before replying.

"At the bottom of the lake. I was swimming. I fell off the dock."

"I'll make you an appointment tomorrow. Is that my bathrobe?"

"Yes. I'll do laundry tomorrow. I'm tired. Love you. Goodnight," I say, turning toward where I suspect my room might be and blundering into a bookcase by the phone table.

"I have a spare set," I say, before my mother can ask

I'm not certain I have committed a crime, but as I bed down, I have the detached feeling of something left undone, as though Eleanor were an item forgotten in a train station. Not guilt exactly, but a defined sense of responsibility. She couldn't have cared less. She did all of it for me. So something bad must have happened. Because she should have been there, hunched naked in the bracken on the hilltop. Waiting for me.

I'm briefly troubled by the thought that she might find her own way out tonight, wondering why I did not call the police when I couldn't find her. That would be even more embarrassing than calling them straightaway. I'm in a difficult position, and there is only one solution. Tomorrow, after work, I need to find her.

*

June 2nd, 2006, North Calais, Vermont

She hadn't called me. I discovered Eleanor was home eight days before I lost her in the forest, when I received a group email that read: "Finally home. Parents in P-town for the next two weeks. Going shopping in Burlington. But hey! VT folks call me---> 802-(phone number)." Though I tend to believe everything in life emerges from absurdity rather than fate, and even if the message had been sent to fifty other people, it seemed auspicious. It had been a long time, but how could I not call her? For the sake of my nerves, I went to the tree house and served myself a tumbler of gin before dialing.

Eleanor and I hadn't spoken for a year. As with Irma, our relationship developed during high school, and failed afterwards. She was a grade ahead of me. After she graduated and went to school in New York, I saw her only once or twice on break. During the interim, we exchanged dull messages via email. I sent a few mix CDs to a mailroom in Brooklyn. Then I graduated, and messed around for a year before going to school in Ohio. During my period of messing around, she came home from New York a few times. But neither of us returned the other's calls. Or we may not have made any. Either way, it wasn't tragic. Again, as with Irma, it made sense that whatever remained between us would fade to nothing.

I didn't exactly miss Eleanor. But she was pleasant (my father's word), willowy, and we amused each other. Her hair was so red, that when she wore a shirt of similar color, her burgundy mane resembled a hood. Freckles littered her pale skin like flakes of red pepper settling over thin, milky chowder. Her features were winsome and avian. We were never overwhelmed by our attraction to each other. Instead, we were drawn together during high school by a tacit acknowledgement of our mutually limited possibilities. To be plain and hormonal during adolescence is to learn compromise early, and each of us was indeed the best the other could do.

Eleanor knew several boys before me. None were significant, except for a psoriatic bassoonist she met at a music camp in Shelburne (she played the flute, quite well) who took her virginity several months later. They coupled on the floor of a guest bathroom in the home of a mutual friend on New Year's Eve/Day (East Montpelier, 2001). He lost his erection after several minutes, and squatted facing the wall between the toilet and the sink trying to revive it. Though he wore a full winter parka with its hood up (that particular section of the house had been shut for the season to save on heating) and no pants, his modesty remained intact. Several times, he asked her nicely not to watch him while he diddled. But after ten minutes, they agreed to take a break and try again later. She said it was his talent and passion for his instrument (the bassoon) that attracted her. I didn't understand this (but accepted it), and was pleased when he strayed from Eleanor while on tour with a youth orchestra in Austria, where he met a Viennese percussionist named Verena. Her passion for the cymbals matched, if not exceeded, his for the Bassoon, and together they made peculiar music. I know this because of the erratic emails Eleanor shared with me.

I was slightly more experienced than Eleanor, but this was only because her standards were higher. I lost my own virginity years before, on a windy Halloween night in Montpelier. The party where it occurred was held at a house on Cliff Street. The domicile sunk in the side the titular escarpment (the "cliff" in Cliff Street) had a generous deck, on which Amelia found me dressed as Santa Claus (I arrived on site without a costume, which caused the host to balk, and retreat into the attic, before emerging twenty minutes later with a box labeled 'XMAS DECORATIONS.' The rest can be inferred). She was Bill Clinton (he had just been impeached).

I discovered Amelia was pretty only when she pulled the presidential mask over her forehead to light a cigarette on the deck. We were quite drunk, and in retrospect, the sex was remarkably rote for a brace of virgins. The only notable aspect of our coupling was that we retained the better portion of our outfits during it, out of respect for those revelers who came outside to enjoy the autumnal current in the air and lights of Montpelier below. Since Amelia, there were a few relationships and more sex. But I always had the feeling Eleanor was expecting something different from me, and I was nervous.

Years (and one juice glass worth of gin) later, I remained nervous. A raven or crow croaked through one of the windows in the tree house, which seemed to augur well for the call I was about to place. I recorded the number on the interior of my forearm, and was barely able to distinguish its characters in the failing light.

*

June 11th, 2006, Pitkin, Vermont
Waking in the morning with a perfect knowledge of what happened the

night before is sometimes worse than being able to recall nothing. But even if this were the case with me, the hole in the interior of my cheek is a sanguine reminder of yesterday's ineptitude as I drive toward work in Pitkin. The wound is healing, and will not bleed unless I poke it with my tongue. But since I seem to possess a propensity for self-punishment, I've been exploring it with my lingua since I awoke. By the time I reach Pitkin Union School, I'm spitting blood in the parking lot.

For all his shortcomings on paper, Gustav is remarkably observant. As I enter Mr. Shiver's class (eleventh grade homeroom), and sit beside him, he squints through a pair of massive spectacles while shifting a frame similar in shape and appearance to a two-man tent, or half-melted snowman (depending on the season). Everything about him, the cushion-like contours of his shoulders, his bejowled face, and even the ring of flesh surrounding his middle above the circlet of his belt like a flotation device, appears to spill toward the floor in a slow cascade of soft tissue.

"You look different, Marlowe."

"I am different," I say, nodding to myself. I'd like it to be true.

He combs an oily strand of black hair from his field of vision, which settles on a patch of regurgitated blood on my collar.

"Is that blood?"

"No. It's chocolate."

"You eat chocolate for breakfast?"

"Yes."

"I want to eat chocolate for breakfast. My mom says I should eat fruit. Do you eat fruit?"

"Yes, Gustav. I like bananas," I reply idiotically, meeting the haggard eyes of Mr. Shivers at the head of the classroom, who appears ready to begin class. Gustav remains fixated on my collar.

"It looks like blood," he says.

"It's not."

"But it looks like blood."

"But it's not."

"But it looks like blood."

"But it's not. It's chocolate."

"But it looks like blood."

"Gustav, you're…"

"Good morning everyone. Everyone!" shouts Mr. Shivers, looking directly at me, not Gustav.

"Today," he continues, turning and plodding toward his chalkboard. "We will be continuing our discussion of *The Odyssey*. I trust you have all completed the reading."

He snatches the text from his desk and waves it at the class as though attempting to cast a malignant spirit (me, possibly) from his homeroom.

"Now," says Mr. Shivers. "Who can tell me what happens after Odysseus meets the witch, Circe?"

None volunteer. Mr. Shivers performs a bit of amateur theater while searching the classroom, before his eyes settle on me.

"Gustav. Perhaps you and Marlowe can enlighten us."

"Perhaps, we can," says Gustav, pushing his book away and standing up. Like Mr. Shivers, Gustav has a dramatic inclination. "When Odysseus' men eat some cheese and wine, Circe turns them into pigs. Hermes gives him a drug to resist her magic. And then…"

Gustav looks at me. I nod for him to continue.

"And then, Circe and Odysseus have sex for one year."

The other students chuckle. Gustav sits down. A cloud the color of raw sewage appears over Mr. Shivers.

"Right. Yes. Well. Thank you, Gustav," he says, turning to a bank of windows on the far side of the classroom as if they might offer an escape. "Okay. Look, quiet down. Let's move on. Can anyone tell me the name of the drug Hermes dispensed to Odysseus?"

One hand aside from Gustav's rises and is called upon.

"Gooballs?" says the student, Arnold, whose paraprofessional, Dane, is sitting beside him, asleep at the wheel, and attempting to hide beneath the broad-brimmed, olive colored hat which he insists on wearing even while working with students.

"Goo…what? What do you mean, Arnold," says Mr. Shivers, briefly losing his composure.

"Pot butter, diffused in peanut butter and chocolate, sometimes cookie dough," says Arnold, adding, "Delicious!"

"No!" bellows Mr. Shivers. "That is the wrong answer!"

"Pigfucker!" replies Arnold, which stirs Dane into briefly doing his job.

"Arnold. Come on, man. You know that isn't very cool."

"Get him out of here," says Mr. Shivers.

"That's not so cool either," replies Dane. "Come on, Abe. He didn't mean it the way it sounded. Right, Arnold?"

"Wrong!" says Arnold, pointing a finger at the ceiling.

"He goes! Now!"

Dane moves lugubriously, placing a nicotine-stained hand on Arnold's shoulder, and locking eyes with Mr. Shivers as he speaks.

"Come on, Arn. The Man says we have to go."

Dane speaks as though he spends his weekends falling from the back of a moving van which, when coupled with the absurd hat, the general odor of fish and cigarettes emanating from him regardless of season, and a shiftlessness that only becomes more pronounced when he attempts to conceal it, reminds me that I only have this job because the school district is desperate. Two weeks after returning from Ohio, my father grew tired of watching me occupy a recliner in our living room for the better part of the day, sipping coffee, reading one of his books, and removing myself from this emplacement only to smoke on the front porch. He suggested that if I planned to live at home for a while, I should probably get a job. I agreed, and did nothing, which I think he expected, because one week later, I was employed at Pitkin Union School on his recommendation, and given to Gustav as something between a tutor and a servant.

Dane and Arnold leave, and Gustav, having absorbed the scene as though it were staged for his benefit, turns to me.

"I like your new glasses," he says. "They look like mine."

Though the prescription is accurate, the frames of my 'spare set' are so large they feel like goggles, and the configuration of the lenses appears to have been borrowed from a blueprint used to design small aircraft. This, combined with the stains on my clothing and the fact that I woke up late and neglected to shower, has me bearing an unhealthy resemblance to Gustav, who is still watching my collar.

"Is that blood?" he asks.

Pitkin is a small village whose major attraction, a Quaker school, Greatwood College, closed several years ago. It was the sort of college where you could major in anything (foosball, tree-climbing, Mesmerism) provided you paid your tuition. The campus remains tucked on the edge of town, manned by a skeleton crew of grounds people and administrators. Over the years, they've had trouble with accreditation, but they still host the odd colloquium, summer seminar, or concert. The best summation of the school's character is found in the admissions building, the walls of which display a dozen or so class photographs taken of the staff and students during the sixties and seventies. The portraits are normal in every respect, aside from the fact that all those posing are naked. Naturally, many alumni remained in town after graduation, bought homes and had children, thus embedding the Greatwood ethic in the town for generations. As a result, Pitkin is something of an enigma amid the greater map of America. In all other respects, it is a typical, relaxed Vermont college town without a college.

Mr. Shivers is a pious, miserable man who does not match the location in which he is employed. It's obvious to his colleagues that he is mostly waiting to retire. But if you ask my father, he'll say that Mr. Shivers retired years ago. For the past two decades, he has employed what librarians call 'The Rule of 1965' in his classroom. Aside from the haircuts and sneakers worn by the students, his homeroom in 1980 would be as it is today, and in it, they would be discussing *The Odyssey* while Mr. Shivers victimized a student, and his (or her) paraprofessional.

Mr. Shivers excuses the class for lunch, but asks me to stay, so I tell Gustav I will see him afterward, and remain in my seat, feeling more student than staff. Mr. Shivers sits with his head in his hands until all the students leave, at which point he begins speaking to me through his fingers.

"Are you familiar with Matthew 9:17?"

"No. Is it a sports thing? A batting average or something?" I say, attempting to plant levity where none will grow.

"No," says Mr. Shivers. "No. It's not a sports thing. It's a passage from the gospels. 'Neither do men put new wine into old bottles: else the bottles break, and the wine runneth out, and the bottles perish: but they put new wine into new bottles, and both are preserved.' "

We both wait for the other to say something.

"Is there something you want to ask me?" I offer.

"This is the second or third time this week that Gustav…"

He removes his head from his hands and looks at me.

"That Gustav has disrupted my class. I understand his situation. And I'm not blaming him. I'm blaming you, Marlowe."

"He had the right answer," I say. "I mean, we went over it together. That's what happens in the story of Odysseus, and his men. And Arnold…"

"This is not about Arnold!"

I say nothing more. He continues exploring his face with his hands as though searching for the catch that will remove it.

"My students are new bottles," he murmurs. "They need focused study free of distraction. This is how children learn. I know you have had some trouble with your own education, so you might not understand that. But after decades of doing this, I know what works and what doesn't."

"Are you saying Gustav is an old bottle?" I say, wondering what exactly he might know about my education.

"I'm saying that it's not up to me. It's your responsibility. And that leaves me with little hope. I know his IEP has him in a classroom for part of the school day. And I think that's a good thing. I'm just not sure if having you with him is."

He stands, and begins shuffling papers, indicating that he is done. I remain sitting.

"Look," I say. "It's not my fault that people had sex back then. All your new bottles have the internet at home. They don't need to learn about this stuff from old Romans."

"Greek," says Mr. Shivers. "Homer was Greek."

"Right. Well. Okay. But the Bible has plenty of that. And they hand it out on street corners."

"You can go now."

"What about Lot? And his daughters? The Jackson-Whites have nothing on them. Or Abraham wife-swapping with Pharaoh? Or Judges? There is some gross stuff in there."

"We're through here."

"You can't pick and choose," I say, gathering my things. "The bible invented pornography. And you go around quoting it."

I leave the classroom, and wander into my father's office down the hall. It's lunchtime, and he is eating a portion of (what looks like) silage from a segmented tray on his desk. Several strands of vegetable matter are caught in (what I call) his cuirass, a gray goatee shielding his mouth. He listens as I relate my interaction with Mr. Shivers, nodding and masticating as I speak.

"He needs to change a poster," says my father. "Or get a hamster. Anything. That classroom is like an oubliette."

"Dad. You have some…something, whatever you're eating. It's caught in your cuirass."

"My what?"

I circle my mouth with an index finger.

"Oh, I see. Thank you."

He wipes his mouth. The flora remains.

"Listen, try to do what he wants. He's the teacher. You're the help. But if what he expects is unreasonable, meet him halfway. Did you say anything else?"

"I told him the Bible invented pornography. Was that wrong?"

He puffs his cheeks and exhales.

"Well, at least school ends in a week. The three of us won't have to see each other for three months."

"He hates me because he hates you. That's what it is, right?"

"Something like that. We got off on the wrong foot. When I first started here, I took his parking space."

"He has an assigned space?"

"Of course not. This is a school, not a brokerage. Abellard has a space where he prefers to park. And I took it. And that kindled what has become a withering rapport."

"And how does he know about Ohio?"

My father removes his glasses, which dangle by a length of rubberized cord from his neck, and folds his hands on the desktop. Behind the cuirass, his face is somewhat grave.

"I didn't tell him anything."

"Then how does he know?"

"Well…I may have mentioned it…to a few people…in passing."

I'm about to speak, but he raises a hand.

"Look, people here like you," he says, as though this is amazing. "They ask how you're doing. You can't expect me to lie to them. I have to work here."

Silence (mine). He continues.

"Don't worry about it. You have nothing to be ashamed of. He's a bitter old man. Everyone sees the work you're doing with Gustav. It speaks for itself. By the way, what are you guys doing this afternoon?"

"I thought," I say, gauging my words, "that we might go for a hike. Around the lake. You know, it's the last week of school. Beautiful day. And I can't spend any more time at the Berlin Mall."

"You don't find that place depressing?"

"I do. But Gustav likes the arcade. I give him quarters, and read a book."

"Well, just make sure to bring water. And some snacks. That will proba- bly be enough to get him into the woods. You're continuing with him over the summer, right? We need someone on-site at Food Barn."

"Yes," I say, standing up. "I'm not doing anything else."

This last statement causes a grim downturn in the cuirass. He stands also, walking around the desk to put a hand on my arm.

"We can figure out the fall. You have time, Marlowe. Use it to get an idea of what you want. Your mother and I are glad you're here. But one try isn't enough. Think about it."

He pats my shoulder. I thank him, and leave the office to find Gustav, and if I'm lucky, Eleanor as well.

3.

June 2ⁿᵈ, 2006, Middlesex, Vermont

When I finally reached her from the tree house, Eleanor acted as though she expected my call, and told me to come over if I was in any shape to drive. I set my glass of gin beside the leg of my folding chair, and inquired of the raven or crow perched on the sill. He (I judged it male) had watched me imbibe during the call, shuffling his talons and croaking murderously from the window ledge.

"Your judgment?"

He tilted his head as though asking me to repeat. I was suddenly seized with a desire to touch him. His silky pinions drew my hand from my side and though the bird was looking directly at me, I had the sense that I might succeed in ruffling his feathers if I proceeded slowly.

"You are important," I insisted, stretching one finger, than another toward his back.

I am not an explicit fool. I half expected the bird to savage me, but just to touch him once seemed worth the risk. Imagine my surprise when the raven or crow ducked my grasping paw, and hopped from his station at the window, to my wrist. His oblique eye surveyed me, perhaps trying to judge whether or not I was edible or otherwise useful. He nibbled my wrist, pooped on it, and croaked once more before flapping out, into the coming night.

I took this as an affirmative, and stood, knocking my chair backward and stomping out of the woods. I would see Eleanor tonight. This was certain. We might have little in common aside from the shared memory of the other naked. But that would be enough.

Eleanor's home sits on the slope of a small mountain outside Montpelier, and was originally a geodesic dome, but there is very little left of the original structure. Two broad wings extend from it to the north and south, joining beneath in a palatial lower story. If seen from above, the building would resemble a wristwatch (with its band undone) laid flat on tabletop. Since the entire structure clings to a ridge, a narrow and elevated walkway, like a drawbridge that doesn't draw, extends from a driveway where I parked my car that first night, to the front door. I clomped up it, pondering the fifteen foot drop to either side of an entirely too low railing, and feeling very much as though I was still in high school. This was our formula. Her parents disliked me from the beginning, so I often arrived just after dark (Count Marlowe) while they were bedding down in the lower story.

The time we spent apart had treated Eleanor well. She was radiant and very adult-looking when she answered my knock at the door. Her hair was daringly cropped, and hung from her scalp in loose crimson strands like a mangled Chinese flag. She had just showered, and it appeared darker. The muscles in her arms were supple, and those in her legs rolled in perfect, mechanical definition as she led me inside. Eleanor was always slim, but her new body seemed trained and fit. Her behind was generous without diffusion. She looked strong and healthy.

She wore some sort of athletic outfit, with tights that ended at the knee and a leotard top cut low in the back. I'd heard she had started dancing again in New York. I meant to ask about this as we sat down in the living room. But instead, I lurched forward and hugged her.

"You look amazing," I murmured, pressing my nose into her conceptual haircut.

She patted my back, and gently pushed me upright.

"Oh my, Marlowe. You're inebriated," she said, sniffing the air between us. "And you smell of…I'm not sure…What is that exactly?"

"Juniper berries?"

"No. Fouler."

"Ah. Likely bird poop then."

"I see. Would you like a shower? Maybe a coffee?"

"You're parents are…?" I asked, glancing around.

"Cape Cod. For Fleet Week or the Blessing of the Fleet or something. Relax. Please bathe. You smell terrible."

"I would like a coffee and a cigarette on the veranda before I shower on my own," I said as though translating. Eleanor blinked and stood, walking towards the kitchen. And after the coffee, she followed me to the bathroom, handed me a towel, and sat on the toilet.

"You can use my toothbrush."

I ignored her, standing on the bath mat in my shoes, waiting for her to leave.

"Eleanor. In a moment, I will be naked."

"I know."

A glass of deep red wine swished in her hand, appearing from I knew not where.

"So…I should…Take these off?" I said, flicking my wrist at my attire.

"That's right."

I sat on the edge of the tub and began unlacing my shoes. Something about the process irritated her. It could have been my timorous pace. Or the fact that I kept looking up, expecting that she would be gone.

"Do you want me to leave?" she asked.

Rather than answering, I plucked the glass from her hand, finished the wine, and then made a circle with one finger in the air above my head.

"You want more?"

I nodded, tossing my shoes into the hallway. She leaned down close to my face and said, "I want to see you. Do you understand?"

I gulped, and tried to kiss her. She palmed my forehead.

"No. I want to see you. Do this for me."

I was ashamed of my body. It sagged. I had the feeling we no longer matched as we had in high school. Aside from my left arm, which usually hung from the window of the Volvo, my skin was pale as the underside of a land-going snail. I had a soft middle, and skinny arms. My penis swung like a hanged man between the titanic gallows of my legs.

"I'm afraid I've aged," I said, turning from Eleanor to twiddle the shower nob.

She took a sip of wine and shrugged.

"It's not so bad. If you worked out, you would be handsome."

"And as is?"

"You'll do."

Eleanor seemed to be saying there was hope, for us, or perhaps just me, but she wanted to humble me first. Certainly, she knew she looked good. And she was always deliberate. The clothing she wore, the insistence that I bathe, the clinical interest in my nudity. Her behavior assumed a charitable aspect, as if I had not realized when she opened the door that if there were no history between us, I would not have a chance. It was important to her that I understood that.

*

June 11th, 2006, Pitkin, Vermont

After leaving my father's office, I go to the parking lot, where I'd arranged to meet Gustav by my car. But when I exit the building, I find Dane standing beside the vehicle instead, his olive colored hat positioned at an angle which is pleasant only for the way it conceals the most suspicious part of his face. I'm worried that he might either want to borrow money, or the car itself. But when he speaks, it's obvious that his proximity to the vehicle is only a coincidence.

"These SPED kids…I don't know, man."

I sense an earthy, reflective confession funneling itself through the dreary tunnel between his mind and mouth. Dane withdraws a rolled cigarette from beneath his hat, and requests a light.

"You know smoking that here is a felony, right?" I say, handing him my lighter, which he uses and pockets as if it's all the same to me.

"These SPED kids," he repeats. "Arnold's a real pistol…I'm saying, I've been doing this gig for a while, and it's the ones that look all normal. Them are the ones that make it a job."

"I see," I say stiffly, reaching around Dane to unlock the car, and trying to imagine what my father would do if he overhead even part of this conversation.

"You're lucky, Marlowe," Dane continues. "You got Gustav, a total downy. I like downies. They're gravy. Eager to please. Yup, I've worked with a lot of downies. I've been doing this a while. They're always the easiest. Just make sure to feed them, right?"

"Wrong," I say, slamming my door, and drowning out Dane's chuckle as I pull the Volvo around to the main entrance to find my 'downy,' furious with myself for even listening to Dane, career parasite, and interpersonal event horizon.

When I leave Pitkin Union School with Gustav, we drive to Danville to get picnic supplies. Our destination is a bakery operated by the Theodora Collective, a cooperative composed of between fifty and hundred women (they come and go) who have endured some sort of trauma. The Collective owns over hundred acres in the hills between Cabot and Danville, on which is planted a vast compound consisting of a working farm, an Eden-like vegetable garden, orchard, vineyard, dormitories, and a sort of nondenominational chapel. Men are forbidden. They recently purchased a storefront in Danville adjacent to the town square, and converted the former feed store to a bakery ("Guidance: Fine Wine & Cheese"). It is here that the less fair sex (myself, and Gustav, for example) may sample T.C.'s produce.

Gustav has never visited the place, and when we enter, he balks at the sight of three pert young woman in aprons, their forearms dusted with flower and their fingers slick with oil, bustling behind the counter and arranging confections in a glass case, the head of each shaved bald.

"Do they have cancer?" he asks quietly, tugging at my sleeve.

"Yes," I say, withdrawing a baguette from a basket beside the door, allowing the pastry to distract him. I select my cheese, as Gustav chooses his sweets.

"And this one?" he says, pointing to an éclair, oozing custard on a paper cozy. "What is this?"

"An éclair with banana custard," answers the attendant.

Gustav looks at me, and I shrug.

"It's a sort of fruit, Gustav."

As I place the bread, and an acrid goat cheese flecked with grape skin and chives, on the counter, a fourth woman emerges from a back room to tally my purchases. She is younger than her coterie, and, even without hair, her face has an unabused, diverting beauty. Her eyes are the color of a darkly ripening fruit, and when her lush mouth pouts the total, I ask her to repeat. Her pate shines without a hint of new growth and is slightly red. A recent acolyte? I accept my change and ask if she is new to the area.

"I'm from Connecticut," she says, and turns away. I can think of nothing else to say, so I usher Gustav out the door, and we drive to the woods beside the lake.

When Gustav falls in the brook, I'm already up the hill where I was supposed to meet Eleanor the afternoon before. Everything is the same, only drier. The defile sits like a paper cut above the lake, and within it I have laid our repast upon a bed of still moist pine needles lining the bottom. But when I hear him bellowing from the direction of the brook, I leave the food where it is, and run back down the hill.

At the bottom of the slope, he is crying and breathing through his nostrils, but also staring at me as though he has met with an injustice, and it is now my task to put it right. But I'm more concerned that his leg, which is twisted between two slick rocks, is sprained or broken. This means I would have to carry him back to the car, a task for which I am neither prepared nor capable.

Though he is a foot and half shorter, Gustav outweighs me by a hundred pounds. The weight is only part of his problem. Even if he ate well, he would still be a blimp, a condition Dane seems to believe I am lucky to be managing. Oddly, his (Dane's) one blessing amid a mélange of curses is that watching him be terrible at his job cements my work ethic. Thus, I try to do what I imagine is the right thing for Gustav as he flounders in the shallow water of the inlet.

"Don't move," I say, kneeling beside him. "Tell me where it hurts."

He says nothing, but continues weeping.

"All right. I'm going to move these. If it hurts, tell me to stop."

I reach into the brook and shift a rock. He withdraws his leg from the water, and sits on the bank. His shin is scraped, but appears fine otherwise. I help him up.

"My shoes are wet," he says.

"Right. There's food at the top of the hill."

Gustav weighs this bargain (briefly) before trundling up the slope. When we reach the peak, I separate from him to prowl the woodland for signs of Eleanor. Twenty steps into the pine scrub, something inorganic crunches under my foot, and beneath my shoe, I discover the unfortunate carcass of my former spectacles. The arms fold crookedly inward against either oculus, the empty frames as brooding and morose as the skeleton of a recently burnt house, but finding them is a relief. In the event that Eleanor is dead, it's best to limit the amount of personal articles strewn about the forest (or crime scene). I tuck the ruined frames in my pocket, and continue walking through the trees.

The problem of my wristwatch remains, which, alive or dead, Eleanor is wearing. If the body is discovered, completely naked aside from the timepiece, it will certainly be considered evidence. I can't recall where it was purchased. It may have been a gift from my mother. Would she have used a credit card? Does something as simple as a watch contain a serial number by which it can be traced if stolen, or found on a corpse? Surely, if I find the timepiece attached to her dead body, and remove it, I would not be tampering with evidence. As with the spectacles, I would simply be reclaiming property.

Up ahead, I see what looks like a swathe of flesh through a low stand of scrub pine, but it's only a patch of exposed quartz mellowing in the sunlight. I place my hand on the mineral, and find it pleasantly cool. I lay my other hand upon it, and finally my cheek. The temperature is elemental. The massive deposit must be sunk deep in the hillside, left by a passing glacier. That was how the lake formed. The striations against my skin are ancient. I touch them to my lips.

Just as I consider how strange it would be for someone to happen across me in the middle of the forest, kissing a rock, I hear the sound of a camera shutter, opening and closing. And this is the only sound. There is no rustling, no snapping of twigs. I jerk upward. I have no idea from which direction it came. I turn around stupidly in the clearing.

"Hello?"

No noise. No clicks. I don't breathe.

"Gustav?"

Of course, he isn't there. Instead, he is planted with his hands folded upon his stomach like some Asiatic fetish, watching the water when I return to the ravine. Most of the cheese has been consumed, and all that remains of my bread is one round end.

"You were gone for a long time," he says, not looking at me. "I got hungry."

I snatch the soggy elbow of bread from the ground and clamp the remainder of cheese upon it as though plugging a leak. I take a bite, chewing furiously, my eyes darting from Gustav to the surrounding foliage, the culinary wreckage, and finally settling on his school bag, which he insisted on bringing.

"It's fine, Gustav," I murmur, kneeling and unzipping the backpack. "Did you enjoy your meal?"

"Why yes, thank you," he quips, still not turning around.

"Good. I'm glad."

I keep my eyes on his back, while blindly shuffling through the items in his bag. Books, pencils, a bottle of water. No camera. Not that I expected to find one. I suddenly feel very silly, and begin zipping the bag closed when I notice a familiar item poking out of the front pocket. A swatch of pale yellow fabric closed in the zipper. Eleanor's underpants. Gustav has been digging in my glovebox. It's my fault. I should have been more careful. This was a problem at the Food Barn as well. In fact, it is the entire reason his IEP needs someone (me) on-site. You might not see it right away, because Gustav is generally pleasant and most people are unwilling to attribute malicious intent to the disabled. He must have swiped the bloomers when we stopped for gas in East Calais. I left him at the pump for a little too long while I bullshitted with Irma (another campfire tonight, apparently). I can't just take the underwear, because then Gustav would know that I was digging in his bag. But one way or another, I'll have to reclaim them before depositing him back in Pitkin.

I unzip the front pocket, dislodge the fabric, and push it inside before refastening the compartment. I couldn't stand to leave it jammed obviously in the zipper. I walk out of the gully and stand beside Gustav, chewing my meager share of the meal.

"Have you been sitting here long?" I ask.

"Maybe."

I roll my eyes. Riddles.

"Have you seen anyone else, Gustav?"

"There were some people in boats."

"Yes, people in boats. But did you see anyone on shore here, though? Maybe someone walking around with a camera? Anyone like that?"

He shakes his head.

"Nope. Just you and me," he chirps, smiling to himself.

Yes, I think. And someone with a picture of me making love to a stone. Another item on my list of things to uncover before the week is through. A tourist probably took the photo. The lakeshore is a plague of summer homes, and this is the season during which people begin to occupy them. Speedboats tow obese children, their bulk augmented by puffy yellow life preservers, on inflatable tubes, carving the passive surface upon which beer cans bob in iridescent patches of gasoline. The air fills with cinders, and smells corrupt. At night, I hear music and shouting. Fireworks blossom through the trees at the edge of my parent's property. The meaty odor of whatever they're cooking or burning reaches me as I lie in bed.

But, for once, I'm glad they're here. If one of them photographed me, the picture will serve as an oddity in the family album rather than evidence in a court of law. A local hill person caught engaging in some heathen ritual deep in the forest. I don't know who else it could be. The place on the hilltop is a private location. It is where I take women. I only brought Gustav here because I needed to search for one of them.

After our picnic concludes, I drive him back to Pitkin. Gustav lives with his mother, Lucia on a hillside overlooking the town. The address is recognizable by a snarl of Tibetan prayer flags strung in the branches of a tree beside the mailbox. On the way, I stop for cigarettes in North Montpelier. Since Gustav has already purloined the most embarrassing item hidden in the car, I'm morbidly calm when I return to the vehicle with the intention of reclaiming it. I sit in the car without turning the key, quietly doing nothing in order to make Gustav nervous. The battle for Eleanor's underwear has begun.

"Are…we…going to leave?" he asks.

"That depends."

This seems to confirm something dreadful for Gustav. He crosses his pudgy arms and sits back in the passenger seat.

"Do you know what it depends on?" I ask, wishing I had not ended the sentence with a preposition. Gustav rolls his planet-like head on its invisible neck.

"I'll just tell you then," I continue. "It depends on you. I know you have something of mine. And I want you to return it."

"I don't know what you're talking about."

I could reach into the backseat and withdraw the yellow panties from his bag, but part of my job is to encourage good decision-making. Though I did this during our picnic, doing it in front of him might constitute a breach of some kind, and if Lucia found out, it would be bad.

But this is not the first afternoon I've wasted attempting to reclaim property from Gustav. While at the arcade in the Berlin Mall last week, he swiped a pair of sunglasses off the top of a ticket dispenser beside the ski ball chute. The ensuing disagreement placed me between Gustav and a three hundred pound hayshaker with a shirt that read 'If It Moves, Shoot It.'

"My fuckin' shades. That lil' retard got my fuckin' shades," he said, pointing impatiently at Gustav, who was actually wearing the sunglasses as he fed quarters into an arcade game.

"Please. Let me talk to him," I begged.

"You get five minutes. After that, I bust the lil' retard's pointy head."

"He'll do it," his girlfriend assured me like some backwater oracle.

"Five minutes. Fine. But if we could please stop with the word 'retard.' It's not appropriate," I said, fully aware that this was the wrong thing to say.

"Not appropriate?" he guffawed. "I'll tell you what's not appropriate: letting 'em run wild!"

I approached Gustav, engaged in his game and oblivious to the coalescing shitstorm.

"Gustav. Give me the glasses."

He raised a light gun, clacking the trigger at the screen.

"They're mine. I found them."

"They're not yours. The owner is standing over there. He would like them back."

"I found them," repeated Gustav, swinging the barrel of the plastic gun within inches of my face.

"Gustav, unless you want to get into a lot of trouble, you will give me the sunglasses."

"Two minutes," shouted the hillbilly from behind me.

"Two minutes," mimicked his girlfriend. "Then it's between you and Toby."

"Gustav," I pleaded. "You need to listen to me. This is serious."

I should have just grabbed the glasses, but I'm supposed to be encouraging rather than forcing good choices according to Gustav's IEP. In any case, it was too late. Toby's two minutes was my thirty seconds. He charged into me like a snowplow, and I fell against Gustav, and both of us tumbled to the floor of the arcade. The sunglasses flew off Gustav's face and clattered to a stop by the claw crane. One lens popped out.

"Aw, shit on a shingle," said Toby, extricating himself from us and retrieving the spectacles. He plucked them gingerly from the ground, examining the frames before pronouncing a condition report.

"They's fucked. You…"

He pointed to me. I closed my eyes and braced for impact. I had never been punched in the face properly. It was perhaps my time.

"You're like some kinda teacher, right?"

"Yes. Something like that," I said, opening one eye, then the other.

"Well, mister teacher. I demand compensation for these here shades."

"How much?" I asked, removing my wallet.

"Three hundred and ten."

"Bullshit," I said, putting my wallet away. Gustav raised an eyebrow.

"Isn't so. It's what they cost."

"I can't pay you anything right now. But…"

I scribbled the main number for Pitkin Union School on the back of my liquor store punch card and handed it to Toby.

"Call this number. They will see that you're taken care of," I lied, combing the remainder of Gustav's tokens into my hand and edging toward the exit. We were out of the arcade and in the atrium heading toward the parking lot when I heard Toby shout a warning.

"They better compensate me. Else it's your ass! And I'll whip you good!"

"Your ass!" squawked his attendant harpy. We ran to the car. With this in mind, I'm grateful that the current problem is only between us. I still have not started the car. The engine ticks.

"I'll ask once more, Gustav. Please return my belongings."

He ignores me. The only thing to do is bluff him.

"All right. If you won't listen to me, then maybe you'll listen to your mom."

I start the car, and begin backing out of the parking spot.

"My mom?"

"Yes. If you won't listen to me, than I'll have to tell your mom. You know how this works."

I swing the car onto the road, driving slowly toward Pitkin. Gustav lowers his arms and glares at me.

"Fine!"

He turns furiously, and snatches the pack from the backseat, and begins digging through it badger-like (using both hands), his careless anger sending items between the seats, and onto the mat between my feet. A water bottle rolls beneath the brake pedal.

"Here!"

He offers my cell phone (grudgingly), which I didn't even realize was missing. I pretend this is what I expected, and thank him.

"That's a good start, Gustav. But we both know there is something else I want."

I'm becoming nervous, because we're getting dangerously close to Lucia's house. The mailbox is less than a quarter mile. And I can't very well ask that Lucia force Gustav to return the panties he stole from my glovebox. I slow the car to the speed of a Protestant luncheon.

"Gustav, I am giving you one last chance."

We're close enough to see not only the prayer flags, but the Four Dignities as well. I stop the car.

"Give me the panties."

Gustav knows he's caught, but takes his time removing the garment, holding it between his stubby fingers, feeling the fabric, lingering on its unfamiliar (I assume and pray) utility. For a moment, I worry he might drape it over his face.

"Thank you, Gustav," I say, losing patience. I snatch the underwear from his grasp just as Lucia appears outside my window.

She is a squat, graying women. Her hair is twisted atop her crown in an unkempt bob. Around her neck hangs a ponderous collection of mela, and an enfilade of tarnished bangles ferrule either wrist. Her body is draped in colorful fabric that appears to have no outward fastening (a sheet, perhaps), and leaving her shoulders bare. On one tan scapula (the right), a rendering of Shiva performs a jig. If she were deployed in an arrivals lounge, she would look very much as she is: a spiritual tourist with an expired visa.

"Namaste, Marlowe," she says, predictably. "I was out for a walk. Everything all right?"

Her serene gaze falls on the panties in my hand, which I begin using to obviously mop my brow, jamming them in my shirt pocket as an encore.

"Yes. Yes, absolutely. Terribly hot, though."

"Hello, Gustav," she says, bending and waving. "Why are you stopped here?"

"Well…" I scramble for something, anything, and find it. "Gustav's backpack came open, and this…"

I pluck a water bottle from the floor.

"This little guy here rolled under my brake pedal."

"Oh, my."

"Yes, so…that's why…I stopped here…In this place."

"Your dad said you guys were doing some hiking?" says Lucia (to me).

"And a picnic!" says Gustav, opening his door.

"Well, isn't that nice!"

He runs around the side of the car, and buries himself in Lucia's curtain, eyeing me from the shade of his mother's body. Will I uphold our agreement? I pass Lucia his backpack through the window.

"Everything went well today?"

"Oh, sure," I lie. "Yes. Perfect."

Gustav visibly relaxes.

"I understand you'll be with him over the summer at the grocery store," says Lucia.

"That's my understanding. Food Barn is on board. It's paperwork, at this point."

Lucia smiles at the space behind my head.

"Well, we'll certainly look forward to that."

It's only when she and Gustav walk away that I realize he's wearing Eleanor's (red) sandals.

4.

June 3rd, 2006, Middlesex, Vermont

Eleanor never asked why I was home. At first, I assumed that she wasn't interested, but it's possible Eleanor assumed I had never left. It fit her template (the at-home dullard). We had stopped communicating long before I left for school in Ohio. But the details of my life were not important to her. I may have been without a history of my own before I called from the tree house. And when she asked what I was doing now (to be polite), and I explained my employment at Pitkin Union School, subbing classes, and working individually with Gustav, she became immediately bored. To be fair, she tried to identify, relating an anecdote about a friend who won a fellowship, and now taught art classes in the Bronx.

"He has health insurance," she said. "The money is a joke, of course."

"Of course" I said, having little idea to what I was agreeing. "The zoo is excellent."

This was my only association with the borough, an association I'd formed at the age of ten when my parents took me there.

"Zoo?"

"Yes. It has a Skyfari. And a King Cobra, I believe."

This took place the night after I called. I left to go to work and came back to see her again because I was lonely. I was accustomed to spending time by myself, and up to this point, it had not been a problem. But after I saw her, I needed to see her again. I remembered the tentative comfort in being granted entry to a home and a life (both hers). Everything was now permitted.

The second night, I arrived at her house after school released, and knocked on the door for several minutes without answer. In my hands, I held some treats from Guidance (a bottle of red wine, assorted pastries), and a few flowers stolen from a planter on the State Street Bridge in Montpelier. I was dressed poorly, but she expected this. Altogether, I felt I was in a fine position to renew her impression of me (from the previous night). I arrived sober, so that was a good start. But when she didn't answer the door, I was suddenly seized by a combination of extreme jealousy and murky self-loathing. Surely, if she was not answering the door she was with someone else, perhaps busy (at this very moment) pleasing this phantom within her chamber, while I, the cur-like fop, stood with my wilted bouquet on her doorstep.

Out of impatience, and a certain greed for her company, I walked around the house and Eleanor was there, taking the mid-afternoon sun naked on the back deck. She wore only sunglasses. Her lithe figure was treated with a collection of florid cosmetic oils arranged in a peculiar phalanx at the foot of the chaise upon which she reclined. Her hand extended in a hazy greeting when she saw me. I touched her fingers, and entered the house through a siding glass door to fuss with my purchases in the kitchenette. I arranged them on a plate, poured two glasses of wine, and set the mess on a tray with the dead flowers. I laid it on the deck beside her chair without a word. She sipped the wine, nibbled a pastry, and sniffed at the bouquet. I was sitting by her feet. She curled her fingers in my hair, and tugged it, soft, then hard. This is how we began our second evening together.

"I never liked zoos," she said. "It makes me sad to see things in cages."

"As long as they're happy," I said.

This is not how I imagined our time together. The second night she was bleak as a forgotten exhibit, and I wanted her more for it. Had she always been like this? Mute, determined, crucial in her movement. I felt alone in each room of her home, even when she was on top of me. And when we changed positions, and I climbed aboard her body as though it was a bicycle with an unusually high seat, our eyes met, the acquaintance of considerable green (hers) with drab brown (mine), and I said "New York has changed you," and instantly felt as though I had just emerged from a jalopy with one strap of my overalls undone, and inquired in which direction I could pick fruit for money. But I excused myself later, because I spoke from the corner into which I was drawn. And she sank her teeth into my neck, loving me for it. I could have asked whether the buildings were tall, or the pizza any good. The result would have been identical. I was her provincial failure.

The next morning, when I sat on her couch, sharing my limited knowledge of New York City, and pronounced 'Houston Street' as though it were named after a city in Texas, she padded from the kitchen and planted herself in front of me.

"Everyone makes that mistake," she said, savoring this correction. "Once."

"Oh. Yes. I see."

She bent down, kissed me on the mouth and said she loved me. Though it was a lie, it did not seem to come from an evil place. I felt less ugly, and slightly more important.

*

June 11th, 2006, North Calais, Vermont

At home, my father (still in his shirtsleeves) is grilling salmon and asparagus on the deck, and my mother is setting plates on an outdoor table. Both wave as my Volvo appears in the driveway, and I wonder briefly how two such well-adjusted, healthy people with advanced degrees could have produced me. I park, and open the glove box. Aside from the sandals, nothing else appears missing. I try to derive a measure of comfort from this fact.

Inside, I help my mother with the place settings. She asks about my day.

"Gustav fell in the river. I had to fish him out."

"Is he all right?" asks my father, poking his head through the deck door.

"As far as I can tell. Scraped his knee maybe."

"We're ready to eat."

He begins forking steaming portions of fish onto a platter and hands it to me as I step outside. I set it beside a pitcher of ice water in which bobs a solitary, vivisected lemon, and we sit down. The deck is attached to the house's second story, and commands a view of the lawn, and a swamp bordering the property. The musical sound of peepers (tiny frogs) emerges from it, reaching my family at our meal. A breeze from the lake a quarter mile through the trees carries vague, human sounds to our table. A bit of food instantly attaches itself to my father's cuirass. Everything is as it should be.

"How was your hike?" he asks.

"Gustav fell in the river."

"Yes, I know. You said that. Anything else?"

"It was nice. I prefer it to the arcade in Berlin."

"Sure, of course. Speaking of which…"

My father raises a cloth napkin from his lap, and dabs his cuirass.

"My office fielded a few calls from someone named Toby. I meant to ask you earlier when you were in the office, but you got me on Abellard and he's easy to talk about. Someone named Toby. He kept talking about sunglasses and reimbursement of some sort. Said he ran into a teacher in the mall who gave him the number."

I don't say anything.

"You wouldn't happen to know anything about that, would you?" he prods.

"No," I say. "But it sounds mysterious."

"What did you guys do in the woods?" asks my mother, bored with shoptalk.

"We had a small picnic. Gustav ate nearly everything while I wasn't looking."

"He'll do that," says my father. "You always need to watch him. Or your food."

"What kind of food did you bring?" asks my mother.

"Stuff from Guidance. Cheese, bread, a few pastries."

"Oh, right. The Collective. They make good stuff. I see people from there frequently."

My mother works as a community therapist for the Vermont Department of Health and Mental Hygiene.

"I do guardianship evaluations there from time to time," she says. "Strange place. Like a cross between a convent and kibbutz."

"This is the place with all the bald women, right?" asks my father, of no one in particular.

"Yes," I report.

"So…They use the hair to make shirts or something?" he jokes.

My mother rolls her eyes, and uses my father's praenomen to irritate him.

"It's not a cloister, Thomas. It's just a group of women who don't want to be around men. What's the problem with that?"

"No problem, Heloise. If they want to have a political preserve on a mountaintop in Danville, that's their business."

"You know," my mother says to me. "They almost got shut down a few years back."

"I never heard anything about it."

"Yes, it was kept pretty quiet."

"What happened?"

She tips some water into her wine glass. A firework explodes down by the lake, after which, a dog barks, mightily.

"Well, there was a murder in St. Johnsbury. This woman killed her husband. He was the curator at the Fairbanks Museum. You heard about this."

"Oh, right — She pushed him off the upper gallery by the Tyrannosaurus skull. But he didn't die, right?"

"Right. She strangled him with a rubber snake from the gift shop. And this was in front of people. There was a student group visiting from the academy, and a preschool program from Montpelier. It was ghastly."

"Do we need to talk about this now?" asks my father. My mother ignores him.

"But apparently when the husband was not running tours for school children, he was doing really vile things to his wife. He made her write essays, really long, academic papers, praising his…his parts."

"Heloise, come on!" says my oddly squeamish father, again invoking my mother's first name, as though it is a benediction. Again, she ignores him.

"The police found dated binders full of them. It had been going on for years. He would lock her outside the house naked for hours, sometimes in the pouring rain. There were neighbors who saw her in the backyard, begging to be let inside. Isn't that horrendous?"

"Yes," I say, nodding like a ventriloquist dummy. As I look down, I notice Eleanor's panties arranged carelessly in my shirt pocket. I try to change the subject. "But what does any of this have to do with the T.C.?"

"Well, that's where she hid out. She ditched her car by the ballfield in Cabot and hiked up to the compound. They offered her asylum, and since no men are allowed on the property, the police had to get a bunch of female officers together from all over the state. Even as far as Brattleboro. I got called in as a liaison."

"Really? Why was none of this on news?" asks my father.

"I'm not sure. But I know whoever funds the T.C. has some kind of influence. They managed to keep the story out of the papers, and none of the local news stations touched it. I only spoke with the woman they chose as a press officer or something. It was generally weird. We drank tea in the chapel until they agreed to surrender the woman. I had to sign a confidentiality agreement. We all did."

"Can they do that?" I ask.

"They did it. A few people with the state police refused and even went so far as to file charges against the T.C. They tried to shut them down. But, obviously, that didn't work."

"Where's the woman now?" asks my father.

"Newport. Northern State Correctional," says my mother, appearing to become bored with her own story. "When they brought her out, she had already shaved her head."

"I can't believe you never mentioned this to me" says my father.

"It was years ago, Thomas. I didn't think much of it at the time. And compared to visiting Belinda on Elm Street, it was a pleasant afternoon. Her bedsores have become so infected that she has begun to smell…how can I put this? Rotten. She smells of rot."

"This is me leaving," says my father, standing up from the table.

"I'll clean up," I say, standing as well. I only realize Eleanor's panties have escaped from my shirt pocket when I see them spread across my empty plate. My Mother notices instantly. My father pauses in his migration.

"There is…an…interesting story…behind this," I say, without looking at either of them, instead addressing myself to a stand of trees beyond the deck.

"Those aren't yours…" says my mother, sipping from her glass.

"No," I say. "No. They are not mine."

"No, not your color," says my father, peering over my shoulder.

"Who do they belong to?" asks my mother.

"Eleanor," I whisper.

"Oh, Eleanor's back from school?" says my mother. "You should have told us. We could have had her over tonight."

"I liked her. She was very pleasant," says my father, watching me. "Any reason her underwear is in your pocket, Marlowe?"

"She left them in my car," I say, without thinking. My mother snorts into her glass.

"We had gone swimming!" I clarify. "We had gone swimming and I… she…Eleanor changed into her suit. And left these behind. I planned to return them today. I was going to leave them in her mailbox. But Gustav was in the car, and I panicked. So…"

"You were going to leave underwear in her mailbox?" says my father.

"If you want to drop them in the basket by the basement door, I'll make sure they're clean when you return them to her," offers my mother.

"Thank you, mom. That's very nice."

I begin gathering the plates on the table, and, unsure of where else to put them, return the underwear to my pocket. My father kisses my mother on the top of her head, and asks if she would like to go for a swim. I use the momentary distraction to slip inside. I drop the plates in the kitchen sink, and run water over them, trying to recall if I have ever seen a film or read a book in which parents were forced to act as witnesses against their children.

I decline joining my parents at the lake. After they leave, I open two beers (so I will not have to get up again) and take them to the deck. I sit facing the swamp with a laptop across my knees. The hum of their car on the lower road fades to silence. Peepers peep. Crickets crick. The sun descends behind the trees.

All of Eleanor's messages are archived in my email account. I don't know exactly why I'm doing this. I suppose, I didn't give her missives much thought when I received them. They arrived every week or two, and it was nice to know she was thinking of me. Only her final message interests me tonight, a message that contains no words, but a link to a video filmed on a rooftop in Bed-Stuy. She and three other women perform a 'dance' they choreographed. The piece is untitled. The dancers stand in a square and begin by beating themselves across the breasts, like women in mourning. The two in front fall backward and are caught, then thrown forward (roughly) onto the ground. The two dancers that remain standing move to the front and begin beating themselves again. Then they fall backward, are caught, and thrown forward onto the rooftop. The 'set' consists of a screen-printed banner behind them, which seems to show a dog with unusually large feet with a motto or something printed beneath it. But I can't make it out. The video is an hour long. During previous viewings, I only managed to watch the first few minutes.

But as I begin a second beer, I manage to stomach the entire performance. I have no photographs of her. The video is the only visual evidence of Eleanor's existence I possess, and watching her movement, grotesque and removed as it is, conjures the actuality of her the day before, and the proximity of the body in the video to my own. The word for this is loss, but a strange loss when its peculiar impact is felt nearly two days afterward, like recalling a favorite jacket left on the back of a chair, in a restaurant to which I do not wish to return. It's a the sense of incompletion that prevents my mind from settling on a more cheerful subject, and thus, the only remedy is to find out what happened in the woods by the lake.

But first, I need to go out to her house in Middlesex to make sure there is no evidence linking me to it. It's been nearly two days since she disappeared, and in less than a week, her parents will return. And once they discover their daughter is gone, it won't take them long to work back to me.

But clearing the house of anything that might help them reach this conclusion should afford some time, hopefully enough to find her on my own.

Of course, it's also possible Eleanor is alive, and at home right now, angry with me, but alive. Maybe that's why she didn't call. The curator's wife in St. Johnsbury managed to outlast her partner's folly. Maybe Eleanor did the same. Either way, I won't be able to sleep unless I make sure.

5.

June 11-12, 2006, Middlesex, Vermont

I reach Eleanor's house around 11PM, ascend her perilous, guttered driveway, kill the headlights, and ease the vehicle gently into the lot beside the house. It's likely that no one is here. Still, I would prefer to draw a minimum of attention to myself if this proves incorrect. The house appears empty, but when has that phrase ever meant anything?

I walk slowly up the narrow ramp between the house and the parking area and am surprised to find the door locked. As long as I have lived with them (most of my life), my parents have never locked their door; the reasoning being that anyone willing to come all the way out to where they live to pilfer things would not be precluded from doing so by a dead bolt. Eleanor's family is situated similarly to my own, and I've never seen her lock up. And the last time she was here, I was here too. In fact, we left together. Could I have missed her doing that?

I search for a spare key in all the places one would normally be. I lift several potted begonias from their trays, displace a happy-looking Philodendron, reach above the door and slide my fingers along the transom, raise the welcome mat, and find nothing. I jiggle the handle stupidly, unsure of what to do next. I could break a window. But I am not completely sure I could do this without injuring myself. In films, people usually wrap their hand in a jacket. I have only a t-shirt, and using this would be like substituting a latex glove for an oven mitt.

But if I can find an open window, I won't have to break anything. And already I see one. About three feet to the right of the front door. Granted, there is a fifteen-foot drop beneath its sill. But it is a large portal, and if I can somehow jump from the outside of the railing (girding the drawbridge which does not draw) to the house, there is a good possibility of flinging my body through it. My confidence that this will work is neither great nor abysmal. Surely, dumber things have succeeded.

I haul myself over the railing in order to determine the best angle from which to jump. If the land were two feet closer, I would have a straight line to the window. But since it is not, I have to leap from the porch diagonally over the moat, and toward the house. Either that, or turn left in mid-air. I'm confident that if I miss, the drop will not kill me. But it will hurt, so the first try must be successful. I bend my knees as much as is allowed by the railing, and leap out, into the night.

As soon as I jump, I know something is wrong. My left foot slips a bit during takeoff, which leaves the entire leg without traction. It now dangles feeble and useless behind my body while the right is fully extended in front, which has me performing an exemplary goose step (or reverse pirouette) in midair. But what I pictured was more of a two-footed leap, in which legs and body slip through the window effortlessly, as though it is a trap door. I also forgot the possibility of an interior screen, which I only apprehend fully when my foot crashes through it, engulfing my right leg up to the thigh. My left slaps the side of the house like a shutter made of flesh, and I land squarely straddling the sill, with the full weight of my body on my testicles.

I'm in too much pain to scream. Nausea radiates from my genitals to the back of my throat, and before I even have decent purchase on the frame, I vomit beer and grilled salmon on myself. My right leg is still buried in the screen, thus suspending the limb at shoulder level. My genitals are the only body part on which I can rest, and with each attempt to free my leg from the screen, they are pressed and dragged along the sill. I cannot let go, because if I fall, I will land on my head. How fitting it would be for Eleanor's parents to return from Hyannis or wherever they are, and find me covered in vomit, wedged in the canyon between their house and the car park. They would say they had seen it coming, but did not expect my demise to take place on the property. If nothing else, that will surprise them.

My hands are slick with sweat and vomit and it seems like a fall is the only outcome available at this time. I have no knowledge of prayer but if this is in fact my last moment alive, I would prefer to be more comfortable. I gingerly remove one hand from the frame and extract a crumpled pack of cigarettes from my pocket. I withdraw one with my mouth and place the carton on the sill. I need to switch hands to retrieve my lighter, which nearly falls to the ground during ignition.

There is a small body of research that suggests cigarettes temporarily sharpen mental acuity, and this is perhaps the reason I remember the car keys in my pocket. I remove the ring, and place the largest in the hole below my leg. Sawing through a window screen is not fast or easy work, but it's fortunate that my car is a Precambrian Volvo with an ignition key like the lower jaw of crocodile. After several minutes, I manage to create a rent large enough to drop my leg on the floor within. This happens with some immediacy. The leg swings down, wrenching the remainder of my body through the window, and I am so happy to be alive that I barely feel my head clonk wickedly against the frame on the way through it. I'm completely satisfied. My plan worked. I'm inside.

I'm not fond of this house. But objectively, it's quite nice. The furniture and appliances are tasteful, and expensive. The residual portion of the geodesic dome is now an atrium of sorts, through which sunlight shines during the day, and the stars at night. The two additional wings are expansive, and enjoy a complement of large windows and delicate, inoffensive paint. A realtor might describe the abode as 'bright, airy, and welcoming.'

But I've never felt welcome here, and Eleanor's parents are responsible. Like figures taken from a Gothic portrait, their eyes seemed to follow me wherever I went, even when they were on the opposite side of the house, or absent from it. And even now, when I know with certainty that they're likely taking the sun on the porch of rented bungalow along Shore Road, with Pilgrim Lake at their backs, and the Provincetown Harbor glittering before them, even now, Eleanor's mother and father intend a menacing, wraith-like station in each corner of the house.

Her mother is a slight, shapeless woman with a merlot colored bowl-cut (when I saw her last), so inoffensive, and easily concealed, that she often startled me by appearing places I did not expect (issuing like demonic smoke from between the floorboards, for example). Her father is short, and roughly pear-shaped, with thinning, long gray hair that he censures in a samurai-like topknot (similar to Lucia's). Though this composite requires nothing further, he also maintains (when I saw him last) a dreadful Fu-Manchu through which he would, on occasion, adjudicate. I learned to fear them early, him in particular. But I am inside, they are not, and I have work to do.

In the kitchen, I remove a black plastic garbage bag from beneath the sink, and begin collecting anything in the house that might indicate I've been here. I unscrew the damaged window screen, and wipe vomit and cigarette ash from the sill. I can't replace the thing, but the absence of evidence is not evidence (I hope). Outside, I comb through the grass at the bottom of the gully, searching for my cigarette butt. I've heard they can pull DNA off these, but my search yields nothing. I could always say I stopped by and no one was here. A butt, if discovered, proves nothing (I hope). I should really focus my attention indoors.

I take the entire trash from the bathroom, because there might be a condom (or two) hibernating within it. A bar of bristling soap and Eleanor's toothbrush (I used it on the first night) go in the bag as well. In curating this growing collection of incriminating items, I appear thorough. But somewhere between the bathroom and Eleanor's bedroom, it occurs to me that I probably should have worn gloves. Though I've never been arrested, my fingerprints are filed with the sheriff's department in Montpelier, since my work for Pitkin Union School required bonding. Too late now, but I can still minimize my chances.

In the kitchen, once again, I remove two smaller plastic bags from beneath the sink, and pull these over my hands. I cinch them at the wrists with rubber bands, and do the same to my feet to ameliorate the risk of tracking trace evidence around the house. My breadth of knowledge involving the actual constitution of evidence is derived entirely from hearsay, and a forensic anthropology class I took during my first (and final) term in Ohio, a body of knowledge slightly better than nothing.

In Eleanor's room, I dig through her laundry basket while trying to recall the exact pairing of undergarments she wore during the nights we spent together. It's a humbling exercise, since Eleanor was in the habit of changing her outfit several times a day, and women's underwear all looks the same to me. Defeated, I tip the entire hamper into the bag, figuring I'll sort through it later, and return anything unincriminating. And then I hear a noise. A step, followed by a rustling drag, like a bare foot on a wooden floor. In the mirrored face of a closet door across the room, I catch the furtive reflection of a round head and narrow shoulders retreating through the bedroom door directly behind me. I stand, dropping the bag and swaying a bit. Could this stranger be Eleanor? Maybe she escaped from the woods, and was asleep downstairs for some reason when she heard me banging around up here. I need to let her know it's me. She shouldn't be frightened.

"Eleanor?" I say, walking toward the door. "Eleanor, it's me, I just…"

As soon as I step through the egress, something crashes against the side of my head. I make a strangely affirmative noise, and drop to the floor of the hallway. A foot collides with my groin, once, twice, and a third time. I curl into a ball using my bagged hands to protect my face and nether parts from further assault, but none arrive. Instead, the light turns on.

"Oh, shit," says a vaguely familiar voice.

"Eleanor?" I burble, peeking between plastic-wrapped fingers.

Standing above me is the beautiful clerk I admired earlier that day in Guidance, dressed for casual sleep in a tank top and boxer shorts. Stubble has just begun to show on her recently sheared scalp, which gleams beneath the overhead light. In one hand she holds a wooden mallard belonging to Eleanor's father (he collects these), and not intended for use as a bludgeon (though in this case, he would be proud). She blinks behind a pair of thick spectacles similar to my own.

"I know you," I say, pointing at her. "You sold me cheese."

"I'm sorry," she says, setting the mallard on the floor. "I didn't realize…"

"Didn't realize…what?"

She shakes her head, as though just beginning to absorb the situation.

"What are you doing here?"

"You recognize me, don't you? I recognize you."

"Yes, you're sort of familiar. But what are you doing here?"

"I came to look for her. For Eleanor."

She looks at my feet and hands.

"Why are you wearing plastic bags on your hands? And feet?"

"I can explain. Really. I can explain everything. Please."

She removes her glasses, and places a hand on her hip.

"Fine. But if you do anything, or try anything, anything even slightly weird…or weirder, I guess, I have a Taser," she says, sniffing. "God, and you stink like vomit. Take a shower. I'll make some coffee."

She pads down the hall toward the atrium. I hoist myself up and limp after her, somewhat surprised at her lack of surprise, but it is a feeling easily outweighed by the sheer relief of her having chosen the mallard rather than Taser with which to subdue me. I earmark her apology at having mistaken me for a genuine prowler, figuring I'll ask her about it later if she doesn't explain it herself. And since she probably doesn't know that I know about Eleanor's disappearance, she could reveal something important. We don't know each other, and the young woman who sold me cheese earlier today could be anyone. Even the culprit.

6.

January 15th - April 7th, 2006, Julian Falls, Ohio

The village of Julian Falls (pop. 3,917) is one part tourist attraction to two parts college town, and during winter has very little to recommend it. But by mid-April, the two main streets, Corry and Dayton, are a sideshow of motorcycle clubs, exurban families from Columbus, and young, upwardly mobile day-trippers from Cincinnati. The bikers drink and sit on the shaded terrace attached to The Olde Tavern, watching student girls with hairy legs and underarms pass on their way to the nature preserve, Skinny Glen (named for Balthazar Skinny, a slave who purchased his freedom, and some land, in the 1860's and bequeathed it to the town upon his death) across Corry Street with an admixture of desire and shame. The families from Columbus stop at Youngstown Dairy off route 343 for ice cream and a few holes of mini-golf, before coming to 'The Falls' to cool off and shop. And the active young couples with one dog and no children walk the Little Miami (a hiking trail named for the railroad which helped the town prosper) and visit the titular falls set deep in the Glen. An interesting fact: a unique combination of iron ore, copper deposits, and refraction can, at a certain time of day, make the water issuing from between the two stout rocks appear iridescent. In short, Julian Falls is what passes for a destination location in southern Ohio, and is the sort of place Pitkin might be if it had retained its accompanying Quaker school.

St. Margaret University, the college providing the town with a steady influx of students (and money, more or less) was founded in 1853. It is a small, private campus (one mile square) of red brick, black alder, and arborvitae. As the program of studies hinges on a sequence of internships

paired with periods of study, the on-campus population drastically fluctu-
ates between three and six hundred.

The term I entered MU (Spring, 2006), there were eighty-nine students
attending it. It was January, six months before Eleanor reappeared in my life
and then disappeared entirely from it. My class was composed of myself, a
townie attending part time to study botany, and a blind girl with an eating
disorder. I knew enrollment had dropped significantly in the past years. But
I did not realize that the school was also without a president. My entering
class (all three of us) was welcomed by the man acting in this facility during
the interim, Martin Bastarde (rhymes with Bacardi). We sat in a wood-pan-
eled lounge beside the cafeteria, while he waited for the rest of the entering
class to arrive. When none did, he ceased nibbling on his fist, and seemed
to regard the three of us for the first time.

"Hello. And welcome."

The animal he most closely resembled was a kind of burrowing rodent.
His large yellow eyes panned the empty room, as though the world above
ground was alien and potentially threatening.

"This…"

He waved his hand at a large window behind him, through which the
silhouette of Main Building stood like a vacant winter fortress. His train of
thought appeared to have met with an ambush.

"This…is…a very special place…"

The claim sounded tall, if not outright false. But at the time, I was as
lost in my environment as the interim president appeared to be. I had never
visited the Midwest and, being from the Northeast, was stunned by the
amount of flat land, churches, and obese people. My mother drove me
through an ice storm in Pennsylvania, and as our car sped along the empty
road littered with an apocalyptic wreckage of trees, power lines, and hob-
bled vehicles, I felt that I had inadvertently applied for admission to some
polar annex of hell. When we stopped for gas outside Mesopotamia, and
parked the car beside a horse and buggy, in which several Anabaptists shiv-
ered, I asked my mother if we could turn back. It was a bad idea. I wanted
to go home. She patted my knee and told me everything would be fine once

we got to Julian Falls. And, in a way, it was. The town, with its artisanal shops, bookstores, and import salons felt closer to Pitkin than anything else. I could survive here. No matter what, I would make it work.

Four months later (mid April), I was in a disused office on the top floor of South Hall facing Martin Bastarde again. Two diffuse young women, Rage and Douglas, both students and ranking members of the Community Standards Board, flanked the interim president. They (Rage and Douglas) were also dating. The window was open, and through it, I heard the sounds of many people (in call and response) chanting below.

"Whaddawewant?"

"Safety!"

"Whendawewantit?"

"Now!"

Every other verse, the organizer would substitute 'justice' for 'safety.' Martin asked me a question I did not hear. I asked if we could close the window.

"No," he said, glancing to both his left and right. "No, I think it should remain…open."

I slumped in my chair. The night before, I had slept on an old golf course abutting campus. No matter how I sat, I still felt the ground pressing against my body.

"I asked, Marlowe," said Martin, "if you have a place to stay?"

"Yes," I lied, scratching a sunburn, which was beginning to show on my face. The grass was soft on the golf course, but there was no shade. I woke that morning boiled in my clothes, with the sun directly overhead.

"Well," said Martin, shuffling his papers, and buttoning his blazer. "This decision really makes itself then, doesn't it?"

The two hulking woman nodded their agreement. Martin inclined an ear to the shouting beneath the window, and stood, looking at me.

"Marlowe, why don't you leave with me through the back. I can drop you wherever you like."

I shrugged and ambled after him, down four flights of stairs to the small staff lot behind the building.

"This heat is something else. But hey! I have AC in the car," he quipped, unlocking the passenger door for me. I stood dumbly beside the vehicle, one hand on the window. The shouting was moving around the building, toward us.

"We'd better go," said Martin, but I didn't move. He walked around the car, and opened the door.

"There is no guarantee that I can protect you once those people come around the building. You need to get in the car."

I was still listening. I may not have heard him.

"Look, some things are just shitty. That's occasionally how it is. Part of growing up is realizing that nothing you do will be rewarded and punishment is arbitrary. I'm sorry, Marlowe, but you need to get in the car."

"What about winning a victory for humanity. Isn't that in the mission statement? "

"Right, right, right," said Martin, pushing me into the passenger seat. He ran to his side and tapped on the window to be let in. Greer appeared around the corner of South Hall, gesturing and shouting. Martin's tapping became more rapid. I popped the lock and he sat down heavily in the driver's seat, starting the car and spinning it out of the lot just as several more students emerged in Greer's wake.

"Be ashamed to die until you do it," said Martin, turning onto Livermore Street and glancing nervously in his rear view. "Win a victory for humanity. But one man's victory is another man's holocaust. Think about it. Those people believed in an order that isn't there. They proceeded from a false premise. So don't feel bad. Do you know the story of Saint Margaret?"

I shook my head. Martin continued speaking.

"Margaret the virgin was disowned by her father for being a Christian, and refusing to marry Olybrius, the governor of the Eastern Roman diocese, because he demanded that she renounce her faith. So she was tortured, like you do with a martyr. But during this torture, Satan adopted the form of a dragon, and swallowed her. Imagine that. Margaret escaped alive because she had a crucifix that gave the dragon indigestion. My point is that things could be worse for you."

I didn't say anything. We drove in silence until we reached Dayton Street.

"Do you need any money or anything?" asked Martin.

"I'd like some."

Martin handed me forty dollars and his card.

"If you have any trouble, you call me. We're out of here in a few days. You can make it."

"Here is fine."

He dropped me at the corner of Corry and Dayton. I walked across the intersection and bought a twelve pack of beer, cigarettes, and a bag of potato chips at the gas station. I had a flight out of Dayton in a few days. Until then, I did not want to leave the village. Everything in the surrounding area was likely worse, even with the threat of grievous bodily harm factored in. I doubled back toward the college, and walked up the bike path heading for the golf course. It was unlikely anyone would find me out there. And there was enough open ground so that if they did, I would see them coming.

*

June 12th, 2006, Middlesex, Vermont

The beautiful woman who smashed me over the head with the wooden mallard is named Lola, and as it turns out, she has little more right to be in the house than I do. After finishing at the bakery, she came down from Danville to see Eleanor. A friend from the T.C. dropped her at the base of the driveway with her overnight bag. After knocking for a while, circumnavigating the house, and peering through windows, she let herself in (the door was unlocked), assuming Eleanor would show up later.

"The two of you had plans?" I ask, not really interested in the answer at this point. I'm fixing a cup of coffee in the kitchen with a towel around my waist. Lola is sitting on a couch in the atrium, watching me. Our mutual suspicion has faded to something between interest and boredom.

"Well, yes and no. I got in a week ago and settled in at the farm and called her," says Lola. "She said to come by whenever. She wasn't doing anything important. But you saw her."

"Yes, I did," I say, walking into the living area and sitting across from her in one Eleanor's father's armchairs. "But I haven't seen her since I saw her. I got nervous. And…I just assumed the worst."

"So…that's why you were sneaking around here? And digging through her laundry?"

"That's right."

Lola sits quietly, nodding to herself. I sip my coffee.

"That makes no sense," she says.

"Well, I appreciate you being so hospitable, despite the confusion."

"If you were any less threatening, you'd be furniture."

I absorb this, because as far as Lola knows, the circumstance surrounding Eleanor's disappearance has nothing to do with me. I'm merely a concerned, and somewhat supra-paranoid friend whose calls were suddenly not returned.

"How did you even get inside?" asks Lola.

"Through a window."

"But I locked all the ones on the first floor."

"Yes, but a few were left open on the second."

"But…"

"I found a way."

We both want cigarettes, and repair to the deck. Outside, it is an utterly silent, clear night with a balmy summer wind rolling up the hill toward the house. Lola reclines in the chaise occupied by Eleanor only days before. And once again, I sit like a dutiful pet at her side.

"You don't think we should call her parents?" she asks.

"They're in Massachusetts. I don't have a number. And I wouldn't know where to look."

"And you didn't call the police, right?"

"No…" I venture, nervously. "Do you think we should?"

"I'd prefer we didn't. I have a record."

"Like…a criminal record?"

She nods, examining her fingernails.

"Can I ask why?"

"Misdemeanor assault."

"You?"

"Yes, me!" she says, indignantly. "Some kingshit groped me on the Metro North, and I fucked him up. That's what happened. If I had the chance, I would do it again, only worse."

"What happened?"

"I had headphones on. I had hair back then. Maybe I looked more inviting. I didn't see him when he sat down next to me. I was looking out the window. It was some drunk kid from Saratoga on his way home. I think his friends put him up to it or something, because they were across the aisle, watching, like four other guys. The kid tried to talk to me, and I couldn't hear him because of the music, and he went to remove one of the earphones and felt him touch me and that was it. I pulled his card."

"What did you do?"

"I broke his nose with my elbow."

"Sounds like he had it coming."

"And two of his teeth."

"Ah…"

"And bruised his testicles."

"Fine."

The recollection is infuriating her, but my curiosity, as someone who has never been in a fight or arrested, is overwhelming.

"So you…went to prison?" I ask.

"No, I went to jail, not prison. And I was out in the morning."

"What happened to the kid from the train?"

"Nothing. His dad is a former district attorney. The little shit studies American history at Skidmore. I got fined, and probation since it was my first offense. And I'm a student."

"And you're still on probation?"

"Yes."

"So, no police, then?"

"No police. Please."

I don't need a partner in my investigation. But I have to reveal something to explain my unusual presence in the house and divest myself of suspicion. And I couldn't ask for better sidekick in my search. Lola is beautiful, fearful of authority, and suspicious, like a female version of myself (slightly upgraded). She catches my eye lingering on her thighs, but seems not to mind. I ask her what she studies.

"Well, I'm doing a double-major. Women's studies, and accounting."

"Hedging your bets?"

"Don't judge me, dropout," she hisses, flicking a butt onto the lawn.

"Wait…how did you know…that I left school?"

She doesn't respond.

"Lola. How did you know that?"

"Eleanor mentioned it to me."

"Did she talk about me often?"

"No, she didn't talk about anyone often. She just said she had a dropout fuckbuddy at home. I assumed she meant you."

"When was this?"

"I don't know, after I got here sometime. We talked on the phone a few times. She said she was hanging out with you some. That's all."

"What did she say about me?"

"I told you. Nothing."

"I just never thought…"

"You thought she was ashamed of you? That she wanted to keep you a secret?"

"Yes. Something like that."

Lola snorts.

"Eleanor was never good at keeping secrets. Even her own."

Lola and I continue talking late into the night, graduating from coffee to wine (to whiskey by 3AM), and speaking almost entirely about Eleanor's life during the year of silence between us. I assume she and Eleanor are classmates, but Lola says this is incorrect. She (Lola) attends school in Bronxville, and only goes to the city once or twice a week, and rarely ends up in Brooklyn. She met Eleanor through a dance company, though company is not the right word. It was a loose affiliation of young, single female transplants that called themselves an arts collective.

"It just made sense. Eleanor had so many friends with common interests," says Lola. "There were derby girls from Iowa. Rooftop agriculturalists from Montana. Circulation clerks from Michigan. One of them knew a few people in Long Island City who were into graffiti and they knew someone else in East Williamsburg who had a performance space and was familiar with a group of people who liked to get together and talk shit in Scarsdale."

She continues her index of places I have never been, and people I have never met. The point is that the group convened regularly at The Artery on Oxford Street because the bar was a neutral location that allowed smoking on a back terrace.

Lola says they had trouble finding a name for the group. Black Girls was suggested, though all the members were white (the name quickly drowned in its own irony). Les Miseradical (a few had a background in musical theater). The Baby-sitters Club. None really stuck until Bench, a lesbian plumber and multi-instrumentalist who lived at C Squat in Loisaida, suggested Femammals. Everyone seemed to like that.

"A Polish girl from Greenpoint silk-screened t-shirts, and patches," says Lola. "A pair of computer science students at Stony Brook made a website and Facebook profile. And the graffiti team in Astoria and lower Manhattan tagged a few locations with our logo." The logo is a kind of deranged looking Hyena with high heels and a purse, and constitutes the odd backdrop in the video of Eleanor dancing on a rooftop in Bed-Stuy.

In short, a hobby was born. According to Lola, if you live in the city, you might have seen them among the vendors in Union Square or Prospect Park on weekends. You might have heard someone reading poetry through a bullhorn ("Your face is a toilet / Your heart is a rape," that sort of thing) while several young women in costumes (animal, usually) or leotards, danced and posed to the unmusic. Make no mistake: the Femammal's work was not overtly political. Instead, it occupied a hazy, no-man's land (none allowed, apparently) in which a bystander might infer a topical undertone if it pleased them, or they might not. The performances were often ambivalent and didactic at the same time. Whether the subtitle appearing beneath the Hyena developed as a sort of mission statement before or after the work established its tenor is a mystery. In any case, for all those who seek to penetrate (wrong word) it, a quick glance at any of the t-shirts, patches, or badges produced by Grushenka on Manhattan Avenue might prove edifying: FEMAMMALS NYC: IT'S NOT OUR JOB TO EDUCATE YOU!

Lola writes poetry and dances. She tells me it was the prospect of being able to explore both interests among a group of strong, supportive women that brought her to Brooklyn. The lines quoted above are her own, from a poem entitled "I Spit on His Grave." It is published in Femammal Report #10 (someone knew a woman in Borough Park with a printing press). When I mention the video I received before Eleanor ended all communication with me, Lola knows the exact performance it documents, because she is in it. Lola is the dancer directly behind Eleanor, though I excuse myself for not recognizing her, because in the video, she has hair. She also helped choreograph the performance.

$$7.$$

.

June 12th, 2006, Middlesex, Vermont

It's Saturday morning, and I'm stirring a coffee (intended for Lola) in the kitchen by the sink and watching a hummingbird vibrate around a feeder outside the window. Since my clothing stank of fish, sweat, and vomit, I'm naked, aside from a ridiculous pair of Eleanor's yoga shorts, while my clothes tumble in a dryer downstairs. The shorts are impolite to say the least. The legs are short and banded with elastic, which has the benefit of preventing my parts from dangling below them. But the waist is quite high, the ass baggy, and the color a stubborn shade of orange. Since I do not intend to leave the house this way, no harm done. But as I pass a mirror in the hall on my way downstairs, I cannot help but feel like the poolside attendant of some troubled dowager empress.

The morning is lovely. The house's 'light' and 'airy' qualities flood even the lower story with sun and oxygen filtered through the verdure outside. I tap lightly on the door of Lola's room, (once again) checking the space on my wrist where a watch should be. Judging by the arc of sunlight invading the kitchenette, it's likely around 9AM. I tap again, and feel stupid. I'm holding a cup of coffee, which I plan to present to Lola. If I retreat, it will get cold and the cream will congeal on the surface. I turn the handle, muttering gently.

"Good Morning, Lola…"

In a wash of sunlight from the sliding doors, Lola reclines on the bed, softly nude as a Modigliani. One of her unshaven ankles is crossed over the other, the knee bent at an acute angle toward the door as though indicating it. Her arms rest across her breasts, which, I note with a certain greed, are round as pumpkins and capped with stem-like, slightly too long nipples. I catalogue the hair beneath her arms, ranging wild in contrast to that atop her head, which is absent, recall. The weightless inhalation of her slumber rolls from her lungs to her belly, which is taught, bronzed, and inviting. Like the cool stone deep inside the woodland, I wish to rest my face upon it. In following from underarms to calves, it only makes sense that the mound of her pubic bone should be grown over, tangled and black as a Teutonic nature preserve. Perhaps judging the chance of a prowler as statistically quite low after my midnight incursion, she has left the terrace doors open, and through them, a moist wind carries the briny, slept-in scent of her from the bed to my nostrils as I stand upon the threshold.

I'm unsure what to do next. Walking over to the bed and shaking her awake is out of the question. My scrotum has experienced enough in the past twenty-four hours. I could shout to wake her up, but that seems crude. Leaving is always possible, but I like it here much better than upstairs. The problem resolves itself as I notice her watching me in the doorway. Lola's dark eyes observe my nervous tenure for only a moment before she speaks.

"Is that for me, Marlowe?"

Briefly, I think she might mean the bruised penis of average size concealed within my ochre diaper. But her gaze is focused on the cup steaming in my hand.

"Yes," I say, without moving.

"Do I have to come get it?"

"No."

I pad across the carpet and set the mug on the nightstand before turning mechanically and walking back to the doorway. She sips the coffee, her eyes remaining focused on me.

"You're not shy," I say, attempting levity.

Lola reclines, recrossing her legs with the cup in her hand.

"This is the body's natural state. Sexual modesty is the provision of idiots."

"I see."

"You can look at my cunt," she says.

"Thank you," I reply, wincing at the idiom, and trying to find something else to look at.

"That word bothers you?"

"No. Yes. I don't know. It's crude."

"If a cock were called a cunt, would it still be crude?"

"I don't know."

"But you don't feel the same about the two words. Cock is…sexy?"

"A cock is also a farm bird."

" 'I want to suck your cock.' Is that sexy? Does it turn you on?"

"Yes. I'm sorry. Yes."

"Don't be. But if I told you to 'eat my cunt,' what would you say?"

"Yes."

"No, no, I meant how would you feel?"

"Privileged."

"That's flattering, but not what I'm getting at."

"Please, Lola. Don't use me as a deconstructionist trampoline. I haven't had breakfast yet."

She sets the cup on the bedside table and stands up, arching her back and inclining her torso in my direction.

"I'm going to shower," she says, looking me up and down. "What are you wearing?"

"Something of Eleanor's. My clothes are in the laundry."

"You look bizarre. Are those yoga shorts?"

"I am bizarre. Yes. I think so."

"You know," says Lola over her shoulder as she walks to the guest bathroom. Her strangely tan buttocks are smooth as the backs of two recently clubbed seals drawn fresh from the surf. "If you stopped drinking and falling through windows, you might not be so bizarre. You should work out."

"Can I watch you shower?" I ask, hopefully.

"I'm going to take a shit and read a magazine first. So there will be a wait."

I go back upstairs and remove my clothes from the dryer. I slip the shorts off by the washing machine and examine myself, pinching my soft middle and feeling my vestigial biceps. I could stand to do something with myself. Eliminate all the conditions and join the limited ranks of attractive people. But women seem to like me well enough in my current shape. And what would I hope to gain? As long as they remain willing to settle, and I remain happy with what I can get, there is no reason for anything to change.

I offer to drive Lola back to the bakery in Danville, mostly because I'm glad of her company. When she comes outside an hour later, I'm spraying flecks of the previous night's dinner off the side of the house with a garden hose. She says nothing, but gets in the car.

Since she is unfamiliar with the route, I extend it by driving through Worcester. I keep waiting for her to start a conversation. After the morning's familiarity, the silence is surprising.

"So. You're at the bakery today?" I ask, knowing the answer.

"Yes."

"Will I see you again?"

Lola ignores the question, watching the landscape pass through the window.

"This isn't the way I came. Do you know where you're going?"

"Yes. I go there all the time."

"You're not taking me into the woods to cut me up or anything?"

"No," I declare, locking my eyes on the horizon. "Absolutely not."

We continue driving in silence, but as we begin to approach East Calais, I ask Lola how she became involved with the Theodora Collective.

"I'm an intern. Or I should say, I'm interning."

"For, like, credit?" I ask.

"Right. I help out wherever they need free labor. Mostly it's the store in town."

"The school I went to did that. Internships, that is."

"A lot of places do it."

"Yes, but there it was part of the program. You couldn't escape."

I see the cupola atop the first house before you enter the village of East Calais.

"Where did you go?" asks Lola, searching for something in her bag.

"St. Margaret University."

Lola pauses in her hunt, regarding me.

"That's the place with the…what is it? The sexual offense policy? It was on T.V. in the eighties."

" 'Preventing Offenses, Opening Paths, Ending Rape.' "

"Right," says Lola. "That's the one. You were supposed to gain explicit consent for every base right? You couldn't just charge around them."

"You were supposed to."

"You didn't?"

"No one did. The only thing anyone asked for when you got them in bed was to please not ask every time you remove a sock. It murdered the mood."

"A man would say that."

"I'm not gay. These were women. Women with me. In my room. Of their own free will."

"Right."

Lola continues digging, but notices the sign for the general store up ahead.

"Can we stop here? I'd like a coffee."

I put on my turn signal. Lola pauses in her rooting.

"Do you have a pen?" she asks.

"Probably somewhere. Try in the glove compartment," I say, without thinking. Lola reaches forward and twists the nob.

*

November 17th, 2004, North Calais, Vermont

Though Eleanor might have blamed me, I never felt the circumstances surrounding our parting before she left for New York were entirely my fault. Her parents certainly did. But in this case, it seemed that in order for me to shoulder the responsibility, I would have needed advance knowledge of events to come.

For instance, I would have known that Frank Huff (a college friend of Eleanor's parents) probably woke that morning at his home on Liberty Street in Montpelier, looked out the bedroom window, saw the fresh snowfall glittering in the sun, and resolved that no Sunday was as good as this one to take his wife (Cora) and their two small children (Ray and Veda) on an excursion to the woods beside the lake. He could have chosen any place. Hubbard Park was within walking distance, and Groton State Forest was a short drive. What made him choose the lake? No one could have predicted that.

But the geometry of a disaster is always perfect in retrospect. When Eleanor told me later that Frank attended Greatwood College with her father and mother during the seventies, and that since the age of thirteen she spent many weekends at the house on Liberty Street, looking after Ray and Veda (though after this particular Sunday, the engagements ended abruptly), it seemed the events that took place later in the afternoon couldn't have been better designed to foster our disunion.

While a snowy Sunday in November meant a family excursion for the Huff household, for me, it meant dressing like a woodsman, donning snowshoes, and disappearing for several hours in the woods beside the lake with Eleanor. But, had I known what was coming, why wouldn't I have postponed our excursion? Later, during the assignment of blame, I was treated as though I had failed to consult my pocket oracle, or in doing so, heard its warnings perfectly, and chosen to ignore them.

But I was unaware that my choices on that snowy Sunday invited the venomous mouth of blame to close upon my head (like a garter snake swallowing a field mouse), which is why Eleanor was naked and shivering in the snow, during our last afternoon as a couple. The hair on her head and between her legs was a brilliant red exposed against the pale middle ground of the clearing in which she stood. Her flushed skin was only a shade darker than the snowfall. Her back was straight, her legs wide (and anchored by snowshoes), and her hands on her hips. She watched me.

I sat across the clearing on log, watching her. Her breath was a cloud, the vapor escaping her lungs the only movement between us. I rose from the fallen tree and tromped over to her in my own snowshoes. I was wearing dungarees, a (red and black) checked woolen shirt, and a bright orange stocking cap. I had not shaved for several days. Stubble budded on my chin and neck.

"What you doin' here?" I asked, affecting a certain homespun twang.

"Nothing," she replied, cocking her head.

"You know this ain't your land?"

"Really?"

"Nope. This here land's posted."

"I don't care."

I put my hands on my hips, and leaning back in my snowshoes.

"Now look here, missy. I hold no quarter with that sorta smartmouth."

"Fuck you, appleknocker. I do as I please," said Eleanor, turning to go.

"Afraid not, missy. I've had about enough of that lip."

I grabbed her wrist, spinning her away from me.

"Unhand me you shitheel!" shouted Eleanor. She tried to pull her hand away, but I held it tight.

"Sorry, missy, but you need a lesson. Turn 'round."

She spit on my shirt, and I grabbed her other wrist, spinning her arms into a basket hold.

"Good girl. Now lean up on that there birch and shush."

I released her hands, which she wrapped around the birch tree I'd suggested. I put a hand on her lower back and pushed it down, so that her rump tilted upward, toward me.

"Now be a good girl, and keep your hands where I can see 'em."

Her breath remained between us.

I assume Frank's plan was to picnic at the inlet. There were wooden tables left out by irresponsible summer people. With the houses cold and vacant on the shore, and the frozen surface of the lake dotted here and there only by a clapboard shanty housing a solitary, alcoholic ice-fisherman, it was cozy, and quite private. Unless two groups of people choose to converge upon it. Then it is no longer private. But apparently, this did not occur to Frank or Cora. It was likely that the family would enjoy their meal alone.

Eleanor and I ate earlier. We were near the beach, and could see the pale expanse of ice through the trees. She was still bent against the birch. Papery bark curled between her fingers. The muscles in her back moved like the winnowing folds of snow across the ground. I had a hand in her hair, tugging the red coil as though ringing a stubborn bell. We spoke little.

The wintery cloak surrounding our congress swallowed whatever sound escaped it, but the fact that we did not hear them is extraordinary. Ray and Veda were gamboling about the forest, shaking the snow from trees and throwing it at each other and their parents, who walked calmly behind, speaking in a medium tone. Which of us saw the other first is hard to gauge. I know I met Frank's eyes while still inside his children's babysitter.

In short, the Huff family picnic was ruined. After this unfortunate sight, Frank gathered his family and returned to the car, bundled them into it, and drove back to Liberty Street. I doubt he wrestled much with his role in the afternoon's events. Of course, both Eleanor and I were of age. But theory is as much a departure from practice as a photograph is from its subject. Eleanor spent time around his children. He made the call.

"I just feel…that I needed to tell you, because…Well, frankly, Oliver (Eleanor's father's praenomen) if Ray or…my god, if Veda were…doing that…you know…Doing that where people could see…I just…Well, I wouldn't want to know, but I should know. A parent should know. I guess I would want you and Lydia (her mother's) to do the same," said Frank.

"I understand, Frank…You said he…You said he was wearing…some sort of outfit?" replied Oliver.

"Right, yes. Like…Do you really want to know this Oliver, I mean it was vulgar. Really just, strange and…vulgar."

"Just tell me."

"Like…some sort of lumber…like…someone paid to cut down trees. A logger?"

"A logger."

"Right."

"That's fucked up, Frank."

"I know, man."

"I mean…we did some wild stuff…when we were at Greatwood…"

"Right."

"But…"

"But she's your daughter."

"Yes. She's my daughter."

"Are you okay?"

"Yes. Not thrilled. But fine."

"I thought I heard a whimper. Or like, a whine or something…It's okay…You don't have to act fine with me if your not."

"No, like I said. I'm fine. I just need to have a talk with that pervert. And her.

"Maybe Lydia should handle that. Do you want Cora to call?"

"No, that's fine, Frank. I can handle it."

"Are you sure you're all right, man? That whimper again…Your asthma acting up?"

The 'whimper' was in fact my own, and it was not a whimper. I was holding my breath to keep from being heard. But some of it squeaked out. I had picked up the spare line downstairs to call my own parents and would have hung it up again, had I not immediately grasped the thread of the conversation. Eleanor insisted on going straight home after the debacle in the woods, unsure of whether or not Frank would call, but wanting to be present in case he did. I had some unrelated errands to complete in town, where she was planning to drop me after a brief stop at her house to un-plug the answering machine. But her parents arrived shortly after us, and since we drove in Eleanor's car, they had no idea I was in the house, eaves-dropping in an anteroom in the opposing wing, my ear sweating against the receiver.

Eleanor returned from the bathroom as I was dropping the phone deli-cately back in the cradle.

"I need to leave," I said. "Right now."

"Was that Frank?"

"Your father wants to have a talk with me."

"It's two hundred yards to the road if you go straight through the woods. I'll meet you there."

As I snuck through the house's lower story, I was terrified at any mo-ment that Lydia would emerge from behind a potted plant and apprise Oliver. I inched the sliding door open and clomped across the deck, sprint-ing the fifty or so feet through the snow to the tree cover just as her father appeared on a Juliet balcony attached to the second story. He had not seen me, but he heard me yelp like a kicked dog when my shoe caught on a root just inside the trees, and I rolled like a fleshy barrel into a snarl of brambles. I lay in it for some time, attempting to delicately extract myself, but lost patience, wrenching my body from the frozen thorns, and leaving strips of skin and clothing behind as I plodded down the hill to the road.

Eleanor never met me. I walked the five miles to Montpelier and called my mother from a pay phone beside city hall. It had started to snow.

*

June 12th, 2006, East Calais, Vermont

I manage to park the Volvo outside the general store before Lola asks any questions. Instead, she stares at the bunched collection of Eleanor's clothing in her lap, which exploded from the dash compartment like a death's-head jack-in-the-box. I switch off the engine and undo my seat belt in case she tries to run away. She is probably faster than me, and even if I caught her, I have no idea what I would do next.

"What is this?" Lola asks, holding the skirt and tank top in either hand. She examines a stain on the skirt. "Is this…blood?"

"Yes," I say without thinking. Lola looks horrified. I clarify. "It's my blood. From my mouth. I tumbled into a…hole…of some sort."

Lola remains speechless.

"Look, I didn't hurt her. I wouldn't do that. She disappeared. It wasn't my fault. She was supposed to meet me. And when she wasn't there…"

"Why are her clothes in your car?"

"She left them. With me. She did. I can show you the place."

"The hunting thing?" Lola asks incautiously.

I open and close my mouth a few times like a dog catching raindrops. Words escape me. Lola should not know about that. I stare through the windshield at the store's façade, thoroughly shamed.

"She told me," Lola says.

"Why did she tell you?"

"It came up. We were at the Artery, drinking and discussing men. Girls talk."

"Eleanor shouldn't have done that."

"Maybe you shouldn't have left her in the woods."

"I didn't leave her in the woods. There was nothing I could do. I looked. I went back. Someone even took a picture of me while I was out there. I just…"

Lola grabs my jaw in her small hand, wrenching my face to the side. She is looking at me, and autonomically, I pucker up, because who knows? A kiss may be likely.

"God, you're disgusting," she says, giving my head a shake. "Look at me. You swear, you promise, that you didn't hurt her. She is not a lampshade in your house."

"I live with my parents."

"That's not the right answer."

"I wouldn't hurt her, Lola. I cared about her. She was very special. I wanted her."

She releases my face, tossing it backward into the window.

"I almost believe you. All told, you're too dim to be truly malevolent. Buy me a coffee."

As we enter the store, it's obvious Irma believes Lola is terminally ill. Her flat, black eyes linger on Lola's bald head, pass over me, then back to Lola, then back to me, and once more as though weighing her capacity for empathy against my apparent dearth of it.

"You pay," says Lola. I nod dumbly, counting out change on a placement advertising chewing tobacco. She indicates the laminated photo of a beard-ed man, dressed in a checked woolen shirt and orange cap dipping beside a stand of white pine. "Was that part of it?"

"No," I say, handing Irma the money. "No, that stuff gives you cancer."

Irma looks appalled, but still invites me to the lake later that night.

"Yes, Irma, maybe," I say over my shoulder as I follow Lola outside. We sit in the car, and I roll the windows down. She helps herself to one of my cigarettes, and waits for me to light it.

"So…What now?" I venture.

"Take me to where you lost her."

"But I thought…The bakery?"

"No. It doesn't matter. Take me to the woods. I want to see it for myself."

"Please don't hate me or anything," I request as we pass the dump. Wallace hails us from his post beside a blue compartmental dumpster.

"Just don't be useless," says Lola.

8.

June 12th, 2006, North Calais, Vermont

In the defile by the lake, Lola suggests we split up. She goes off into the woods, and I descend the opposite way toward the shore, intending to scour it for clues, I suppose. The water is loud. People accelerate past the peninsula in motorboats, causing an abnormal tide, which laps the shore beside my feet. The vulgarity of what passes for normal, seasonal recreation. It's fortunate that the wooded peninsula from which I watch and judge, and much of the land around it, is part of a trust established by a business-woman named Annalisa (Inc.), who lives on a sprawling homestead nearby. When I was in elementary school, her son, Hermes, and I were close, or as close as it was possible to become with the sheltered, inward male child that he was. His parents were often away on business-related excursions, and my parents were tasked with caring for him during these long weekends. Still, if his mother had not taken it upon herself to act as steward of the woods beside the lake, the entire stretch of forest in which Eleanor disappeared would likely be a passionless mirror of the far shore, vulgar strings of summer homes and innocuous private beach.

Lola shouts my name from the top of the hill. When I reach her, I notice that she's holding my watch.

"Do you recognize this?"

"Yes. I gave it to Eleanor. So she would know when to meet me."

"So, the last time you saw her, she was wearing it?"

"Yes, Lola, where did you find it?"

"Back there," she says, jabbing her thumb toward the trees. "Looped around a branch."

"Do you think she left it? Like, as a message of…trouble?"

"I don't know. I also found these."

She holds out her hand. In it is a crumpled bit of paper, and half a condom wrapper, colored a friendly green.

"You touched that?" I ask.

"There's nothing in it. People don't wipe their dicks on these things."

I gingerly take the wrapper in my hand, trying to examine it without touching the foil to my skin, which is impossible.

"I know this brand. Well, it's not a brand exactly. I mean, you can't buy them in stores. Wow, been a while."

"What do you mean by that?" asks Lola.

"Well, the label. 'Green Sleeves.' Like, Green Mountain? It was this campaign. The state health department wanted to make birth control available to everybody. So they ordered a shitload of these. You used to see bowls everywhere. In the general stores, the booths at the farmer's market, even the concession stand at the movie theater in town. Every Vermonter my age wore a Green Sleeve the first time they got their ashes hauled."

"Are they actually green?"

"Yes. Extremely verdant."

I hand it back to Lola, and she turns it over in her hand.

"It's expired."

"I would suppose so. They stopped handing them out a while ago. State cuts."

"Any place you could still get them?"

"I don't know. Probably. Like I said, they used to be everywhere."

"What about this?"

She hands me the paper, which is actually a receipt from the general store in East Calais.

"Two cases of Champlain Boathouse Ale. Someone had a big night."

"What is that?"

"A beer made by a microbrewery in Burlington. Expensive, and tasty, but you should only drink one. It's high gravity."

"So, someone buying a couple cases would be…unusual?"

"Maybe."

Lola runs a small hand across her scalp, thinking. She looks at me.

"You know that girl."

"What girl?"

"The tired-looking one at the store."

"Oh, you mean Irma. Yeah, she wants me," I say, nudging Lola with my elbow.

"You're absolutely revolting," she says, raising the receipt. "Do you think she might remember this?"

"Worth asking."

"Let's go."

As Lola descends the hill, and tromps through the brook, sweat rolls in translucent droplets from her bare skull, and as I follow close on her heels, the sharp odor of her, toiling and driven as a galley slave, suddenly makes me glad that Eleanor is gone. I want to see her again. But for now, she can be missing.

Back in the parking lot of the East Calais general store, I stretch the beer receipt between my hands and smooth it on the steering wheel as though I intend to insert it in a soda machine. Lola watches impatiently. It is now mid-afternoon. The day became dry and hot while we were canvassing the woodland that had seemingly consumed Eleanor. A trickle of sweat, like a pearl attached to filament, descends from the space beneath Lola's left breast.

"You're just going to hand it to her and ask?" she says. "Can you do that?"

"I don't know. Is it confidential? Do clerks keep secrets?"

Lola looks uncomfortable.

"Ermine probably won't tell you."

"Irma. And she might."

"Why would she?"

"Because she desires me."

Lola snorts.

"Yes, you mentioned that. How can you tell?"

"Looks. Invitations. Invitations in the form of looks. Need manifested as helpfulness."

"She could just be a nice person."

"Is there a difference?"

Lola looks horrified.

"Yes, there is a difference."

I pause for a minute, considering the paper between my fingers.

"I suppose it depends on what you want out of it. Hand me a pen."

I turn the receipt over, and am about to write, but I hand both the stylus and the paper to Lola.

"I'm going to dictate. If you could please write what I say on the back of that paper."

"Why me?"

"Because my handwriting is terrible. And Irma might recognize it."

This appears to mollify Lola. I begin.

"Hello. I'm leaving this note because I accidentally bumped your car and some people saw me. I want them to believe I am a good person, doing the noble thing and leaving my contact information. However, I don't feel I should have to pay for the damage because you parked badly, and at the end of the day, I just don't care. Good luck, and best wishes."

Lola finishes writing and hands me the note. I exit the car.

*

November 17th-February 15th, 2004-2005, Montpelier, Vermont

After Frank's phone call, Eleanor and I did not see each other as much. Eleanor used all the influence a child can exert over a parent, and managed to prevent her father from calling my parents. They had never met, and it would have been an awkward introduction. He had apparently stomped about the house with the portable phone in his chubby fist, top-knot waiving, decrying my presence in his daughter's life and impugning my proclivities like King Lear imploring thunder to unmake the world. I had to concoct some completely implausible fable to satisfy my mother's questions as to why I was bloody and practically hypothermic on the steps of City Hall when she picked me up.

"I decided to walk. Eleanor had a family thing."

"Where is your coat?" my mother said, touching my cheek with the back of her hand. "You're chilled, my god. Are you crazy? And you're bleeding."

"I was bleeding. It stopped. I'm okay, mom."

"Why are you bleeding? You look like you were attacked by wild animals."

"No. I fell on the ice."

Eleanor and I started seeing other people gently. It was not a decision we reached after a long discussion. Since I could not go over there, and she could not be anywhere near me in public (Frank or Cora might see), our meetings were strained and clandestine. The few times we were able to meet, it was just for sex, which was fine, but we had grown to enjoy each other in a certain way. I brought her a glass of water in bed. She did not ask. I liked doing it. She wore new clothing and asked my opinion. We watched movies and discussed them. I cooked badly for her. Small stupid things that bring people close. But it was no longer easy, so we put it on hold. And besides, her bassoonist was home from Austria for Christmas. Whether he was still seeing his Viennese cymbal maven was unclear, but Eleanor told me over the phone that it did not concern her.

"I would be happy to watch his hands. On his instrument."

"When was the last time you played yours, Eleanor? I doubt the two of you will have much in common anymore."

I was not prototypically jealous. I was frustrated that she had found a replacement for me before I had found one for her. Either way, she sounded finished with me.

"We never had much in common."

She hung up, and I tried to determine whether she was talking about me, or the bassoonist. I still don't know, and shortly afterward, she left for school in New York.

In January 2005, I started working as a page at the Montpelier Library. The person whose purview I occupied was a girl my own age (seventeen, at the time) who had worked at the library shelving books for the past year. She was abnormally tall (much taller than me) and built like a farm girl, with wide, round hips and broad shoulders. He middle was trim, and her limbs were thickly muscled, more suited to churning butter than shelving books. She maintained an outlandish shock of blond hair that she piled atop her head, adding several inches to her already imposing stature. Her clothes were peasant-like, yet complimentary. Long skirts which clung to her generous bottom, and flowing, embroidered blouses that accentuated the heaving of her breasts as she lifted an overfull book cart over the lip between the elevator and the first floor rotunda.

I was certainly attracted, but there was nothing to immediately suggest her as a replacement, other than her name, which was also Eleanor. The librarians put her in charge of training me, and I followed in her wake, glorying in her sharp and soft odor, which seemed composed of fresh bread, and ripe ginger.

Eleanor (2) (Known as 'El' from hereon) was from the town of Northfield, a vaguely Calvinist, overtly bellicose enclave unevenly straddling both banks of the Winooski River. It is an authentic mirror image of Pitkin in that the notable components of each match the other in function but diverge in terms of ethic. Whereas Pitkin hosts the skeleton of a Quaker school, Northfield is home to a military college (Norwich University). It is a town with many flags, and little irony.

El's father, Dexter, was the Northfield town general practitioner ('Doctor Dex' among his patients). He was a mild, olive-skinned man who, even when dressed casually, resembled a Mediterranean lounge singer. He was gently disinterested in his work, and spent most of his spare time on either a bicycle or pair of skis, depending on the time of year (of course). I met him during late fall or early winter (depending on your disposition), a difficult season for Dexter. The weather was chilly. The valley encompassing the town was cut with gusts of arctic wind unsuitable for even the most avid cyclist. Yet the slopes at Killington and Mad River Glen were barren, and he was agitated. When we arrived in El's car, he waved from the front door of the house, signaling for his daughter to cut the engine. I stepped out in the driveway, and raised my hand in a greeting as I approached the porch.

"Hi, I'm…"

"Get back in the car!" shouted Docter Dex, gesturing frantically at the vehicle. I stood stupidly, unsure of what to do. El blinked.

"Daddy…"

"Honey, stay where you are. You!"

He pointed to me.

"Whatever your name is, do what I said. You want to get hurt?"

"No, sir," I said, getting back in the car and shutting the door. I turned to El. "Your dad seems nice."

"I don't know what…He isn't usually…"

Doctor Dex seemed reluctant to come all the way out of the house. His hand was extended toward the car with the palm raised, indicating that we should stay put. He was watching something beyond our periphery. El rolled down the window.

"Daddy. What's going on?"

He did not remove his eyes from whatever he was watching.

"Honey, I know you can't see it from where you are," he said. "But there's a goddamn emu the size of a phone booth just around the corner of the house. I got to call Randall to come and get it. Just sit tight."

The emu farm, owned by a Mr. Randall Dinornis, is likely the most interesting portion of the town on western side of the Winooski. There is a rest home which looks like a minimum-security prison, and a well-appointed cemetery at the top of a hill past El's house. Other than that, it's mostly mobile homes and Rottweilers until you get to Brookfield. Randall eventually came and got the animal into a horse trailer, and we were able to leave the car. I spent the remainder of the evening following El's father around the family's vividly restored farmhouse with my hand extended in front me like a beggar, hoping that at some point, he might ensconce it within his own.

Whether he was reluctant to welcome a male into the household, or had simply confused me with one of the numberless bowls of potpourri his wife had stationed upon every horizontal surface within, Doctor Dex failed to introduce himself. He was preoccupied by the bird. El tried several times, and eventually gave up. We retreated to her bower on the second floor.

It seemed that rather than a step forward or back, I had accomplished a lateral movement. Both Eleanors were smart, attractive, middle class young women from good families. But from the first moment, in the library basement, when El asked if I would like to get a coffee after work as we sorted newspapers, I sensed a power I did not have with Eleanor. I knew El had the potential to love me violently in a way that Eleanor never could. There was something in the muscles surrounding her mouth, an inchoate dependence searching for a home. Sweat beading delicately along her golden hairline. This was new to me. I was intrigued, and easily conquered by the novelty of being a conqueror.

9.

June 12th, 2006, East Calais, Vermont

Despite what Lola might think, I still find Irma attractive. Her lips remain full, and her hair is black as the underside of a raven or crow's pinions. Granted, the darkness girding either socket is authentic, and her skin, once ruddy, now seems inscrutably tarnished. Her vaguely exotic bearing has faded to the confident decrepitude that comes with early motherhood. She appears at least five years my senior. But still, as she examines the note, and my face, and the note again, stretched between her fingers (dirt, beneath the nails) I recall a time in eighth grade when I watched her maneuver a plastic tray heavy with an overhelping of chicken barbecue between tables in the cafeteria, the impact of her heels on the tile floor shaking her half-grown breasts in a loose t-shirt commemorating First Night (Burlington, 1998), and an urge to do something with her, anything, though I could not express it, to myself or my dining companions. To be overwhelmed as a young man is to be underwhelmed as a slightly older one. Each time I look back, I become sad.

"You said where again?" Irma asks, assuming an ugly hunch.

"Fishing access by the lake. I was…canoeing. Fucker left it under my wiper."

"You canoe?" she asks. I assume it's a joke.

"Oh, yes. I do canoe. And so should you. Too."

Irma appears to be wishing a wall between us. I pick up a jar of gummy fish and pretend to examine it.

"I take the boat out occasionally."

She watches me with her mouth and her tongue pressed inside her left cheek.

"Well, Marlowe…This here is from last Saturday."

"Yes. I saw the date."

A vague yet depressive silence appears between us.

"Should I know what that means?" I ask, hopefully.

"Well, see, thing is, I don't work Saturday."

"You don't?"

"Naw."

"But today is Saturday."

"I'm covering."

That silence again. It occurs to me that Irma might be hijacking my query in order to spend more time around me.

"Irma. Who was working last Saturday?"

"Wanda. Wanda works on Saturday."

"Of course she does. Where is she today?"

"Barre. Getting an AIDS test."

"A what? Why?"

"Just felt like it I guess. She'll be at the fire tonight. Out at the lake."

"Do I know her? Have we met?"

Irma looks at me like I asked for directions to my own house.

"She went to school with us. Don't you remember? Real skinny. Pretty, too. Quiet."

This isn't helping. Irma leans forward slightly.

"Exit Only?" she whispers.

"Wait. No," I say. "Her name's Wanda?"

"Yup."

"Does she still…Is she…The test, is that why?"

"You've never had one?" says Irma.

"Well…Yes…of course…But does…Surely, she…"

That goddamned silence has returned. I've run out of things to examine on the counter.

"Is there like a question you want to ask me?" says Irma.

"I guess I'm curious if she still only…does things…the way she did…at one time."

"How would I know that?"

"You guys work together."

"We don't discuss that stuff."

I leave the counter to fix myself a cup of coffee, even though I don't want coffee. I just need to do something while I try to remember whether there is anything else I need to ask. How can one simple task become so bizarre? All I need is a name, the name of the customer who bought the beer, and dropped the receipt in the woods in which Eleanor was last seen, but it is completely impossible to do that with Irma pouting at me. She charges me for the coffee, which I knock all over the counter when I hand her the money.

"So, she'll be there tonight? At the fire?" I ask, as Irma sops of the mess with a paper towel.

"Like I said."

"She doesn't need to rest or anything?"

Irma pauses, regarding me like she cannot tell whether I'm serious or not.

"It's an AIDS test. Not an abortion. Go get yourself a refill."

"Right, of course."

Outside, I hand Lola the coffee I do not want and sit in the driver's seat without starting the car.

"What happened? Did she recognize the beer?" asks Lola, sipping at the cup. "Why is there so much milk in this? It's like half milk."

"I was distracted."

"What did you find out?"

"The person we need to talk to will be at a thing down at the lake tonight."

"What sort of thing?"

"A fire. They have these fires. Often. Local people."

Lola shifts her position, propping her face on hand.

"What kind of fire? Not like a guy with a guitar and no penis sings old folk songs while we sit around drinking microbrew and congratulating each other? I've been to that fire. Jews with dreadlocks. Someone always brings a tabla they can't play."

"Wow. No. This is not that. I can go by myself after I drop you at the compound."

"It's not a compound. And I want to come."

"Won't they miss you at the…the farm?"

"They're not paying me. My time is still my own. When should we be there?"

"After dark, I imagine. In the meanwhile, we might head back to Montpelier and see if we can't find some Green Sleeves. If we find a place that still has them, we might get some idea of where the kidnapper likes to hang out. It's a long shot but…"

Lola nods, settling into the seat and lighting one my cigarettes.

"It's your show, Marlowe," she says.

*

January 8th-May 2nd, 2005, Montpelier, Vermont

Over what turned out later to be our first date, El revealed indirectly that she was an excellent athlete. It made sense. Her stature coupled with a savage (I would learn later) physical acuity made her an obvious menace on a sports team. She had played soccer since she was young, and swam on the Northfield school team. In her spare time, she skied with her father during the winter, and cycled with him during the warmer months. She had her own kayak, which she would place on top of her car as though it were bag of groceries. But I didn't see her do this, or even so much as kick a soccer ball, until many months after accepting her first offer of coffee after work.

"I'd like you to see me play," she said, and I was afraid she saw something in my face, a darkening across the brow that might indicate my low estimation of sports and those involved with them.

"That sounds interesting. What position?"

She blushed, and I over-corrected.

"Pardon me, I meant what position do you play?"

"Mostly defense. Fullback. Sometimes goalie. But I hate that. I do it mostly as a favor. You have beautiful skin. Did you know that?"

I snorted into my coffee, spraying some of it onto my glasses. Though I admired her for being forward, this was the first conversation we had shared during which one us was not holding a book, and the immediacy of her desire startled me. I removed my glasses to polish the lenses, and she giggled.

"Nobody has ever told you that before?" she asked.

"No. Not at all."

"You do, though. It was the first thing I noticed about you."

"Well, I have the body of a little boy. And I kiss like I'm trying to scare a raccoon off a front porch."

"I doubt that," she said, lowering her eyes from my face.

The first opportunity I had to accept El's invitation (to attend one of her soccer games) was on a balmy day in May, several months after our initial expression of shared interest. Things between us were going well, and the sex was good. The newness of her enchanted me, compared with the somewhat ancient quality of Eleanor, with whom congress had always involved a martyr-like aspect. In order to achieve it, one of us needed to mount the cross carried by the other. I had forgotten the difference, which consisted entirely of my being an object of desire. El wanted me greatly, and I knew my desire did not equal her own, which prefigured me as a sort of dominant custodian during our coupling. No matter what happened, I would remain in control.

But how can I explain the feeling of watching El knock a girl from the opposing team (Bristol, I think) off her feet with a shoulder to the sternum, pitching her like a wilted toy into the grass, and sending the ball to the other end of the field. It was one animal motion. El's long blond hair was set in a plait which twirled around her head like an extraordinary lariat, and even from the side line, I could see drops of perspiration fly from her skin and evaporate in the heat shrouding her magnificent body. I wanted to both press my mouth to the side of her damp red neck, and laugh at the girl she had bulldozed.

And ten minutes later, it happened again. The girl was even smaller this time, and didn't get up after she hit the ground. The game stopped. Several people ran onto the field. Her coach and the referee spoke to the girl quietly for a moment, before helping her up. Her mouth was bleeding. They walked her to the bench and sent in a sub. Two spectators passed, one saying she had bitten into her tongue. And El was there, unmoved, breathing like she had just savaged a matador. Her breasts rose and fell, her hands were on her hips, her thighs were bright red below her blue athletic shorts. I stifled a laugh.

When the game ended, I waited for her by the gate to the parking lot. The game had been played on a field that was part of the Norwich campus. Several cadets in fatigues were hanging out on bleachers nearby, watching the teams break up. El emerged from the line of girls shaking hands. I waved from the gate and she began walking toward me.

"Hey, I like your hair," said one of them. "You want I can comb it for you."

His retinue tittered.

"You want to get a drink, soccer lady?" said another. "I got a handle in my room. I can take you away from all this."

El blushed and I didn't think she would say anything back. But she did.

"I'm in high school, lowlife," she said. "Shouldn't you meatsacks be killing kids in Iraq or something?"

Silence from the bleachers.

"That really simplifies…our position," said one of them, slowly. El took my arm and led me toward the parking lot.

"I like you," I said.

"I'll drive," she said, clicking her key ring and unlocking the doors. "I like you too. I'd prefer to bathe before you touch me."

"I am fine with it. You smell like violence. And comedy."

She tossed her gym bag in the backseat and watched me for a moment over the roof.

"You want to take a drive?"

"Yes. Are those guys going to fuck up my car if I leave it here?"

"No. My father has had a finger in each of them. They'll leave you alone if they want proper coverage."

"Don't you want to bathe?"

"I have a place."

I didn't know what that meant. We passed beneath the town's solitary traffic light, blinking an ambivalent orange, and across the Winooski. The rest home sat quiet and dark, and the emu farm appeared similarly shuttered, though it was only late afternoon. El's driveway was just ahead. I undid my seat belt. But she passed the turn, and continued on up the hill toward the town graveyard.

"El. Where are we going?"

"I thought we might take a walk."

"And your shower? I don't mind."

"I have a place."

We ascended the hill, loose stones clinking in the wheel well, and a low heat rising from the valley as the car climbed higher. El said nothing until it stopped. She told me to get out.

*

June 12th, 2006, Montpelier, Vermont

Contrary to popular opinion, drinking in the middle of the day is actually fine, and (in the right circumstance) can even be salubrious. At the base of Langdon Street, I sidle into an eponymous taproom, intending to lubricate my faculties after a long, fruitless search for the formerly ubiquitous rubbers. It's been a mostly shitty day.

I've cased (a word I hope is appropriate) all the streets of downtown Montpelier, visited the Capital Apothecary, a failing record shop ('Sound Judgments'), three bookstores, a Laundromat, a pizza restaurant, and even the movie theater, where I was ejected by the usher without discovering a reserve supply of Green Sleeves (to say nothing of Eleanor). And in fifteen minutes, I have to meet Lola in the parking lot behind City Hall and reveal my failure.

The interior of the taproom is dark and cool as a root cellar, with sparse pods of people deposited throughout the narrow room, using computers or reading (in the hand of one, I spot a fresh copy of *Beyond Coitus*, Theodora Press, 2008: Windsor, VT). An eerie, tinkling music issues from a speaker jailed in a far corner, which I recognize as Noah Howard's 'Queen Anne'. The actual bar is without traffic. I plop my ridiculous body on a stool, order a Champlain Boathouse Ale (for the sake of thematic or quotidian consistency. Possibly both), rush through it, and order another, which I attempt to nurse while deciding how best to explain my failure to Lola.

We both know the facts, or what seem like facts, since we have nothing to disprove them: Eleanor is missing. In the woods where she disappeared, we found the receipt for the same beer I now guzzle, which will be investigated later at the bonfire, and a wrapper from a formerly common brand of regional prophylactic. These things would not appear on their own, and must have been transported to the woods by a third party (or parties), and our foremost task at the moment is finding this person, because if we find them, there is a chance we will find Eleanor.

But this afternoon's failure leaves me feeling guilty, because this is usually the feeling that arrives after disappointment. And through the shameful, descending mist of one drink followed by another, I wonder if it is possible that I have more than one body, that this collection of bone and gristle into which I now pour alcohol is just one part of the aggregate. Sometimes I have the sensation of watching myself, of witnessing my mundane activities through a window, or simply through a glass, darkly (Corinthians, I think. Mr. Shivers would be proud). I'm not abdicating responsibility for anything. Both what happened in Ohio (of which, more later), and with Eleanor, are my fault. Because I watched myself do those things. I was both the witness and the perp. In other words, I made no move to stop myself. The blame should be on my head twice, if not more. As yet there is no one to assign it. And so I'm free. But for how long? I'm so involved in my thoughts that the bartender has to ask three times if I would like another beer. I look down and notice the bottle containing my Boathouse Ale is empty. When did that happen?

"Aren't you supposed to cut me off?" I joke, sliding the empty bottle toward him.

"You look like this is normal for you," he says. "I try not to get between people their habits."

A good barkeep, I think. He's around my age, but in better shape. His slim build is compact. The veins in his tattooed forearm are raised and healthy. He sports an inchoate beard, and a pair of fashionably obvious spectacles. But most curious is the tattoo I notice on the inside of his left wrist when he hands me the refill: a hyena in heels, with a handbag.

"Interesting ink," I say, aiming for casual, but coming off somewhere emotionally proximate to high-strung. He glances at his forearm as though he has forgotten what's drawn upon it.

"Oh, thanks…Which one?"

"The hyena. Are you from New York?"

"Yes. Well, no. I went to school there. I'm from Connecticut."

"Sure. You like the Femammals?"

"Oh…Yeah. Sure. They're pretty awesome," he says, growing slightly withdrawn and frowning to himself. But he continues recounting, as though not wishing to make me feel bad for asking. "Yeah, I used to see their stuff around the city. They were out on May 12th. Had a band and everything."

"I'm sorry, I don't understand."

"Well, there was a big protest around Battery Park. You know, because shit's fucked up. They were out with this marching band they put together, and we all got behind them and plowed down Water Street. It stopped traffic. You didn't hear about any of this?"

"No, I guess not."

"Really? There were like twenty thousand people."

"No, sorry. Missed it entirely," I say. "By any chance do you remember if there was a flute player? You know, with the band?"

"Oh, you mean Eleanor. Yeah, she was there," he says, turning away from me to draw off another beer that no one ordered. With each question regarding the Femammals, he becomes more withdrawn, so I allow the conversation to end. I sip my fourth or fifth beer, and he polishes glasses behind the counter.

"How long have you been in town?" I ask, after several minutes.

"A few months."

"You just working here or you doing anything else?"

"No, I mean this gig's just a stopgap. I'll actually be working for Montpelier Underground. You know, the teen center in the basement of City

Hall. But my contract hasn't started yet, so I'm doing this in the meantime."

"Wait, the teen center? I thought that place closed?"

"It was for a few years. But it opened up again. I guess someone wrote a grant or something."

"Yeah, I used to hang out there when I was in middle school. Not a bad place."

"No, man, it's good. Kids need that. Just somewhere for them to go, have a snack, shoot some pool, and pick up a few rubbers."

I choke on my beer, and starting hacking into my sleeve.

"Damn, maybe I should've cut you off," he murmurs, leaning away from me, as I wipe my mouth.

"No…No, down the…the wrong tube…What did you say? About Montpelier Underground?"

"Oh, I was just saying good to have a place where kids can go. Stuff like that."

"Sure, sure. But they're still handing out condoms down there?"

"Yeah," he says, suspecting a challenge. "What's wrong with that?"

"Nothing," I reply, dropping money on the counter and swallowing the rest of my beer. "Nothing at all. Thank you."

He combs the cash into his hand and I tip overconfidently from the bar stool, walking fast toward the door. It is around 4:30PM. If they still have the same hours, I should have thirty minutes. I am slightly inebriated on the sidewalk, but my sense of purpose has returned. I part the curtains of drunkenness as though slicing a bed sheet with a fencing foil, and allow the mercurial sensation of an unexplored lead to somewhat sober me as I leave the bar.

I wave an unsteady hand when I spot Lola leaning on my station wagon in the lot behind City Hall, doing my best to conceal the pleasant wash of ebreity guiding my uncertain movements. But she notices anyway.

"You're drunk, Marlowe."

I lean a hand on the chassis, but spastically withdraw it, as the metal is overwarm from sitting in the afternoon sun (now fading over the roof of the building).

"I have drank," I reply prophetically. Lola caps her sunglasses, resting them on her barren pate.

"It was an hour. I left you alone for an hour."

I raise a finger to silence her.

"I have made a discovery. Come with me."

I take her arm (more for my benefit), and lead Lola around the side of City Hall to a minute courtyard nestled in its northern flank. Within, someone has planted flowers, violets, begonias, and a solitary, unsociable-looking croton. Two unoccupied picnic tables brace a low door set in the foundation. Beside a set of stairs leading to the portal, a whitewashed plywood sign advertises the space within rendered in bright, homespun calligraphy: 'Montpelier Underground: Teen Center, Come On In!'

I must smell like a public house, because at the base of the stairs leading inside, the nostrils of a lithe, sunburnt slattern plopped on a stool begin to twitch. She notices us, marking her place in another new copy of *Beyond Coitus*, and stands up. A ginger braid like the tail of an unnaturally large cat swings from the top of her narrow skull, as disapproval mars a collection of features, which, if she were a house, could be described as 'sturdy.'

"We don't allow that here," she says.

"Allow what?" I ask, leaning on a coat rack I mistake for a vertical heating pipe. It crashes to the floor (black and white tile, like a chessboard), and the only thing that saves me from following it is Lola's hand on my wrist.

"Drinking. You're obviously drunk. This is a place for young people. You need to leave."

"I will," I say. "But first, I have shome…some questions."

"You're not understanding me…"

"I am understanding you…"

"No, you're not. Get the fuck out of here or I'll call the police!"

"I need condoms!"

"What?"

"Condomsh! Where are the goddamn condomsh, you crossh-eyed twat?"

"Leave!" shouts the clerk, but her lips do not move, which puzzles me. This is because Lola is the one demanding my exit. She spins me back toward the stairs with a hand in my back, and I mount them reluctantly.

"I'll be back!" I shout, knocking my head against the top of the door as I lurch through it.

"No, you won't! Stay outside!" says Lola, following me up the stairs, and latching the portal.

"Fuck you!" I say to no one, plopping myself on a picnic table among the beds of freshly planted flowers. Was this not the same place where Ursula Snopes and I mashed braces, and pawed each other several hours before a Toxic Narcotic show at the Unitarian church on Loomis Street, (August, 1999)? What tangible excitement. She wore a spiked dog collar, and my hair was sculpted with stolen wood glue into a decorous and variegated plumage. I wonder what happened to Ursula. I think she went to school in Colorado and is now independent and employable. And I am still here. At the picnic table.

I am not sure whether Officer Stool notices me before I notice him. The police station is across the parking lot, adjacent to the courtyard where I now sit drunkenly examining glyphs etched in the wooden pallet of the table ('JBA IZ DA STREET DREAM,' 'FTW!'), so it's likely he has been watching for some time. Rounding the garden gate, he stops, about to speak, but hesitates, squinting and examining my face.

"Wait…I know you, don't I?" he asks. The utilities girding his circumference make low, plangent noises as he shifts his weight. I make an absurd motion to indicate that I have no idea what he should and should not know.

"Yeah, Marlowe, right? You went to school with me."

"Yesh," I slur, and then it hits me. The vaguely ichthyoid lips. The oily crop of hair so dark and flat it appears painted on his skull. The body suspended between narrow, sloping shoulders, like a sack of day-old bread hung from a tree branch. Arthur Stool.

"I thought so!" he exclaims, helping himself to the opposing bench. "You and I ended up a couple places together, didn't we?"

"Yesh," I say, examining the badge crookedly pinned to his khaki uniform. Arthur leans back, pleased in confirming this memory. Other than his canker-like presence during smoky car rides between empty houses, I can recall nothing of him during our high school years. So we sit in a silence broken only by the occasional hiccup from my side of the table.

"So, Marlowe," he begins. "What are you doing back here? I thought you went to Illinois or something."

"Ohio. For shkool."

"For what?"

"School. College."

He nods, leaning in a little bit.

"Well, it's great to see you. Sure is. Let me just ask though: You been doing a little drinking?"

Arthur's question catches me just as I am drifting unconsciously to one side (I recall myself earlier, regarding Champlain Boathouse Ale: "…you really only drink one. It's high gravity."), and I quickly slap a hand on the table to balance myself, though a bit too hard, startling him.

"Steady big fellow…" he murmurs, rising slightly from his seat.

"Why would you ask that?" I say, retaining mine (my seat).

"Well, a couple reasons, but mostly cause you smell and look like it. Now, be honest with me otherwise it's perjury. You had a little drink or two maybe?"

"Perjury happens under oath. I'm not under oath."

"Now, see, that's smartmouth, and I don't really want to hear that. You best get up and come along with me."

"Where are we going, Arthur?"

"That ain't your concern."

"I think it is."

"And I'm an officer."

"Of what?"

"Of the law! Now get your ass off the table."

"It's not on the table. It's on the bench."

He walks around the side of the table or bench, and grabs one of my arms, while trying to force the other around my back. I keep my hands clamped between my knees, and since he is about as robust now as he was in high school, Arthur quickly becomes exhausted. Sweat drips from his chin onto my cheek.

"Now, see, you're resisting. Don't do that."

"I'm not resisting. You're just not trying hard enough."

"You want me to try harder?"

"If you like."

He touches his hand absently to the pepper spray sheathed at his hip.

"You going to shrpay me with that, Arthur?"

His hand pauses.

"No. No, I suppose not."

"What's going on here?"

The question comes from Lola, who has emerged from the nether annex. Arthur is obviously taken with her despite himself, or her, more exactly. A long, elegant bronzed flank extends from the low door as though inviting appraisal, and draws his attention away from her scalp. She comes out leading with her breasts, which are barely muzzled in a tank top rolled to expose her midriff, and the point of either hipbone.

"Everything she does is on purpose," I say, but neither of them hears me.

"You know him?" asks Arthur.

"Yes, I do."

She plants herself between us, placing a hand on my shoulder.

"I'm his wife."

"You didn't tell me you was married!" squawks Arthur, breaking what he might think of as his composure. He slaps my other shoulder. "Well done, friend!"

"Thanksh."

"Any reason he's drunk outside the teen center at five in the afternoon, ma'am?"

"Yes, officer…is it Stool?"

Arthur nods, more at his nameplate than Lola.

"We've just come from a funeral. Marlowe's Aunt Eleanor passed just this past Friday, and it came as quiet a shock to the extended family. They're still trying to regroup."

"Yesh, we are," I agree. Her hand squeezes the back of my neck.

"It's a large, healthy family thank goodness, and they do get to drinking when the occasion strikes. I was the designated driver of course, but I made the mistake of abandoning my poor husband while I ran a few errands. I'm sure he just needs a nap. Come, darling…"

Lola lifts me to my feet by the back of neck and steers me out of the gate. "Let's be off."

"My condolences," says Arthur, who seems unsure of his place in all this, and so follows us at a distance.

"Keys!" Lola hisses when we reach the car. I fumble in my pockets without finding anything, and am obviously moving too slow for her. She hooks a finger in my belt loop and spins me around, patting my pockets until something jingles. Her hands on my body, even at their most economic, stir me, and a small, delicate moan escapes my mouth.

"Oh, gross," says Lola, snatching the keys and jamming them into the door.

"How come he's got the keys if he's been drinking?" asks Arthur from a distance of several parking spaces.

"He often holds my things," yells Lola, and, thinking better of it, adds, "No pockets."

She pats her bottom in his direction. Arthur turns to leave, but makes inadvertent eye contact with me. He points two fingers at his eyes and then at me.

"I'll be watching you."

"Watch my nuts, Arthur," I say, as Lola ducks my head inside the passenger side, rather like Arthur would if he had apprehended me farther from the station.

"Aunt Eleanor?" I say, as Lola sits in the driver's seat and starts the car. "You had to use her name?"

She doesn't answer. Instead, she holds out her hand, and in it is a wrinkled bit of emerald foil containing, of course, a Green Sleeve.

"There were a few at the bottom of the bowl. The apothecary made a donation and Russ just filled it when she got in this morning. They're still cleaning the place out. It had been that way for a while."

"Sho…So, whoever dropped the Green Sleeve had to have access to the teen center?"

Lola nods, swinging the car out onto Main Street.

"Unless we missed something, the condom probably came from there."

*

May 2nd, 2005, Northfield, Vermont

The car remained on the road, and El was in the water. Her hair loosed from its plait was a golden fan upon the surface, trailing her body in an unbroken radius as she stroked toward me on shore. When she reached the shallows she stood, tilting her head to ring it out. She was naked. Her soccer uniform was piled beneath a fatigued willow, weeping from the shore. The water sat below her hips at an obscene level exposing most of the tawny space between her legs. She squeezed water from her hair, twisting the strands, the muscles in her arms and beneath her breasts twitching.

"Come on in."

The pond was small, and set back ten minutes from the main road. I was not completely confident in its privacy, but was naked anyway, touching a toe to the surface. El backed up, the water drawing around her body like an absorbent shade. The sun shone through a low stand of elder and ash on the opposite shore. She did not look at my body. She watched my face. The water reached her chin, and was very cold.

"If I come out that far, I won't be able to stand," I said.

She moved toward me, and placed a hand on my stomach. Her powerful body pressed my own. But in the touch of our skin, I felt a relinquishment past the normal yielding of flesh to flesh. El drew her lips across mine as though tasting me.

"I watched you destroy someone today," I said.

"I want to be around you," she murmured. "That's what I want. When we were in the mysteries upstairs and you touched my back to get by, I wanted to do what I'm doing. That was how I felt."

"It was biographies."

"What?"

"It was biographies. We were in biographies. Or memoirs. Whatever they call it."

“It doesn’t matter. Do you like this? Does it feel good?”

“Yes”

“Will you touch me?”

“Yes.”

“Like I’m touching you?”

“Yes.”

“Please.”

I did. She kept talking.

“I love you, Marlowe,” she said, twining her legs through mine beneath the water.

“I believe you,” I replied, bracing a hand on her hip.

June 12th-13th, 2006, North Calais, Vermont

What I hear is laughter, or music, or laughter and music. But I can't seem to reach it. Or I may be imagining it. Do I see fire? Or are those headlights? How do I separate where I am from where I should be? Because I shouldn't be here, wherever here might be. It's obviously my car. But I'm on the wrong side. I'm a passenger. Or I was. The car is no longer moving. And it is very, very dark. The window is open, and I have been resting with my head leaning out of it like a dog. My seat belt is fastened. But I'm going nowhere. I'm awake now. I was dreaming. I was dreaming of Eleanor when she was alive. That's all there was to the dream. Her, alive. She could still be alive. It's possible she is just missing. This is what Lola is trying to find out. But where is she?

I open the door and try to step out of the Volvo without unfastening my safety belt, and for a moment, I'm throttled in my seat. But my eyes adjust. I understand my location. The car is parked at the fishing access by the lake. I raise myself from the seat, and my head begins to pound. I somehow feel both sick and ravenous. There is no food in the car. Unless Lola bought something. I rummage in the back seat and find nothing. I am also quite thirsty. I wander down the boat launch to the lake and kneel at the shore, cupping and slurping huge mouthfuls of tepid, sun-warmed water into my mouth. I stumble back toward the car and vomit all of this out beside the wheel well, which leaves me even hungrier.

I know that when Ignatz is sick, he eats grass. Granted he's a cat, so he doesn't do a lot of drinking, but still, it could work. I lurch to my feet and find a patch of grass beside the dirt parking area, and begin plucking handfuls of it from the earth and shoving them into my mouth. It's not bad. The grit is unpleasant, but the blades have a pleasing consistency and are slightly sweet. I eat several handfuls more, until I feel fit to stand.

The light I saw from the passenger seat is definitely a fire. It flickers at the tip of a peninsula extending out of from the lot, about a five-minute walk from my position. It's probably Irma and her friends. If Lola is anywhere, that's where she'll be. I set off down the access road, the water shimmering on my left as a low orange moon emerges from behind a thickset cloudbank. A loon howls. I must have fallen asleep after we left Montpelier. But that was hours ago. What has Lola been doing since then?

I hear laughter again, and the sound of country music. They've built the fire in a small clearing with a generous view of the lake and directly beside a granite war memorial, which was planted all the way out here before I was born. A few fresh flags, their poles the size of pencils, are stuck at its base, as well as several clutches of handpicked flowers. Irma is standing, telling a story, while four other people sit on folding chairs and sections of waste lumber, all holding beers. I see Lola's pate thrown back in laughter as I enter the circle of light cast by the blaze.

"Here he is," says Irma. "We heard you started early, Marlowe."

I gesture hello to everyone and sit down. I know them all. We went to elementary and high school together. There's Cyrus, who dropped out in tenth grade. His dad delivers my parent's firewood. His huge ginger head nods to me beneath a camouflage baseball cap as I sit beside him on a length of log, upsetting a picket of beer cans (his, I think). Across from us is Irma, of course, and Bernard, the only homosexual in East Calais, and beside him is Wanda, prim, plain, but friendly enough.

"Yes," I say. "I started early."

"Is that…What is that on your face?" asks Bernard. "Is that…grass?"

"Afraid so," I hiccup, nodding to Lola, who is not looking at me and doesn't see. I feel the need to shift the attention from myself, so I turn to Cyrus.

"How's it all going, Cyrus? Long time."

"Surely."

"You been well?"

"Surely."

"How's your family?"

"What you know about them?"

I'm not sure how to answer his question so I turn to Irma, hoping she'll prove more neutral.

"Nice spread you got here, Irma."

"I think so. Want a beer?"

"Drastically."

"Not the Busch," says Cyrus. "Give him a Steelie."

"I'll take a Steelie," I say amiably.

"You sure will."

"Yes, I will."

"What?"

I stand to take the wet can from Irma, and change my seat, since Cyrus seems best left to himself. I sit down next to Bernard, a little too close for his comfort. He shifts into Wanda, who tips from the log like a drawbridge.

"Jeezum crow," she murmurs, picking herself up and wandering over to sit beside Cyrus.

"Musical logs," I say cheerfully, and no one laughs.

A pall seems to have descended as a result of my arrival, and I begin to wonder why Irma would consistently invite me to join in these things if all her friends hate me. Lola still hasn't looked in my direction, and I shrug, opening the tall can of lukewarm bum beer and lighting a cigarette.

"I heard you went away, Marlowe," says Bernard as though he wishes I had remained, as he says, away.

"I did. I came back."

This seems to satisfy him. In search of some topic that might unite us in a mutual agreement, I remember Arthur from earlier.

"So, I ran into Stool today. He's a lawman now."

"That a fact?" asks Cyrus.

"Sure is. He tried to arrest me."

"What for?"

"Being drunk, I suppose."

"He ticketed me for jaywalking. On a Sunday. On a street that was closed to traffic," says Bernard.

"It's the perfect job for him," I say. "He was always hard to avoid."

"He ain't the only one," says Cyrus, wrapping his arm around Wanda. Someone laughs but I can't tell who it is. Perhaps emboldened by the beer, I speak directly to Cyrus.

"Is there something you want to say to me?"

"Not yet."

"I'm just asking. You don't seem to want me here."

"You're just a faggot is all."

"Am I?

"Cyrus, shut up," says Irma.

"Sure are."

I look to Bernard for support, but he is apparently unbothered by the slur, and is even smoking one of my cigarettes though I don't recall offering.

"Well," I say. "I'll be on my way then. I just have a few questions for Wanda if you don't mind. Before I go."

"She don't have to say anything to you."

"Why not?"

"She's through talking tonight."

"Is that so, Wanda?"

"Yes," she says quietly, nestling into Cyrus' coat. I glance around to try and judge if this behavior seems weird to anyone else, but no one even looks at me. Except Lola. There is motion in her face. Her eyes are trying to tell me something I can't decipher. I mouth 'Should I?' across the flames, and she shakes her head. But that doesn't make any sense. How are we supposed to find Eleanor if I can't even ask this ridge runner's lady friend a few questions? This is why we came to the fire. To find out if Wanda remembers who bought the Boathouse Ale, because if she remembers, we will have our third party, or the person who probably saw Eleanor last.

"Wanda," I begin. Lola shakes head vigorously. "Do you remember anyone buying two cases of Boathouse Ale at the store? Maybe a week ago? It's important."

"You still work with retards?" answers Cyrus. "Because you sure are act-ing like one."

"I don't know Cyrus. Do you and I work together?"

He seems to be rolling something around within his red head, mumbling quietly to himself, and nodding once before standing up. He lifts a thick flannel shirt, unfastening his belt and withdrawing it from the loops.

"You going to rape me, Cyrus?" I ask, even though I'm no longer sure that it's safe to provoke him.

"You'd like that wouldn't you?" he replies, more to himself than me.

"If I were you," whispers Bernard. "I'd apologize."

"For what?" I ask as Cyrus begins to lumber toward me.

"Oh, for fuck's sake, Cyrus. Can you ever just take a break?" says Irma.

He is now standing in front me. The belt is in his right hand.

"Stand up."

I hesitate which causes Cyrus to lose what little is left of his patience. He reaches behind my head, and with one huge hand lifts me to my feet by collar, and rotates me in the direction from whence I came, out, toward the darkness. I understand he wants me to leave, but the point is truly brought home when Cyrus brings the belt down on my back once, twice, three times in rapid succession. It startles me, and I make a sound somewhere between a shout and a whistle and try to pull away, but I'm caught in the concrete grip of an angry lumberjack. Even when he switches his grip to my hair, and tells me to lower my pants, I still can't wriggle out of his hands. I try kicking and swinging my fists backward, but Cyrus' reach exceeds my range, and each time I try anything his belt falls somewhere on my back with a crisp and painful report.

"Drop your pants."

I hesitate again because now I really am afraid he will turn me, like Wan-da, into an Exit Only, recall. But I might as well fear the wind for all my power to prevent it. He hooks his belt hand into my waistband and yanks the pants around my thighs, and I feel the pleasant warmth of the fire on my bare ass. But then he brings the belt down upon it several times, counting to himself, reaching five, then ten, then fifteen and then Cyrus steps back, planting a foot in my ass and sending me over the log onto my face.

No one laughs. And I don't turn around or buckle my pants when I stand up. I hobble out of the firelight and remove them. No one says a word. The only sound now fading as I walk back down the access road is the same country music playing from a hidden stereo, a music I recognize as a lisping Ernest Martin singing 'Sugar Coated Love.' I find the car and sit down without thinking and immediately stand up because my entire backside is on fire. I lay face down in the back seat.

Ten minutes later the driver's side door opens, and the overhead light switches on. Lola says nothing until she starts the car.

"Some nice friends you got back there."

I don't reply.

"You're probably the dumbest person I have ever met."

I still don't say anything. The car is moving along the road, and I can tell by the series of turns and changes in elevation that we are heading toward my parent's house.

"Do you know someone named Hermes?"

The next morning, I awake to the sound of laughter once again. I slept as if I was shot from behind and left for dead, which seems strange until I roll over, and nearly scream. My back and ass feel sunburnt, and when I examine myself in the bedroom mirror, I see both are jaggedly scored in red stripes. A closer look reveals that each reddened shadow of the lash upon my skin bears the design impressed on the leather which (from my vantage) reads 'SURYC.' Of course this how country people spend their money. I should have guessed. I have been branded.

With tears gathering in my eyes, I pull a shirt (which feels like a cilice), over my head, don my goggle-like spectacles, and leave the room, following the sound of laughter billowing like a set of good-natured curtains from the dining area down the hall. Perhaps as a result of my late night flogging, or the grass I ate beside the fishing access, I am pleased to find my faculties in perfect working order as I enter the living area of my family's home. I also find Lola breaking a jovial fast indeed with both parents. How did this happen? They don't notice me at the end of the hallway. My father is relating an anecdote about New York City and its environs.

"…the same alley in 'On the Waterfront.' It runs parallel to Washington Street, although when we were living there it was more of a sailor town than anything else. Not stroller city, as it were. Me and a buddy got two pitchers of beer from the Clam Broth House and walked all the way down it one night, just to see where it went. It was fun to be in those places. Can you imagine?"

"Oh, sure," says Lola, sipping from a glass of orange juice, and wiping her lip delicately. "A friend and I once followed Jim Carroll for twenty blocks before we realized it was just some homeless white guy with a weird haircut. But by the time we realized it we were on the street where Melville worked as a customs clerk, which is actually mentioned in one of Jim Carroll's poems. Weird right?"

My mother notices me lurking in the doorway.

"Well, good morning, Marlowe. Want a pancake?"

"I coulda beena contenda," says my father to Lola.

"No thanks, Mom."

I sit down at the table, and begin buttering a piece of toast, though I am not hungry.

"It was yoo Chahly," continues my father. Lola giggles for (likely) the first (and last) time.

"Sounded like you had a rough night last night," says my mother.

"Oh?" I say, gnawing on my dry bread.

"You should be careful. You're lucky you had someone nearby to get you home."

"Yes…" I hiss, beginning to absorb the narrative Lola has constructed for the benefit of my parents while I slept. The cold toast rakes my throat, and I'm amazed that it makes it all the way to my stomach without become lodged in my windpipe.

"What were you doing drinking like that in the middle of the day, anyway?" asks my father. "And why are you sitting that way? You're not in church. This is the breakfast table."

"I was thirsty…?"

"You don't drink ten beers because you're thirsty!"

"I was having a rough day."

"What happened?"

"I lost…something."

My father wipes his cuirass and stands with his plate, forging toward the sink.

"You'll lose a lot more than that if you're not more careful."

"Would anyone like a pancake?" suggests my mother, brightly. No one does.

Outside, the day is already warm and the verdure surrounding the house is forged in a summery golden green, redolent of heated earth, and what I imagine as the kinetic scent of large insects, beating their wings. A chirping symphony of frogs rises from the bog beyond the lawn. A raven or crow belches from the bracken. If there is a cloud in the sky, I do not see it.

Lola suggests we take a walk by the lake since we haven't decided what to do next, and I agree. We pass shoeless beneath an apse of maple trees shrouding the driveway, and turn left on the packed dirt of the road, the water already reflecting sun in the short distance between it and us.

"Thomas and Heloise are quite wonderful," says Lola.

"What did you tell them? And where did you sleep?"

"In the guest room. I just helped myself."

It is Sunday morning, but already, a motorboat swings in a broad career across the surface of the lake, with bovine children in tow. Smoke rises from the raised decks of several homes along the shore, and, once more, laughter reaches us on the main road.

"I found you on Langdon Street, looking confused, and you needed help. We're old friends."

"How did you say we know each other?"

"I just said we had mutual friends at St. Margaret's. I visited once. Met you. Chance encounter. I'm interning here for the summer. You knew I was around, but didn't make an effort to get in touch with me because you're an asshole."

"They believed you."

"Does any of that sound unlikely?"

"Did you sleep naked?"

"Did I sleep naked?"

She pauses. A pickup truck with several excited looking teenagers squeezed into the bed rockets past us.

"I don't remember. Is that important to you? You're interested in my cunt touching your mother's sheets?"

"I wouldn't phrase it that way."

"Never mind then. You didn't answer the question I asked you last night. Hermes. Do you know anyone named Hermes? Wanda gave me the impression he lives around here."

"He does. Or did. His folks do. It's summer. He might be home."

Now I pause.

"Wait. Wanda told you? You asked all the questions? Without me?"

"You were passed out in the car. I turned your head to the side so you wouldn't choke on your own vomit."

"So, he's the one. He bought the Boathouse Ale."

"That's what Wanda said."

We walk in silence for a few moments. Something explodes on the opposite side of the lake. The sound is followed by a beatific shout.

"So…why didn't you tell me that last night?" I say, suddenly angry. "Why didn't you let me know before I…before he…He beat me! With a belt, Lola! You saw that! Why couldn't you say something?"

"You mean other than shaking my head and saying 'no' over and over again? You mean aside from that?"

We stop walking.

"I thought you were…I just assumed…God fucking damn it, Lola, his name is imprinted on my back. It's almost eighty degrees today, and I can't go swimming because If I take my shirt off in public, everyone will think I belong to someone named Cyrus, and you're refusing to understand why that makes me upset?"

In one motion, Lola seizes my jaw in her small hand again and gives it a shake.

"Listen, stupid," she says, quietly. "Whatever you did to piss off that appleknocker has nothing to do with me. I'm not assuming any blame here. Find someone else. I'm not your fucking girlfriend. The fact that you can't tell when someone is itching to kick your ass makes me hope that you never decide to live in a city. All I know is after I left you in the car, I showed up at the fire, Irma introduced me, said I was a friend of yours, and that's about all it took before Cyrus started talking about what was going to happen if you showed up. Before you did, I was about to go to the car and make sure you didn't. So don't blame me because people hate you. You walked into it."

She releases me, and starts to walk ahead.

"But, wait, what did he say? Lola, what did Cyrus say?" I shout at her back.

She stops walking, and turns around.

"Look, I have no idea. Something about his cousin's sunglasses, and retards, and you being a faggot. He also mentioned compensation of some sort. I didn't make any sense, and he said he wasn't even sure you were involved, but he didn't like you anyway, so it didn't matter. Can we keep going?"

"Sure. Yes. I guess we should," I say, but she is already nearly gone around a bend in the road, the sun no longer reflecting on her bald head because it is no longer quite bald. A quarter inch of new growth has appeared, a moist shadow above her brow, and when she gripped my jaw a moment ago, I wanted to touch it to my face, to feel the bristle against my cheek. I still do, but there is no way to ask, so I keep quiet.

*

April 3rd, 2006, Julian Falls, OH

The morning after Ludmilla Hornblower and I had oral sex in the poolroom above MUSU (St. Margaret University Student Union), I slunk from her hall (203 Bingle) around 8AM and walked downtown to have breakfast by myself in a back booth at the Aurora Cafe.

It was April in Ohio, America. Shoals of dirty snow girded the red brick around campus, water trickled from gutters into beds of moist gravel, and the grass spat with each barefoot step across Main Lawn toward town. Where had my shoes gone? Ludmilla may have removed and stashed them in a location particular to her, in order to prevent me from doing exactly what I had done without waking her. It's possible that I even promised to take her with me to the diner, though this invitation was by no measure formal. It was Saturday and the cafeteria wouldn't open until noon. She would have to wait.

It was the morning of the warmest day of Spring term, and the evening before had perhaps heralded the forecast. Comcil (Community Council) moved the kegger from the Dance Space upstairs MUSU to the steps outside, and installed a sound system beneath the cantilevered roof (should it rain) above which some ambitious, spidery fourth year had stenciled TRANSIENT MODE HOME as a sort of welcome. Girls wore tank tops, guys wore cut-offs, and balmy wind blew in from the direction of Dayton. Trees shook like wild women dressed in sackcloth. If anyone had bothered to replace the flag first hung correctly, than upside down, than removed entirely from its pole, it would have snapped in the tornado air like a bull-whip. The music, 'They Came at Night' by Patrick Cowley, was loud enough to encourage dancing, and in the inexact fluorescent orange glow of a security light above the sound deck, the pagan revelers spun and jigged on the tousled brick patio outside the cafeteria. There was the clatter of a skateboard. Smoke rose from a several overfull standing ashtrays, and one metalloid barrel filled with trash and fire on the perimeter.

This is not where I encountered Ludmilla. After Professor Haemon broke Legitimation and Capitalism early (it was Friday), she followed me around the back of Main Building and suggested we meet later. I had no idea what to make of this. I knew her only from Haemon's class, in which she sat at an indelible radius from me, her thighs slightly parted in a skirt like a pocket square. Above the table, her face bore no trace of the suggestion implied beneath, and in any case, she was not a pretty girl. Her body was long and thin as a sunken jib, several inches too tall to be willowy and too short to be Amazonian. Her face contained a dour, plague-like darkness that she accentuated through the generous application of cosmetics. Her voice reminded me of a screen door repeatedly slamming on a small dog. But though she appeared drawn by Käthe Kollwitz, Ludmilla made it work as one can only on a small campus with a shallow pool.

"I know where you live, Marlowe," she said.

"I see."

And then it became slightly awkward because we lived in the same dorm, and had to walk down the path toward it together after agreeing to meet later for god knew what, but now it became incumbent upon us both to make polite conversation not entirely weighted by, or free of, innuendo.

"So…you like anything late at night?" asked Ludmilla, which seemed like a good way of straddling the fence. It was now up to me to either say something about how sex is nice late at night, or cite a neutral hobby in which we might both participate.

"Pool room will be open. They're moving the party thing outside because of the weather. We should have it to ourselves."

"I love pool."

Did we mean the same thing by 'pool'? I couldn't be sure. MU had it's own language for this kind of thing: Preventing Offenses, Opening Paths, Ending Rape. The day after my mother abandoned me on the frozen campus, I was directed by my orientation schedule to attend a workshop on the sexual offense prevention policy in a media room above the Coretta Scott King Memorial Library. Several representatives from Comcil and Adcil (community and administrative council, respectively) were running the thing, and since the blind girl had gotten lost on the way and the townie went home for dinner, I was the only member of my entering class in attendance. Martin Bastarde, appearing very much the sort of person who was everywhere at once, kicked off the proceedings.

"Well…In light of the fact that we're all probably a bit over-prepared, would anyone here mind if I just give him the thing to sign?"

Rage, an obese black junior, who was one of the members CSB as well (though I wouldn't learn this until much later), shrugged her broad shoulders, shifted a shock of sheer bleached hair, and glared at me.

"You know what is fisting, Marla?"

I shifted in my seat, checking the empty space behind my chair to make certain I was in fact the only new person in the room. I still had to ask.

"Are you…talking to me?"

"Who else?"

"Oh. All right. Well. That is when you…insert…insert…the hand, it goes into the…"

Martin cleared his throat.

"I think he knows, Rage."

"But is he gonna do it right? You."

She pointed at me.

"You understand what is the Silent Duck, Marla?"

"Marla? The Silent Duck?"

Rage made a very odd shape with her hand, not unlike a mallard, and than performed a digging motion. I watched this demonstration, as Martin handed me a clipboard with a single sheet of paper attached to it.

"We're creating dialogue," he said, watching her digging, but talking to me. "That's the central idea here. Through dialogue, we can prevent and eventually end offenses of this nature. If we all understand each other, and are comfortable, there is no reason for a problem. What this requires of you is to gain explicit verbal consent for each step of an intimate proceeding. Stop when you are asked, and expect others to do the same. A sort of golden rule for the bedroom."

"Or wherever!" chuckled Rage, elbowing her consort, Douglas, a woman of apparently similar rank and obvious girth sitting to her left.

"Any questions?" asked Martin.

"So…I have to ask…for…kisses?" I said, feeling imbecilic but not wanting to be any more explicit.

"Yes…" said Martin as though he was unsure whether he had answered the question.

"No free lunch! Or blowjobs!" squawked Douglas.

"Understand," said Martin, "that whether or not you sign it is up to you. Regardless, you will be expected to uphold the clauses contained within the contract. What you're really doing by signing is expressing a solidarity important to any healthy community."

Rage and Douglas watched me, and I realized this was a very important test to which there was only one correct answer. I borrowed Martin's pen and signed the contract.

But in practice, the contract I signed during my first day on campus held very little quarter with the students. So, I wasn't surprised later that night when I felt Ludmilla's claw on my back from behind, then my stomach, and then scrabbling at my belt buckle as I leaned over the pool table to rack. Excitable girl, I thought, continuing to set the balls in a plastic triangle.

"We're missing a striped thirteen," I said. "Should we play anyway?"

"You were right. There's no one here," she replied.

The concussion of the stereo out front ('I Ain't Gonna Run No More,' The Mighty Lovers) of the building redounded off the woodchip burner set outside the poolroom's single row of narrow windows. They were open. Someone shouted. The walls were painted black, and two immersive, tattered couches flanked the table, which inclined unapologetically toward the southeast corner of the room. Other than the floor, every surface was occupied with an empty beer can or bottle, and a thick underpainting of ash. A jaggedly positioned rack balanced an assortment of splintered, tipless cues within its scaffolding, and I mentally selected one from across the room as Ludmilla leaned into my back, throttling my penis from the rear and licking the space beneath my earlobe.

"Does this feel good, Marlowe?"

"Yes," I lied, as she wrenched and dragged my member against the interior denim as though she were painting a mural with the severed leg of a white-tailed deer. There seemed to be little way out of this. But I tried anyway.

I turned around, and kissed her, which tasted like the wine we had been drinking since 8PM, and not much else. She leaned into it, bruising my lips against my dentition, but momentarily released my organ, at which point I released her mouth and stepped back.

"I'm sorry. I should have asked."

She looked at me curiously.

"No. Really. Let's not do all that. Whatever is fine. Just not. You know."

"What? I should probably know."

"In my ass. Please"

"Oh. Right. No problem."

She leaned against the table, the single shaded bulb above it illuminated her body, and for the first time I realized her hair was blond.

"I shaved. Want to see?"

I didn't say anything. I assumed the question was rhetorical. She raised herself onto the green felt, savaging my perfect rack (curse her), and lifted her filmy skirt to expose a narrow pinch of skin skimmed bare of all encumbrance. I nodded, unsure of what to say.

"That's a fine job."

"Kiss me."

I leaned over toward her face, but she moved away.

"No. Kiss me. You know."

"Oh. Yes. Sure."

I needed time to collect myself, and this was as good an opportunity as any. I leveraged my jaw on the raised edge of the gaming table, and buried my face in the porous yawn of her pelvis, reflecting (as one will when living in a closed system) on whom this might later affect, and in what way. She bucked, her pubic bone bonking the bridge of my nose and smooshing my lips closed on my probing tongue which momentarily fixed the imbecilic expression of Persian cat on my face as the door askance from our position swung open, and Greer stood in its frame with a six-pack of Great Lakes porter and a friend who I did not know. Ludmilla cared not, and before I could remove myself from between her thighs the door swung shut and an apology echoed in the hall outside. Ludmilla sensed that I wanted to stand up, and placed her hand on the top of my skull to prevent me.

"They saw us," I gurgled.

"Can you fuck me?"

"Can I…?"

"Will you?"

"I suppose, I mean, yes, of course. Do you have a…a…"

"It's okay. I'm not ovulating."

"I see. Well. I would just…I would feel more comfortable…if we were to…use one."

"Oh. Well. Here."

Ludmilla slipped from the table top to her knees in one motion, flipped my belt buckle from its fastening with one motion further and pushed me onto the table facing her, my ass in the place where my face had just rested.

"I'm solution oriented. Are you comfortable?"

"Yes. Thank you."

"Stay with me tonight."

"We live in the same building."

"So it's on your way."

The architecture of her plot was elegant. She had me cornered at each turn. And when we tumbled through her door, which was oddly positioned one floor above my own, I scanned the bookshelves for something to disdain and discovered instead several volumes I probably should have read ('Castle to Castle,' 'The Melancholy of Resistance,' and something by Thomas Bernhard), looked at the well-hung poster depicting a nude by Caravaggio, and allowed myself to be lulled by the music on the stereo beside her bed (A selection of Bach's suites performed by Mstislav Rostropovich. She claimed it helped her sleep, and it did). It was, of all things, pleasant. And even when we were unable to complete sex due either to the alcohol (the wine had surely gone) or the previous exercise beside the pool table, there was so little shame, so little inhibition, that I surprised myself with the haste I made in sneaking downtown the next morning to be alone in a place separate from the campus. The waitress eyed my bare feet in the rearmost booth at the Aurora, but said nothing because she had likely seen it before. I ordered something exceedingly dull, and sat beneath a bare bulb sheathed in a retrofitted canister (which once contained a gallon of olive oil), and suspended from the ceiling by a chain, and considered the girl across campus in North Hall who I had been seeing almost since my arrival at St. Margaret University. She was the only person who might be seriously bothered by the way I had spent the evening before.

A lack of allegiance wouldn't explain my behavior. We were both new to college, and learning the various disappointments that involved. But I liked her. We spent time together. The problem was my feast or famine approach to romance. When women were good enough to make themselves available to me, I saw no reason not to have my fill of them. Because how long could it last? How long till they became bored with me? Since this was not in my control, it always remained a mystery. But I anticipated an indefinite point on horizon in which any who shared my company would eventually depart from it, because we are all, essentially, alone in our search for what makes us happy, even briefly. Still, I assumed she would be upset if she found out. And she would (find out). I was seen with Ludmilla. And there are no secrets on a liberal arts campus. The best thing to do would be to tell her myself (after breakfast, of course).

$$11.$$

June 13th, 2006, North Calais, Vermont

The one thing I did right the evening I broke into Eleanor's house was waiting until it was empty. Or, until I thought it was empty. Lola was there of course, but who could have predicted that? Unless you intend to assassinate those within, waiting until they are absent from the dwelling would seem the best time to trespass. But later that evening, in the woods on the far side of the lake, I'm behind Hermes' family compound, counting a row of practical European automobiles flanking the roadside through an aperture in a rock wall above the cow pasture, wondering why we would do this now, when there is obviously some sort of soiree in progress.

"This doesn't make any sense, Lola."

The family home across the road is a prototypical Vermont farmhouse with an attached barn. When I was younger, I visited it frequently, though, during the intervening years it has changed. I recall a bulky, somewhat palsied home settled indolently into the hilltop upon which it is built, with an unfinished basement, creaking, dusty stairs, and a drafty barn full of old hay. But as Annalisa (Inc.) began earning money, the house changed. Now, it is a looming, whitewashed structure, with landscaped beds before and aft, a steady, muscular pitch to the roof, and an entirely refurbished wing set in the attached barn. 'Stately' might describe it well.

"They're obviously having some sort of privilege party. Nothing on that road costs less than sixty grand. And I haven't been in that house for years. I have no idea where anything is. Holy Moses, is that an Alfa Romeo?"

An innocuous jazz wafts from a patio (when was that installed?) at the rear of the house. Two more cars arrive, one of which contains two young women and Hermes, who I haven't seen for years. He is tall, taller than me, and quite blond, with a slim, powerful torso, which he now employs in hefting two cases of Champlain Boathouse Ale (What else?) from the hinged boot of a maroon Saab hatchback. There is something Knight-like about him, Galahad-ish perhaps. Hermes the Strong. He says something to the prettier of the two women, who giggles, before shepherding her, the other, and his beer, indoors.

"He looks like a he should be wearing a suit of armor," I murmur. "His jawline is like a tectonic plate."

"He looks like a member of the Schutzstaffel," replies Lola, apparently unimpressed. "Are you going down there?"

"I don't know, Lola. Why would we do this now? When the house is full of people? This is stupid."

"We don't have the luxury of a perfectly-timed break-in. If he has her locked up someplace, we need to know that. Besides, everyone is occupied. You couldn't ask for a better chance."

"You don't actually think…He was sort of a prick when I knew him, but not…not dangerous."

"How long has it been since then?"

"…Ten years or so…"

"That's more than enough time to become a creep. Let's do this."

"What do you mean, 'let's'? I'm going by myself, isn't that right?"

"Yes, that's right. One is better than two. Less chance of…you know…."

"Oh, sure, I know, Lola. How am I supposed to explain myself if they catch me? 'Hello, I am your estranged childhood friend and neighbor here to offer greetings after more than a decade, but oh my, look what you've done with this old barrack, it's no wonder I lost my way in trying to find the party to which I was not invited.' Something like that?"

She pushes me toward the house with her elbow.

"I don't know. I'm not your life coach. Get down there."

But I don't move.

"Lola, I really think we should reconsid…"

She takes my hand in her own and presses it to the crotch of her cut-offs. Her contours are of course hidden by the denim, but I detect a pulse below (my own, as well), which is exciting, exciting enough to leave my protest incomplete (which was surely her intention). I look at her eyes as she releases my hand, and the resignation in them convinces me before she speaks.

"If you do this, you can touch me more."

"Really?"

"Yes. Go."

She makes the mistake of slapping my back (as encouragement), and I make a sound like a balloon losing air, but she doesn't apologize. I stand and begin picking my way toward the large pale manse across the road. Since I have no idea if anyone is watching me, I also have no idea when to duck and hide, thus I cut a peculiar figure, running down the hillside toward the road while hunching low enough to touch the ground with my hands, which dangle mutely at my sides.

I reach the first row of parked cars, and work along it toward the side of the house. The music is a bit louder now, and I detect the chiming of glasses, and silverware set carelessly upon a plate. I scuttle toward the attached barn, and creep along the foundation until I reach a basement door on the side. I'm in a dangerous position. I can see the pond out back reflecting light from a sun fading past a stand of trees girding the yard, and several people chatting by the edge of the water, holding plates. All they need to do is turn around, and I would be done.

I squeeze into the shallow doorway, jiggling the handle, which does not turn. There is a small window set in the door at about the level of a Judas hole, but smashing it is out of the question. Even if I managed to break it without anyone noticing, the portal is too high to allow me to reach through it and unlatch the door from the inside, unless I find someone to lend me a stepladder, and I have my doubts about just wandering through the front door and requesting such a thing. I appear to be out of options, which is amazing because it seemed I had so many a moment ago.

More people congregate pond-side, Hermes among them, and I realize that I need to do something right now. I look around and then up, and notice a bay jutting out above the door, the sort normally containing a window. But in this case, it contains something else entirely: a toilet. Or toilets, I should say. Two holes cut side-by-side overhang the door above me, and were someone to use them at that moment, their waste would fall on my head. I remember them now. When Hermes and I were young, and the barn was still a barn, we used to explore the rambling interior cluttered with rusting threshers and stale hay, and had several times happened upon these tandem toilets nailed to the side of the house, and even used them on occasion (why not?). Perhaps Annalisa kept them as a curiosity, or she just hasn't gotten around to removing them. In any case, the dunny hovering above is my only hope.

I hear voices moving toward me from the rear of the house, which moves me, through several separate types of fear, to act. The bay is set low enough to serve is a kind of odd shelter for the basement door, which is perhaps why they kept it. I jump and grab the interior of the seat with both hands, and through some miracle of strength, manage to hoist my head and shoulders through before becoming caught at the waist. I kick my feet sadly in the mysterious air beneath, trying not to imagine what someone passing below might see: a pair of pale, idiotic legs pedaling an invisible bicycle.

The problem is now twofold. There is of course the weight I've gained and shape I'm in, which does not help, especially as my arms grow tired from bearing it. My belt buckle is also caught on the underside of the seat, and as long as it is in place, I will go no further. I lean as far forward as I can to prevent myself from falling out of the toilet and onto the ground, and twiddle the fastening with one hand while using the other to keep me in position. I've managed to loosen it, which is good, but it a bit too much, which is bad. The shorts, tugged by a combination of the belt, loose change, and gravity fall from my waist onto the ground beneath. On the one hand, I am now able to wiggle the rest of the way through the porthole into the dusty annex housing the toilets. On the other, I am without pants, and though today is Sunday, a day on which I normally do my laundry, I have not done any washing because of Lola corralling me into doing what I have just done, and as consequence of this I have no clean clothing which is to say no clean underwear, which is to say further that I now stand uninvited in a forgotten closet with two forgotten toilets attached to the home of an estranged childhood friend with nothing to conceal the way in which I have grown since the time when securing an invitation wouldn't have been a problem.

But I am inside. No small feat, and considering Lola's promise, well worth it. I place my ear to the door of the dusty closet apportioned for the toilets, and hear nothing. I turn the knob. The door opens quietly into a tastefully austere room. The furniture all appears new or barely used. But the renovations are impressive. They have installed opposing banks of windows along the walls of the former barn, a few of the original beams running parallel to them. A narrow deck is attached to the side of the house facing the party, and through a sliding door left ajar, I hear muffled music and conversation. The light fixtures are delicate and exact. They have left the floor plan open, and I appear to be standing in a living/dining area. But what is beyond?

I close the door behind me, and pad toward another on the far side of the apartment, which must lead to the main house. I hear nothing on the other side and am about to negotiate the egress when I hear a voice behind me.

"Husky boy…"

My dangling scrotum contracts and I turn slowly around. An old women is peeking her head around a doorway I passed on my way through the apartment. Likely her bedroom. How did I miss that? Her eyes, like two bits of burnished meteorite, glitter impishly in the light from the sun falling outside her windows. This must be Annalisa's grandmother, Frieda. I have only a peripheral memory of her, cultivated when we were both younger. She doesn't seem to remember me.

"Hello," I say, clamping one hand over my part and raising the other like an Indian chieftain. "Where are the pants? I seem to have lost mine."

"Husky…"

"Yes. Are they this way?" I say, waving at what I assume is the exit.

"Boy…"

"Ah. All right. This way to the pants then. Well, thank you, ma'am."

"Husky boy…"

I turn and twist the nob, entering a sort of sitting room. I lock the door I entered through from the outside, though a lock can't block sound, and once more I hear Frieda's hissing from the within.

"Husky…"

It sends a shiver through my exposed perineum. How old is she now? Almost ninety, at the earliest. On the far side of the room I spot a sideboard with several bottles of liquor barricading its top, the labels of which I do not even read as I cross the room and select one, guzzling the contents and wiping my mouth on the edge of an overstuffed ottoman on my way to the stairs, which, if I remember correctly, are through the next door. Hermes' room is at the top and to the left.

I have almost forgotten that I'm supposed to be looking for clues of some sort. How strange it is to be wandering through a place you have not been since childhood. I recall the white farmhouse as a drafty, ponderous construction, a perpetual 'handyman's dream' (to borrow the language of real estate once more) with each ancient nook containing dust from the shoulder of Ethan Allen's frock coat and a basement likely home to a ghoulish contingent of the undead. It was a mysterious place, with portions perpetually closed off in order to safeguard against falling through them into the level below. If the house was as I knew it then, I could easily picture Hermes absconding with Eleanor and secreting her away in one of its nether oubliettes. But not now, with each point filed to a soft transition, the walls sheet-rocked and painted comforting, modern colors, and the rooms filled with comforting, modern furniture. I would guess the basement abattoir is now carpeted. It's hard to infuse this tastefully appointed home with any hidden menace.

But still, I find myself in Hermes' bedroom, searching for it. The bunk beds are gone, replaced with a broad bedframe that looks like a bier. A computer sits on a similarly broad desktop set beside the slanted witch window, which I have never seen open (until today). The belief here is that tilting a window forty-five degrees to fit it into the gable also prevents any evil sorceress (They're all evil, aren't they?) from passing through it on a broomstick.

I cross the room to examine a bookcase built into the wall, and on the lowest shelf, I notice several albums shelved sideways. I remove one, shuffle the pages, and there we are, Hermes and I, on a playground structure at Calais Elementary, him, smug, blond, and oddly short, and me taller then, without glasses, and exhibiting a better haircut, but otherwise unchanged. I can't recall who took the picture.

Feminine voices, followed by the light report of eager steps on the stairs, cause me to slap the album shut and replaced it on the shelf. Someone is coming. Escaping through the witch window is not an option in obvious daylight. It seems I need a place to hide. The closet is far too shallow. If they were to open it, and reach for something, they might end up with my penis (and we can't have that). Beneath the desk presents a similar problem. I can hear them (two sets, at least) mounting the final steps, and giggling. It's strange how the sense of order and sound remains with you. I know exactly where someone is at given point based on the sound of his or her foot depressing a certain portion of the floor. How much time did I spend here? Far more than I have to hide myself. But just before the door opens, I duck beneath the bed.

It's not the best choice, but it's the only one I had (so, perhaps it is the best). The space between the floorboards and the mattress can't be more than ten inches, and the thing sags quite a bit lower in places. I have to squeeze and shove it aside in order to fit my body. There is no room to rotate my head, so my choice is between lying face up or down. I've chosen up, with my head turned left in order to keep my nose and mouth out of the mattress (so I can breath). From this vantage, I see large male feet enter followed by two dainty sets that are obviously feminine (lacquered nails, green and red, respectively).

"So, this is my room," says a surprisingly deep voice, which I take to be Hermes.

"Cute. Wow. You have a slanty window. I love slanty windows!"

I drag my face against the mattress, following their feet to the other side of the bed. Hermes stops before his closet.

"I thought I closed this."

"I love your bed!" says one of them.

"It's so big!" says the other. And then her feet disappear from the floor, and I have only a moment to grasp where exactly she is before her body lands in the center of the bed and knocks the wind out of me below it. For all the padding, she may as well have jumped directly onto my sternum from a kitchen chair. I gasp, and make the sort of noise heard when a llama is slapped (half howl, half yodel), which fortunately coincides with the swelling strings opening The Walker Brother's rendition of 'Make it Easy On Yourself' as Hermes switches on the stereo.

"I love this song!" says the one still floor-bound, her feet disappearing immediately after this report. She lands a little further up which, rather than crushing my torso, simply grinds my head into the hardwood floor.

"Come here," says the one sitting on my head (to Hermes).

"Yeah, come over here," says the other on my chest.

"Take of your shirtses" says Hermes, agrammatically.

His feet lumber toward the bed, and if I could clasp my hands beneath it, I would pray that he not jump, which he thankfully does not. Instead he lies down in the direct center of the bed, exactly above me, our silhouettes in perfect alignment. It's like being buried beneath a sandbag. Not comfortable at all, but not as bad as the jumping. I can still breathe, which is a stroke of luck. I hear more insipid giggling, and the sound of kisses being exchanged and flies drawn down. Garments begin to hit the floor on either side of the bed, pants, a skirt, a dress, panties, shirts, bras, a belt, a shoe (last, for some reason).

"You do her," says Hermes. "I'm going to jack it for now."

How colorful. Hermes shifts his position to the head of the bed, and the head of me, as well. I can still breath, but with each rhythmic yank on his part, my jawbone is ground little by little into the floorboards. There is a low, theatrical moan from above followed by a slurping (of sorts).

"Put a finger in Linda's butthole," commands Hermes.

"Um…Herm…can we just…"

"Come on! Or kiss it! Yes, kiss it…"

"I've got an idea!" says one of them. "Let's do you! How about that?"

"Well…Okay, yes, do me…"

There is more shuffling, and the room lapses into a silence punctuated only by a full-mouthed cough or hiccup from the girls or command from Hermes.

"You like that?"

There is a sound of agreement.

"Is it all in your mouth?"

And another sound of more factual agreement.

"Get on top."

I have no time to adjust, and I'm not sure where I would go in any case, before one of the women mounts Hermes and begins bouncing on him and crowing half truths into the coming dark, while the mattress pushes into my gut over and over. My breath is continually forced from my lungs by her pistoning. I turn my head (to see if it's easier to breath that way) at exactly the wrong moment, as the ancillary girl chooses the exact same moment to (I can only assume) sit on the face of Hermes, and just as I drag my mouth and nose across the underside of the bed, it falls a few inches lower beneath her weight, pinning my head to the floor and my face in the bedding. I am now suffocating, but blessedly, so is Hermes above.

"Move. I can't breath with your pussy on my face, Linda."

There is a collective breath catch.

"All right. Mackenzie, roll over."

Yes, Mackenzie, please be on the bottom I silently beg. But perhaps I wish for the wrong thing. There is another low moan, as Hermes is inserted, and the entire bed frame begins to shake with his poundings, which, as it happens, are taking place right above my head. How did he get there? Whenever I attempt to raise my head, a thrust from above knocks my skull back into the floorboards like a stubborn crab dropped by a seagull, once, twice, thrice and then I nearly lose count and consciousness. But it continues for so long that it starts to feel normal, this head hitting this floor, and, like anything else that is regularly painful, becomes just another obligation.

I taste blood, and I'm actually grunting and wheezing along with Hermes above, who is (essentially) fucking my skull. At some point, the girls change places, which provides respite. But soon it all begins again, my chest crushed beneath the mattress, and my head bonking the floor in time with their violent joy.

*

December 15th, 2005, Montpelier, Vermont

Eleanor met El just before Christmas. It was a good season for us. Her father was back in Stowe, which is to say that although the farmhouse in Northfield was bereft of Christmas cheer, it was often abandoned amid the same heaped drifts of fresh snow Dex negotiated atop Spruce Peak. I say 'abandoned' only in the sense that we were so often without supervision that we began to play at inchoate domesticity. We had been seeing each other for nearly a year. It made sense that we went grocery shopping and commuted to the library in the same car. I did my laundry at her house. We took showers together.

When her father arrived home after a long day on the slope, he gave me a nod, cracked a beer and took it to bed. After forty minutes or so, I would enter the guest bedroom in which I was meant to sleep, and tousle the sheets before going to El's room. And she would be there, massive, blond, and clear-eyed as a Nazi oracle between the sheets of which she would raise a corner to expose her nudity (always, she slept this way) in the low light cast from a bedside lamp and I would ensconce myself there, with her, each night.

The librarians were a shrewd bunch, and perhaps suspected us from the first tandem coffee break. But whatever doubt remained in the withered breast of each or any was resolved when we began arriving together in El's Volkswagen. They did their level best to assign separate tasks but it was inevitable in a small library that our work would at some point resolve itself in a nether region of the building, a place where none go for anything, the subterranean town archive (for example), and just as our work had found us here, in this low brick tomb, so would our hands find each other in the sort of reckless boredom only possible between young people without living expenses.

It wasn't unusual for us to leave mid-morning to get a coffee on State

Street, which is what we did the morning they met. I paid the cashier (my treat, this time), turned to hand El her beverage, and there, behind her in line, was Eleanor.

"You cut your hair," I said to Eleanor, and El looked puzzled.

"Did I?"

"No, I mean…I'm sorry…Behind you."

Aside from the hair, (shorter, I think) and the ungainly narcissist at her side, Eleanor appeared unchanged. From the narrowing of her eyes, a prim smile threatening to infringe on her severity, I could tell she was aware of her advantage in this neutral location, though I was unsure how she had won it.

"What are you doing here?" I asked (foolish question).

"What does one do here?" Eleanor replied as though reading from a copy of *Three Guineas*. She turned to her consort, who was examining me with a mild, almost academic interest. "I'm on a break from school. I'm sorry. This is Anders."

I took his hand. The skin was saurian and inflamed.

"Ah. I see," I said.

"See what?" asked Anders.

"Anders is just back from Europe, where he's been playing Shostakovich in Vienna" interrupted Eleanor.

"Austria," he added, as though he suspected I might ask him for a map.

"Well that's…something."

Awkwardness descended like a honey buzzard hitting a bay window. El touched my shoulder.

"Oh my, I'm sorry. Eleanor, this is …Eleanor."

It was not clear whom I was introducing. But they seemed to know. Eleanor extended her hand, and El, towering above her, took it as though testing its weight.

"Pleased to meet you," they said simultaneously, without releasing the hand of the other, their eyes, one blue set and one green, scouring the opposing visage for I knew not what. I looked at Anders, who was scratching beneath his jacket and examining the menu above the counter.

"Should we…get a table?" I asked, though I wished to leave.

"No," they said again, disengaging. Each took a step back.

"Nice to see you," said Eleanor, to me. "Come, Anders."

They took their place at the head of the queue. El took my arm and we walked outside, leaving our coffees on the counter. Snow fell.

*

June 13th-14th, 2006, North Calais, Vermont

The only thing worse than waking up in a bed not your own, in a place you would rather not be, beside someone you dislike or don't know, is waking up beneath it. The third criterion does not trouble me when I awake beneath the voluminous, saggy sleeping place of Hermes the Virile. I know I'm alone because no part of the mattress presses the air from my lungs, or grinds my skull into the floorboards. I lick my lips, tasting blood and, oddly, tears. Have I been crying? It's possible I wept, but my last recollection before passing out is of Hermes the Impetuous asking Linda to collect his seed in her mouth and then repatriate it in Mackenzie's. When this deed was complete, he collapsed on the mattress with his waist knocking my head into the floor so hard that I thought my eyes had been ejected from their sockets like two potatoes shot from a cannon. The bedroom is dark. I have no idea how long I've been unconscious. And I am still without pants.

I leverage my hand on the edge of the wooden frame and draw my body from beneath it. Once free, my neck makes a noise like a gunshot when I turn my head for what must be the first time in hours, and once centered, it (my neck) refuses to return to either position, neither left nor right, I am thus stuck looking straight up at the dark ceiling of the room. As I raise myself to standing, I place my left hand directly on the well-used condom likely left by Hermes the Bold as a tribute to whatever household god allows him to ravage two women at once while developing feelings for neither.

A light is out of the question, so I reach for the cigarette lighter I do not have because my pants and their associated cargo are still sitting in a rumpled heap outside the basement door (or beneath the indoor outhouse). Unless they have been discovered, which would be bad, since they contain my wallet, driver's license, and thirty dollars in cash. No matter. I open the closet once more and begin feeling for something that feels like pants or shorts or anything I can use to conceal my genitals. But the stock suspended in the gloom is only composed of one Oxford shirt after another. I finally lose patience and remove one, tying the sleeves around my waist so it dangles in front, and doing the same with another so that it covers my bottom, fabricating a kind of loincloth (or manskirt).

I creep to the door, which I open slightly. There is light at the bottom of the stairs, and an upbeat music ('Tarzan Boy' by Baltimora) creeping from the sitting room. I few voices murmur, a few laugh. I am trapped by good cheer. I withdraw into the bedroom, searching it for a means of escape, until my eyes settle on the witch window, already open (for my convenience). I pad toward it and pull myself through onto the roof.

It's a warm night, and the breeze feels nice on my face, which is rasped raw by the bedding. I'm in a tremendous amount of pain, and since I cannot turn my head without turning my shoulders along with it, I have no idea if anyone is watching me as I pick my way gingerly along the side of the roof sloping toward the road. Past the pitch, I can hear people talking in the backyard. Perhaps it's not so late, and Lola is still nearby.

I reach a portion of the roof between the barn and the house proper, which I know is too high to jump. But if I can just hang from the gutter, and let myself dangle, I should be able to drop to the ground. I squat facing the gable from which I emerged, and grasp the edge of the roof, tentatively dipping one leg out into the night. I brace my elbows against the gutter, letting the other leg fall, and with all the strength I have in my aching body, I lower my chest and head.

Sadly, I discover the only problem with this plan after I am already hanging by my hands from the gutter. Since my injured neck will not allow me to look down, I could be dropping into a wheelbarrow full of pitchforks. The only solution is to try swinging my body out over landing in order to apprehend whether it is safe to drop. I begin rocking forward and back from the roofline, hoping this will afford me a view of whatever is beneath. And it is in this fashion, swinging from the gutter like a baboon in a business casual diaper fashioned from his clothing, that Hermes the Wise discovers me. A light in the window before me switches on and there he is, facing me chest-to-chest, Herculean and occupied rolling a joint from a sack of marijuana plopped on a table below the window. He glances up to seal the paper with his mouth, and spots me swinging from his roof. We make an odd sort of eye contact with him appearing not very surprised at all to find me as I am, and me, wondering why he isn't more surprised. In either case, the wind picks up and a powerful summery gust rolling up from direction of the pond catches my manskirt. The garment (if you can call it that) flies up, treating Hermes the Unamused to a categorical, face-level cinema of my genitals. We're both frowning, and I, perhaps in solidarity with the man who checks his wristwatch while holding a cup of hot coffee, remove my hands from the roof to cover myself properly and instantly drop from beneath his purview into a rain barrel.

The barrel partially breaks my fall. I land straddling it, but the rim fortunately misses my exposed parts, which occupy the side holding water. It's an awkward, though not exactly painful situation, which (considering the events of the evening) is quite lucky. Hermes the Vengeful is no longer in the window. He is probably on his way outside to discuss my performance, and that's not a conversation either of us need to have. The only way to get out of the rain barrel is to knock it over, and drown the flowerbeds separating me from the road. Any flowers that escape the deluge are trampled beneath my idiot feet, as I flee the property.

The line of cars is somewhat smaller than before, though plenty of guests seem to have remained at the party. I'm nearly to the end of the queue when I pass a well-groomed couple chatting beside their Citroën. The woman spots me first, but the man continues talking until he notices the sound of my bare feet slapping the dirt as I sprint past them into the night, the tails of my loincloth billowing behind me like a dry-clean only oriflamme as I disappear from the broad circle of light thrown by the house.

I'm not sure if anyone is chasing me, but I continue to sprint down Foster Hill Road as though attempting to outrun my own humiliation. The car is fortunately where I left it, backed into a logging road at the base of the hill (Foster), with Lola asleep in the passenger seat. I jerk the driver's side door open, and she jerks awake at what I can only assume is a ghastly vision beneath the overhead light.

"Holy shitfuck!" she gasps, a hand covering her mouth. "He beat you?"

"Not exactly" I say, starting the car and turning it onto the road without looking (because I can't).

"What do you mean?"

"I mean he didn't mean to. It wasn't intentional."

"Don't make excuses for him."

"I'm not, it's just he was on top the bed, you know? And he just kept… thrusting…and thrusting…"

I sneeze and spray a fog of blood across the windscreen.

"Oh no…" whispers Lola. "He didn't…He…I'm so sorry…I shouldn't have asked you to go in there…"

"No, you shouldn't have," I say, without fully understanding what she means.

"We need to get you to a doctor" she says, crossing her arms. "First thing. We're going."

"I hate doctors. I don't need a doctor. I'm fine."

"Of course you need a doctor! When stuff like this happens you need to get tested! We should go right now. We can be there in half an hour. You shouldn't wait."

"Wait. What? Tested for what?"

"For everything, stupid!" says Lola, glaring at me. "You don't know where Herman has been or what he's done or who he's done it with. It's not too late to protect yourself."

I suddenly realize what she's suggesting.

"Lola, his name is Hermes. And he didn't rape me."

"But…the thrusting?"

"I was under the bed and he was on top."

"What?"

"He was on top!" I yell, swinging the car onto Pond Road. "He was on top and Linda and Mackenzie were too and every time one of them bounced on him my head knocked the floor or I couldn't breath and they wouldn't stop giggling and jumping on the bed, for hours, up and down, all night, and I couldn't move or get away and the only reason I'm not looking at you while I'm saying this is because my neck is so goddamn stiff that all I can do is stare straight ahead and did you know that tonight, beneath a rich man's bed I thought I was going to die? Did you know that? Tell me!"

"No," Lola whispers.

"No, I should expect not. From now on, I get to choose how we do things."

Lola hooks a finger in one of the shirts tied around my waist.

"What are you wearing?" she asks delicately.

"Something I made."

A pause.

"What happened to your pants?"

"They slipped off when I crawled out of the toilet."

A further pause.

"Why were you crawl…"

"I'm through answering questions!" I shout as I throw the car door wide and step out into my parent's driveway, tearing the shirts from around my waist and casting them into the yard as I walk inside. I hear her enter the house a few seconds after me; her small footsteps tapping the stairs to the guest room, and then silence. I have completely forgotten her offer.

12.

June 14th, 2006, Barre, Vermont

According to the pictograph affixed to the Wall of Team Leaders behind my head, Varna Madvig has been assistant manager at Food Barn since September 2004. She may have started with bagging, or as a cashier, and worked her way up, but the only information on the plaque (aside from the date, and her title) is a fatigued platitude regarding the importance of customer service ("It's a priority!"). But this phrase appears beneath the name of each team leader, even Louise Ford, the developmentally delayed senior trolley attendant. So when Varna accosts me on the bench beside checkout, I have nothing to balance my assessment of her as anything aside from a moderately ambitious yokel past the age when it is acceptable to have braces.

"Heesh in aisle shix."

Varna is not unpretty. She has a long, athletic frame, small breasts, and black ringlets cut in a clownish bob atop her skull. Her face is placid as a pony, or serene as a bowl of dough (if you like), and aside from an opaque pout about the mouth resulting from her (new, it seems) dental ware, is otherwise Gordian in its inscrutability. It would be hard to determine her feelings if she did not explain them.

"Pleesh. Heesh shitting on the floor."

"He's whatting on the floor?" I say, closing the cover of the only book I had in the car, *Beyond Coitus*. Lola left it behind when I dropped her off at the bakery in Danville earlier, and when I awoke this morning, I was in no condition to select my own reading material.

"Heesh shitting!" hisses Varna through her mouthgear, and a dollop of spit lands on my cheek, just below my left eye. She is embarrassed. "Shorry."

I stand up.

"Aisle six, you say?"

"Yesh."

It no longer hurts to sit down, thank god. The marks of Cyrus' flagellation have begun to fade from my ass and spine. But as a result of my time beneath the bed of Hermes, it now hurts to stand erect, and walking is an ordeal. And turning my head to either the left or right remains impossible. As a result, my walk past checkout to aisle six appears as a sort of eccentric parody of a young man doing his shopping. I take nimble, mincing steps to reduce the impact of my heel on the laminate flooring, because if I step too hard, the force reverberating up through my leg, chest and neck will set my head throbbing. At the mouth of each aisle, I stop, turning my entire body in a robotic, asinine motion like the closing of a shutter, to read the number painted above the index of goods, before reversing the procedure and continuing on my way. The floral stand set without good reason in the center of the thoroughfare presents a unique problem in that I cannot choose whether to go around it on the left or right, and thus must repeat my abbreviated rotation twice. Nicolette Corey (Floral Manager, June, 2004) watches me perform this ritual before the counter, her hand poised in mid-sever above a batch of pastel tulips. My reflection in her shears pivots right, back to center, then left, back to center, and pausing, before pivoting once more and going right.

Gustav is sitting with his back to me in the center of aisle six, reading a collection of frozen pizzas stacked on either side of him. His legs are buckled in a full lotus as he examines the rear of the tablet as if it contains some inclement missive, before selecting another and comparing it. Shoppers inch past him on either side, as though he is merely a clumsy boulder set amid the current of their daily responsibilities.

"Gustav."

He doesn't turn around. I notice the apron, which Food Barn was good enough to provide, is undone about the waist, and slung over his sloping shoulders like a cape.

"Gustav. Please stand up."

He doesn't stand up. Could I have predicted this? Possibly, but when my father called the house earlier this morning while I was evicting a compound of bloody snot from my nostril into the toilet, a keepsake from my time beneath the bed of Hermes, I was not feeling exactly prescient.

"They want to do a training day. Feel it out."

I examined a bruise collecting around my left eye in the bedroom mirror.

"So, what do I do?"

"You pick him up at Lucia's," said my father. His cuirass rasped the receiver. "Bring a book, or something to entertain yourself. They just want someone on site. In case there's an issue."

"I have to drop Lola off first."

"Sure, fine. She's at the house again?"

"Yes."

"You two…seeing each other?"

"Nope. She uses me for my car."

"Well, that could turn out well for you. Either way, since you're not coming to Pitkin today, it's fine to run a little late."

I consider calling him now, but that would probably do nothing, which means I need to handle this. Gustav is now holding two boxes, one in either hand, and appears perplexed by some dilemma involving them. I touch his shoulder, which is like poking a marshmallow.

"Gustav. Listen to me."

"Pleesh Gooshtav," says a voice behind me, and I shiver. "Lishun to him."

"Varna," I say, without turning. "Have you been following me this entire time?"

"Yesh."

I suppose that means she saw me walking like one of my mother's clients around her store. I squat beside Gustav.

"Here's what we're going to do. You have a choice."

I could be a birdhouse or parking meter for all he cares. I continue anyway.

"You can pick up these pizzas and return them to the shelf. And then…"

"Not on the shelf, pleesh. In the freesher."

"Right, thank you Varna. Return them to the freezer. And then we can go back to bagging groceries. Because that's why you're here. Or…"

"No, shorry, excyoosh me. That opshun ish no longer available."

I glance over my shoulder at Varna, whose fly is down, and through it there pokes pastel evidence of some sporty undergarment.

"Seriously? No three strikes or anything?"

"Shorry, no. Training day ish important. He neesh to leave."

"All right, Gustav. We're leaving."

This seems to register. He stands amid his heaped pizzas and removes the apron from around his neck.

"Good. Working is stupid."

"Yes, working is stupid," I agree, folding his apron and handing it to Varna. "Now clean these up so we can go."

He doesn't move.

"Gustav. Clean them up or I'll call your mom."

"You don't have her phone number."

"Really?"

"Nope."

He's right of course. I don't have Lucia's phone number. Fortunately though I have her name programmed into my phone, though the entry remains blank. I conjure this, and show it to Gustav, who immediately sets to returning the pizzas to the freezer.

"Like with like, please," I say, turning to Varna. "Can we speak privately?"

"Oh. Shure. Yesh. My offish?"

"That'll be fine," I say, but we don't move. She cannot seem to remove her dull, mammalian gaze from Gustav. "He'll be fine now that he doesn't have to do anything."

I arrange to meet Gustav on the bench where I was sitting when Varna approached me, while she and I parlay in her office, which is a cheerless, low ceiling room without a window, unless you count the sheet of mirrored, one-way glass affording a view of the checkout line. I sit in a plastic chair before a massive, Stalinist desk upon which Varna folds her hands and looks at me. She knows exactly what I'm about to ask.

"So, Varna."

She inches forward a little in her desk chair.

"What do you like to do?"

"I…what do you mean?"

"Hobbies. Do you have anything you enjoy? I didn't learn much from your picture on the wall out there."

"Oh, that," she says (embarrassed). "Thash jusht…you know… shumthing they make ush do."

"Sure it is. But what do you like to do?"

"I…I like to ekshurshize. Um…"

"I can tell. What else?"

She blushes, slightly.

"Well…I like…dogsh. And Indian cuisheene."

"Yeah, dogs are great. And who doesn't love a good Biryani? Let me ask you something else."

She blinks.

"Do you know your fly is undone?"

She blinks again, and looks down at her crotch before whisking her hands from the desktop to beneath and hunching slightly as she tugs the zipper. She straightens her blazer and the plastic nameplate affixed above her heart before returning her hands to the plane separating us.

"Thanksh. Why don't people tell me theesh thingsh?"

"Well…I just did."

"Yesh."

"Which is not an easy thing to tell someone."

"Yesh."

"So, as I've done you a favor."

"Yesh."

"I'm wondering if you can do me one."

She pauses, examining me. I imagine her thighs beneath the desk, rubbing together in their khaki uniform slacks.

"Gustav is stubborn. But it's just bagging groceries. He can do the work," I begin.

"I undershtand his posishun."

"Sure."

"We provide employment for people of all kindsh."

"I know. That's why PUS continues to work with you."

"But Food Barn cannot be responshible…"

"Look," I interrupt. "Maybe we can discuss this over some Indian food? How would that be?"

She begins to gibber.

"I…I…sure, I supposh…"

"It's just that I need to tell them something about today when I get back to PUS. Can I tell them he didn't do great, but he did a good enough to continue working here this summer?"

"Well…"

"I'll be here. I'll be responsible. I think you and I can work together to solve resolve any issues with Gustav. Don't you?"

"Well…yesh, I supposh."

"Great," I stand up, and hold out my hand. "It was very nice meeting you, and I look forward to working together."

She holds my hand in her own as though it is a remote control.

"Yesh…me too. Do you want my…my…telephone number?"

"Why don't you give it to me next time we come in?"

"Well…all right."

"And when will that be?"

"Wedneshday. I'll faxsh the final paperwork back thish afternoon."

"Excellent. Thanks for your time, Varna."

I leave the office before she can say another word, and recover Gustav who is perched on a bench by the restrooms, eating a stolen candy bar. I know it's stolen because of the speed with which he is consuming it. As the confection is nearly gone, I don't say anything and instead lead him through the automatic doors toward the parking lot.

Recall: Varna is not bad looking. The braces are a little sloppy, but by no means a deal-breaker. But the point here is to secure a certain type of employment, not company. If Gustav can't work at Food Barn, it means I'm stuck acting as an aid at one of the area summer school programs until my father finds another placement, which might not happen at all. If it's a choice between assisting delinquents each day or reading on a bench at the Food Barn while Gustav bags groceries, I'll do whatever I must to ensure that my time is spent doing the latter.

After dropping Gustav at Lucia's, I return home, and am enjoying a cocktail in the treehouse (the raven or crow is nowhere to be seen) when I hear a car plunking up the driveway. My mother and father had plans to see a show in Burlington tonight, and Lola doesn't have a car and, in point of fact, is at this very moment up to her elbows in organic shortening over at Guidance, expecting me to pick her up in an hour. So the rumble of a car approaching the house is suspicious at least, threatening at worst. Aside from Lola and myself, there is no one in the entire state of Vermont to report Eleanor missing, but still, as I creep through the underbrush toward the house, I imagine the sight of between two and five cruisers (perhaps one civilian vehicle) parked at odd angles to one another, and police wandering around back while several remain out front in case he (I, actually) bolts. But this is not what I see.

Instead, a red Saab hatchback is angled neatly beside my own in the small lot, and on the front steps a tall, broad-shouldered fellow holding a plastic bag in one large hand uses the other to tap politely at the door. Hermes the Brave! Of course, since I am up here, hidden in the swarthy forest like a troll, no one answers. He cups a hand against the glass, using it to brace his low forehead as he peers inside. I consider remaining where I am, letting him puzzle out the riddle of my Volvo obviously in the driveway, yet no one home, as he returns toward his car. But I prefer to get this over with now, since there is no one else here, and if I am to receive a beating for my actions the night before, I prefer it take place in private.

"Hermes!"

He turns at the sound of his name, and I emerge from the trees, dragging a scrabbled bit of them around one leg as I jog toward him. Through all this, a glass remains in my hand as I offer him the other in greeting.

"Been a while..." I venture.

He takes my hand gently, his massive head watching my face.

"Not so much. I believe I saw you last night. Hanging naked from my roof."

He drops my hand and proffers the plastic bag.

"You left your pants."

"Is that how you knew it was me? My wallet?" I ask without thinking, blindly happy that he hasn't hit me yet. Hermes blinks, and since I have not taken the bag containing my pants, he places it on the ground at my feet.

"No," he says. "I was not aware that you left your wallet. I knew it was you because I saw your face. When you were hanging naked from my roof."

"Yes. Look. I'm sorry about...all that. Would you...like a drink?"

He seems to weigh this, looking at me, the glass in my hand, and finally the direction from which I came.

"Why were you in the woods?"

"Oh. Well. There's a tree house out there. And it's where I go to...to relax."

I raise the glass.

"Really? Did you just build it?"

"No, no. It's actually been there since before I was born. I don't know why we...why we never...went there."

"Well," says Hermes. "I'd like to see it now."

"Oh. Sure. Yes. We can do that. Right this way."

We pass beneath a row of conifers and over a rock wall hugging the property line. He mounts the steps, ducking his head as he enters the dwelling. The entire structure creaks beneath his weight, and I worry that it may collapse and tumble down the hill into the slough, drowning him in the bog and embarrassing me. But I follow him anyway, sitting on a milk crate as Hermes has taken my chair. We sit quietly, watching the strip of road through the trees below us, and past that, a tendril of iridescent water, the lake, and the flexion of early evening sunlight on its surface.

"A nice spot," pronounces Hermes. I pour him a drink, which he receives without a word.

"Look," I say. "I'm sorry. I didn't mean to invade your home and expose myself to you, in that way, it's just…"

"How did you get in?"

"How did I…? Well, I…I climbed in through…through those…the toilets."

"Oh, yes. My mother likes them. Thinks they're 'country,' as it were. Didn't we used to piss in them?"

"Why, yes! We did! I thought of that when I was pull…"

"Did you meet Meemaw?"

"Did I meet…?"

"Meemaw. My grandmother. You remember her. Her apartment abuts the toilets."

"I…I may have…I…To be honest, I can't quite recall…"

"She enjoyed meeting you. Or, reconnecting, as she said."

This is quickly becoming weird. I take an anxious sip of my drink, clinking the glass off my front teeth and, finding it empty in any case, I pour myself another as Hermes looks out upon the land he owns and not at me. I feel as though I'm meant to confess to him, but he keeps not asking any questions and the suspense is making me uncomfortable.

"Hermes. Would you like to know why I was in your house?"

He makes an ambivalent motion.

"It's just that…A friend of mine disappeared and…we had, another friend, she and I thought you might, you know…know something…about it."

He doesn't say anything. I continue talking.

"I should say that I, for one, no longer think you're responsible, it just doesn't make any sense to me, I mean what with Mackenzie and Linda…"

"They mean nothing to me," he says, rather than asking me how I might have come by their names. "Your friend. Is she very beautiful?"

"Which one?"

"Either."

"Ah, yes. Both. Both are quite, um, stunning."

He nods more to himself than me.

"Will you take me to them?"

"Will I take you…to them…Well…One is, as I said, missing. So it may be…"

"And you think I had something to do with this disappearance?"

"Yes. No, actually. Not anymore. As I said."

"Why do you think that?"

And since this is the first pertinent question he asks, and it may be the only one, I'm quite suddenly divulging, revealing the story from the beginning, as though a floodgate were not only opened but blown off its hinge by an atomic bomb, the entire humiliating tide of my life since Thursday of last week is ejaculated with a magnitude both torrential and precise, as he doesn't appear to have the greatest need for narrative detail and so I try not to overpresent in the hope that Hermes may gather enough of the facts to at least absolve me of my trespass upon his property. And just as I finish my confession, the raven or crow appears on the windowsill, uttering a funereal croak before departing. Hermes refills his glass.

"I can't speak for the receipt. Though since it was for something I bought, and found on my property, I have nothing to explain. What it sounds like to me is you are caught in a pussy trap."

"A pussy trap? What do you mean?"

"It's when you become trapped. By pussy."

"Oh. I see."

"You're trying too hard. She'll turn up. And if she doesn't, someone else will."

"That's…true, I think."

"Now, regarding compensation."

Hermes stands, turning his chair from the window to face me across the wooden floor.

"You have damaged some of my property. But I will refrain from explaining to my mother the actual reason her flowers are trampled and the gutter now sags, if you allow me…"

He pauses, and I lean forward, my anus clinching with a jailhouse dread as I recall Lola's mistake the night before, and wonder whether here, in the closest thing I have to a castle, it will become an actuality.

"If you allow me," continues Hermes, "to come here, to this place, this shack you have, whenever I wish. I quite like the view. And this chair pleases me.”

I relax, and unclench.

“Well…all right. Yes, I can agree to that. It’s a deal.”

I hold out my hand, which he does not take. Instead, he stands without a word and exits the tree house, tromping back toward his car. I set my drink on the floor and scrabble after him.

“Hermes!” I shout from the edge of the forest as he opens the door of his automobile. “And you won’t say anything? To anyone? About Eleanor?”

He blinks.

“Eleanor?”

“Yes…she is the…the…”

He blinks again.

“Fine. Good.”

He is about to leave, but something on the lawn catches his eye. He closes the car door, and walks toward it, and I jog after him. In the grass are two badly soiled dress shirts twisted and stained like the mangled skin of decaying carcass. He frowns at this tableau, and seems not to notice me behind him, but defeats this notion by speaking directly to me without turning around.

“These are from my closet.”

“Yes. I’m afraid they are.”

“You used them instead of pants.”

“Yes, I’m afraid I did.”

He pauses, nodding to himself again.

“You will stock it with liquor as well, Marlowe”

“Yes, Hermes. I will do that.”

“Nothing too expensive. I can buy that myself.”

“Yes, only the…less than best.”

Back at the car, he offers his hand, which surprises me.

“Always nice to see an old friend,” he says through the driver’s side window. I watch his license plate retreat beneath the canopy of branches, trying to judge by the angle of the sun if it is time to meet Lola and whether or not to tell her what I have just done.

*

December 15th, 2005, Montpelier, Vermont

Snow fell on State Street like curled ribbons of ash from the roof of a burning building. Traffic stopped and waited. Clerks and shopkeepers were out with shovels, pushing the snow into drifts on the edge of the sidewalk and dropping salt from white buckets like chicken feed, and with each step, it popped beneath our boots as El and I walked toward the library without coffee. Whether the silence between us was adopted from that which arrived on the frosted coattails of the storm, or simply standing in lieu of our inability to say anything pleasant to one another, I could not be sure.

"Oh. We've forgotten our coffees," I said after we had reached the point at which turning back made little sense.

"You're sleeping with her," said El.

I pulled her inside a convenience store, and twisted two paper cups from a dispenser by the coffee service.

"Not anymore."

If she expected me to apologize, she would be disappointed because I would not. I made that decision as soon as I spotted Eleanor over her shoulder. I had nothing for which to apologize. But just as I became full of the delicious anticipation of self-certainty, El hooked a finger in my shirt cuff and drew my hand within her own.

"You can. If you are. I don't care."

"But I'm not. Any longer."

"Okay. But if you want to again."

"She appears to have someone. The itchy musician. El, why are we talking about this?"

"Because. I want to."

"Why?"

"You should have everything you want."

"I don't want to talk about this," I said, paying for the coffees (once more) and tromping out into what had become a blizzard since we left it.

"Was it bad?" she asked. A car skidded lazily through the stoplight, nosing the rear of another like a curious dog.

"No. We got…bored," I lied.

"Will you get bored with me?"

"I'm not bored with you."

It wasn't the answer she wanted, but I hate speaking in hypotheticals for the sake pleasing anyone. The light changed, and we were about to cross, but El released my hand and stepped in front of me.

"The dean called last night. They accepted me. I'm going in January."

I don't know why El was afraid to tell me. I offered congratulations, and said I was proud of her, but it was too late. Revealing her acceptance cast an aspect of bereavement across the remainder of the afternoon at work. The librarians, intuitive as they are, provided El a wide berth, and I did not reveal the good news to them, and instead proceeded about my rounds with El mooning and glum at my side. And an hour before closing, I lost patience.

"Did you think I would care more, El?" I said, jamming several trade paperbacks into an overcrowded bay. "Do you want me to be upset? Is that why you're upset?"

She wasn't a crier, but when she looked up from the stool on which she had sunk, her eyes were pink and moist, as though she had been crying and I hadn't noticed.

"No. I don't want you to be upset," she said. "But…do you ever feel like…the things we do don't make any sense. And we just do them because…we don't have any other ideas? And it's maybe so much easier to do something instead of doing nothing that we just…we just…"

I was poised in mid-shelve.

"…El? Is there more?"

She stood up, grabbing several books and sticking them on the shelf in no order.

"I think," she said, "that growing up is about taking everything you like to do…the stuff you enjoy, and just setting it on fire."

"So you don't get cold?"

I was joking, trying to plant a sort of levity where none would apparently grow, because El became even more solemn and pointless in her work.

"No. The idea is to have the biggest fire."

When we reached her house that evening it was cold inside and Dex was asleep in a chair. El woke him gently, and he raised himself, a beer bottle clattering about his feet, and waved to me before plodding up the stairs. El and I followed a few minutes later. I raised the sheet and pulled myself into her bare expanse, the collection of large, warm muscles and heavy bones, and what I expected was a talk of some kind, but she was already asleep, which left me curious for the first time as to how I would feel when she left.

13.

June 14th, 2006, Montpelier, Vermont

Four hours after Hermes visited the tree house, Lola emerges wobbling from the Langdon Street Taproom. I wave from across the street beneath the broad brim of what she earlier referred to as a 'racist hat' (perhaps confusing it with a pith helmet) but which is really just an average headpiece, the sort of semi-practical thing you might don in order to kayak (or garden beneath the sun). She steps between two parked cars before lurching in front of a third which breaks gently, the driver, a friendly grandpa sort, appearing puzzled by this extreme looking person leering at him through the windscreen. She drops onto the bench beside me.

"Please, take that stuff off. You're making yourself more conspicuous."

In addition to the hat, I have also exchanged my goggle-like spectacles for a set of yellow tinted shooting glasses I found collecting dust on a shelf in my parent's basement.

"You look like Hunter S. Thompson. If he was a woman," Lola hisses, snatching them from my face and flinging them into the street. She reaches for the hat, but I shift to the far side of the bench.

"When I said we should do things my way," I begin, "I didn't mean that you should start behaving like me. I just meant I would prefer not be brutalized based on hearsay."

"What do you mean?" she asks, burping somewhat.

"I mean, remember when I was drunk? Now you're drunk."

"I had to have a couple. Develop a rapport, you ingrate."

"Did you get his name? At least?"

"Kristof."

"Kristof what?"

"Kristof how the fuck should I know? Why don't you go in there and fool him with your disguise? Show me how it's done."

She gives the brim of my hat a violent tug, which twists my head and makes me wince. This seems to sober her.

"Oh…Oh that's right…Your neck…I'm sorry."

I retrieve my glasses from the street, and return them to my face.

"What time does he get off?" I ask, being sure to stand out of reach.

"Nine is what he said."

"Where does he think you're meeting him?"

"Outside, I guess."

"You guess? Lola, this was really easy."

"Then why don't you do it?"

"Because I do everything and he isn't gay!" I shout, drawing the attention of a clutch of evening goers outside a cafe across the street. My outburst actually seems to please Lola, who reclines regally on the bench locking her purple eyes on mine behind the shooting glasses.

"You know this is completely stupid, right?

"I disagree."

"Just because he maybe works in a place where there's a green arm…"

"Green Sleeve, Lola! And he does work there! He told me! And he has the tattoo! Yes, you're forgetting the tattoo!"

"So just because he works in someplace with a bowl of Green Sleeves and has a Femammals tattoo, you think I should prostitute myself to find out if he has Eleanor's head on a stick in his backyard? It doesn't mean anything. You know how many times I've seen that thing sewed onto some shitking's messenger bag? Just a bunch of limp dicks in practical shoes and hats like that one."

She points to my headgear.

"One big apology tied up with a ponytail. Faggots."

She is saying all this quiet loud, and the onlookers across the street are starting to inch from beneath the awning to hear more. I reach down and take her arm gently, at which time I'm met with an open-palmed, yet still powerful slap, which sends my glasses once again skittering into the middle of the street. The pedestrians make a communal sound of disbelief, and one detaches from the retinue to retrieve the glasses. I meet him in the middle of the street, thanking him and returning them to my face.

"You got yourself a rough one, friend," he says over his shoulder as he returns to his side of the street and I return to Lola, who is tittering to herself on the bench.

"Let's try this a different way," I say, once more placing myself beyond her range. "I'm going to sit on a different bench, because if I sustain any more blows to the head, I will have a seizure. You don't want to go home with him, I can't make you. But when Kristof comes out of there. I'm following him. Come if you want. But I need to find out if he's hiding something. It's too big a coincidence not to investigate."

"Fucking pussy…" she mutters venomously to herself, because I'm already down the street, watching the barroom door and trying to guess the time. I don't understand why Lola is resistant to my plan. Well, probably because it's mine. And the alcohol doesn't help. Is that how I appear to those beyond the confines of my brain? When discussing this plan on the way from Danville, Lola suggested that, since there was drinking involved, I should be the one to approach Kristof, though we did not yet know this was his name. I said I thought it would be better if she did and she asked me why.

"You're a…an…an attractive female…person."

"I don't drink well."

"You can learn to."

She seemed to be weighing this on the passenger side.

"Do you think you're an alcoholic?" she asked.

"No" I said. "Do you?"

"Do you drink everyday?"

"Usually."

"Do you need to drink everyday?"

"No."

"Then why do you?"

"I believe there is a boat in my stomach. Normally, this vessel is stuck in dry dock. I pity it, so I drink because the thought that it is once again sailing on a calm sea of ethanol pleases me."

"Why don't you just drink water?" asked Lola.

"The boat likes liquor!"

This silenced her, and for a moment, I felt bad. Perhaps she was actually concerned, and just trying to help.

"Do you think I should stop? Perhaps go to a meeting of some kind?"

"No. Not at all. It makes you happy."

Yes, that's certainly true. It makes me happy. But watching another person do it does not. Especially when they have descended past the point at which my plan would be appreciated. It's not a terrible idea. Kristof works at Montpelier Underground, the only place in the area still stocking Green Sleeves. He is aware of Eleanor and her clique, the evidence of which is imprinted on his skin. And after my conversation with Hermes the Shrewd, it was obvious that we had exhausted one of our two leads. And when Lola argued that the condom could have been sitting in the bottom of a drawer in some adolescent bedroom from the time when the prophylactic was prevalent, I had no rejoinder other than to say that Kristof was a suspect, and we had nothing else to investigate.

Which brings me to the plan for tonight. I never suggested that she actually sleep with him (Kristof). All I said was that it would be helpful to us both if she could merely suggest that this was a possibility, if only for long enough to gain entrance to his apartment and have a look around. At which time, she could pretend to get sick or something and excuse herself. No harm done. But my face still aches from her hand, and I cannot understand how my plan is any worse than the one I employed the night before, which in all its reckless ambiguity nearly killed me.

Kristof emerges from the Langdon Street Taproom at exactly nine, and waves to me across the street. I respond by tugging the ponderous brim of my practical hat, cursing myself for even bothering to wear it. I hear a snort down the line, which I take to be Lola eliciting smugness, but is actually just a sleeping sound. Without me at her side to abuse, she apparently grew bored and passed out, which is how I leave her as Kristof rounds the corner from Langdon to Elm, and I, after counting to an arbitrary number in my head, follow.

In what light is left in the evening, or perhaps in that thrown by street lamps, most of which are only now igniting, stuttering once, twice, and once more, the courthouse blooms across the street, and it's like I'm noticing it for the first time as a place with the potential to seal my fate if this plan, my plan, does not produce what I hope it will. I've never been arrested, or even served on a jury. The court of law, even this outwardly friendly red brick facade with its Doric columns and unset clock in the cupola, is as mysterious (to me) as a Masonic hall, and inclement as, well, as any structure symbolizing authority beyond my own. When Eleanor's parents return in two days, is this where it will end? Is this where my confession will be entered into my permanent record, and all present will know that I left when I should have stayed, and I dithered when I should have gone to Arthur Stool (for help)? I can see her parents, Oliver and Lydia, shaking their heads among those seated, as I explain what they already understood years ago, yet their faces plied by a renewed disgust in the proclivities I inflicted on their daughter, and god knows how many more innocent young woman.

I've been torturing myself with these speculations for long enough to allow Kristof to nearly disappear around an elbow of low-income housing two blocks away, and I would have lost him entirely if he did not pause and enter one of the end units. I jog toward the buildings, which are all of similar make, three stories of anonymous windows and one door, each unit joined to the one beside it like a sort of decrepit townhouse sans yard, as the entire length of the street is hemmed by the Winooski river in the rear, and the street itself in the front. In every third window or so, a bare bulb burns or the bluish white light of television casts long shadows across dull ceilings, beneath which residents grow old. What is Kristof doing here?

I squat in the shadows across the street, and when he emerges a few minutes later with several people in tow, two young women, both somewhat pretty (at a distance), both interchangeable, brunettes (as it were) and a man, I hunch even lower, and using the row of parked cars for cover and their jovial, expectant voices as a guide, I follow them further down Elm Street. The voices turn left onto a pleasant side street of larger, Victorian homes divided into apartments, and it is into one of these that Kristof and his cohort enter, lingering on the broad, hooded porch while he fumbles a key into the lock, and then I'm alone and lurking across the street, just beyond the pale white purview of its single lamp. What now? The house looms in its darkened lot like a fortress. I have no idea on which of its three floors Kristof lives. A light flickers in a second floor window, but is that proof? After my recent experience with misplacing my suspicions, I need something concrete.

I cross the street and tap up the front steps, absently testing the locked front door. Is this the end? For all I know, Kristof could have organized a torture and molestation party for Eleanor. She could be shackled to a urine-soaked mattress in the basement, her white skin bruised yellow, her green eyes split wide as Kristof and his retinue enter, chuckling, to take their diverse pleasure. I can't stop here. But since there are obviously people within, I can't break the glass, and I have nothing with me that might serve as pick, and still there remains the problem of which floor Kristof rents. The directory beside the rectangular mailbox resolves the last of these issues (1 FL.), but I'm still left without a way inside.

I tug the door again with an ape-like motion, though I'm unsure of what I would do if the portal were to yield. Light appears behind a thick curtain hung in the window beside the door, and I hear several voices muffled behind it. Inching below the sill, I press an eye to the minute space beneath the fabric's edge, which allows a view of several pairs of legs, two crossed (the women) on a couch, one standing, another squatting in front of a what must be a stereo, as music pulsing from the speakers vibrates the glass against my cheek. Even on this side of it, I smell marijuana. Not exactly the sort of inebriant one would expect to preempt murderous sadism. Even so, I can't use that as proof. I can just imagine the conversation with Lola.

"They were smoking pot and listening to music. So I left."

"Fool!"

And she would perhaps follow this with a brand of sadism all her own, a bludgeoning about the face and shoulders, or a simple silent treatment meant to foment the notion between us that I, in all my potential yet un-demonstrated talents, am not an asset to the investigation. Perhaps she has grown as bored with me as I have with her. Even when I remember the color of her pubic hair and sun shining through the sliding door upon the associated quim, the gloriously firm vision of her breasts and nipples, the taut, brown skin of her stomach, and everything else I saw in Eleanor's basement, I remain unmoved, even in memory. The recollection of my hand against her crotch in the field above Hermes' house is just a dream of sun-warmed denim without promise. How odd that desire, when left to dangle, will sometimes retract its tendril like an anchorless length of rope drawn over the prow of a ghost ship. Maybe I'll suggest we spend some time apart when she sobers up.

Since everyone inside is distracted in the front room, it's probably best to sneak around back. Hopefully if the rear is locked, I can locate a base-ment window in the foundation and wiggle through. Then, once everyone leaves or falls asleep, I'll have the run of the house. But before I can stand up, the porch is illuminated by a light set above the transom, and I hear a voice behind me.

"Do you want to come inside or something?"

Rather than raising myself to my feet, I wheel around like a crab to find Kristof with his head outside the front door, watching me.

"How?…One moment!"

I return my face to the window, and still I count four sets of legs behind the curtain.

"Who is the fourth legs?" I ask, and Kristof seems as puzzled by the question as I am in asking it.

"I don't know what that means. Look…"

He steps onto the porch and closes the door behind him.

"If you want to come in and hang out or something, it's just me and my roommate and a few friends. They're nice. It's cool."

I raise myself to my knees, my hands dangling at my sides.

"You're not going to…call anyone?"

"What? Like the cops or something?"

I nod. He smiles and for the first time I notice two of his teeth are missing.

"No. I'm not going to call the police. I saw you following us. That hat kept poking up behind cars across the street."

"But…I'm spying on you!" I say. "I'm…I could be a…a…a criminal!"

Kristof shrugs.

"You just seem kind of…and don't take this the wrong way, man, it's just I remember you from the Taproom…You seem kind of lonely."

I don't say anything, and he opens the front door, and sets one foot inside.

"We got some beer and, you know, other stuff if you want. I'm going to leave the door open. If you want to stay out here, that's fine, but please stop crawling under the windows. It might freak out the other tenants."

He is gone through the door, which he doesn't bother closing, and which I shut as I follow him inside and past a large staircase into the apartment.

The curtain is not a curtain but a sort of Mughal sheet peppered with yawning, vaginal flowers and probing phallic paisleys, and is strung along a length of rope suspended above the sill, and fluttering now, as Amelia (yes, that Amelia) opens the window it conceals, and on the couch is Ursula Snopes (she too), older, a bit porcine and without a spiked collar, but still certainly her, and by the stereo, two men, my own age, who I do not recognize, and Kristof introduces together as Hector and Willow.

A disused fireplace intends one wall, and in it, a miniature refrigerator has been indecorously installed. But who am I to question its use as I accept a beer withdrawn from the coals (so to speak) by Hector or Willow, so cold it burns my hand, and as I beginning tugging from it, Amelia turns from raising the window and her features change slightly in the light which I saw from outside, a low lamp on a low table with a revolving, patterned shade that casts the figures of hobgoblins, imps, and lesser demons on all four walls in a macabre jig, and her own contorted expression, as she struggles to recall where she might have seen me before. Was I so unmemorable?

"I know you…Amnesty, right? Yeah, we were did A.I. together after school! How you been?"

Apparently so. I was harder then, or at least leaner, the diet version of myself, but it appears now that in my soft middle, my receding hairline, my practical, wide-brimmed hat and spectacles like the lens of an aerospace telescope she divines only an aging liberal whose best work is certainly behind him. Yes, of course we wrote letters to our congressman requesting that they free political prisoners malingering in some third-world gaol, penning missives in pursuit of social justice over decaf tea and ginger snaps in the atrium at Montpelier High School, and left feeling we had done a little something for the world. Should I pretend I was the chapter head? Would that help me in any way?

"No, I think you…have me confused with someone completely different, Amelia."

Best not to lie, since there is no benefit. The last time I touched a newspaper was while lining Ignatz's litter box. She is still quite lovely, prim, and excited-looking, an obvious valedictorian. Conversely, I was never particularly attracted to Ursula. In fact, ever since that summer when she forced me to kiss her beneath a crab tree on the State House lawn, the memory of her had been a source of shame. But since I was fifteen years old then, and had no license (and thus, no car), I had no definite means of escape (other than a plan to meet my mother when she got out of work). And it was interesting to have an afternoon girlfriend who would allow me (pardon) to touch her vagina, which, since I was young, seemed like probing the mouth of a toothless, slack-jawed dog. But she acted as if she enjoyed it, and when she touched me, I did enjoy it. It was interesting enough to continue, this new ground broken between us. But it was a small pimple (of all things) that I spotted that afternoon on the State House lawn beneath her armpit (perhaps it was an ingrown hair), which turned me from her, and indirectly toward Eleanor.

"I remember you," says Ursula from the couch, and Amelia turns to her for clarity. "You treated me like shit, Marlowe."

"So you guys know each other," says Kristof, by the stereo. "Great."

It wasn't so much the pimple itself as the fact of it upon her, its yellowish, inflamed sheen unbroken beneath her arm. Not close, but not exactly distant either, from the mouth yawning into my own. When night fell beneath the crab tree, this same mouth would navigate to other parts of me. The novelty of Ursula's willingness was both its own redemption and curse. I expected her to be flawless, but was willing to settle. And only after Halloween, and the mating of Bill and Santa (Clinton, and Claus, respectively), and then the loss of the former both in the world outside, and in that which comprised my private longing for Amelia (more of her), but forgot me as soon as I flung the knotted condom off the deck attached to the house on Cliff Street. It flew out into the frosted October night, which had (during our joining) become the morning of November, and she departed never to return in that particular way. But who remained, who was available, who was willing?

"Ursula. Nice to see you, again. I thought you'd gone…away. To…"

"Missoula. I came back."

"I've heard Colorado is nice."

"It may be. Missoula is in Montana."

Yes, sadly it was her, Ursula, who weathered the ineptitude of this newly kindled desire, this unavoidable next step, this 'getting serious' as she called it. I did not realize she had preserved her maidenhead until after I had robbed her of it in a stand of woods behind the rest home on Heaton Street. As her bare thighs quaked in the cold, and her back settled into a bed of fallen pine needles, I arched stupidly above her, lasting all of five earthbound minutes. Afterward, as we sat, freezing, collecting ourselves, she told me it was her first time, and I apologized. She may have said something insufferably stupid, something like 'We're not kids anymore,' and all I saw, in the blaze of a late autumn sun above the houses hugging the treeline was the whitish pustule sitting in a feverish red areola beneath her arm earlier that summer. Was it still there? There was no way to tell. She had not removed her parka.

"That's an interesting hat," says Willow or Hector. "I have one just like it."

"Oh, how interesting," I mimic.

"Is that a disguise or something?" asks Ursula. "Kris said some sad guy might be following us.”

“I didn’t say sad,” says Kristof, emerging from the kitchen. “I said lonely. And it wasn’t a criticism.”

“Are you lonely?” asks Amelia.

“I am often lonely,” says Hector or Willow to no one.

“Everybody’s lonely,” says Ursula, crossing her arms over her rotundity. She stares at my face. “Do you actually need those to see, or is that like some kind of statement?”

I don’t reply, instead helping myself to another drink from the fireplace and planting myself on the couch beside her.

“Can I ask you something?”

She looks suspicious.

“I’m not sure I want to talk to you.”

“Please it’s not bad. Or I hope it’s not bad.”

She shrugs.

“Why are you so mad at me?”

Ursula opens her mouth, apparently shocked that I would have to ask, and I try to clarify.

“No, no wait! I mean ‘why’ as in what do you remember? When you think of me, what do you remember that makes you so angry? That’s all I mean. You can be angry. But please, tell me why.”

“That seems reasonable,” says Willow or Hector from the kitchen.

“Is this like a dick thing?” asks Ursula. “Do you just want me to say what an asshole you are so you can like be a caricature? The person you imagine you’re supposed to be?”

“No. No, I don’t think so.”

“Wait…” says Amelia, thoughtfully, reexamining my face.

“You were…nothing,” says Ursula. “It wasn’t even that you weren’t available, I mean we were fifteen or sixteen or whatever it was. You were just not there.”

“So…I was stupid?” I ask.

“No. Not stupid. You could obviously think and act intelligently. Maybe that was the worst part. You just kissed me like…like…like I was made of shit. I'm sorry-"

She apologizes to Amelia, who won't stop looking at me, and actually walks over to the couch to look beneath my hatbrim. Her mouth forms an O.

"Like you couldn't be bothered to just…God, this is so hard to explain…I felt like whenever you looked in my eyes, even when we were, you know, it was just so you could watch your reflection."

"So, I'm…vain?" I venture.

"No! It's not vanity; it's weirder than that. It's like there was always two of you, or you were imagining two of you around, all the time, and whenever we were, we were, we were fucking, sorry, Amelia, whenever we were fucking, it was like you were always referring to the other you rather than me, and everything you did, kissing me, or touching me, or saying something nice was all for him or some audience, like you were seeking approval or doing this stuff for them or him even though you didn't want to, you weren't trying to please yourself or me or anything except the person you imagined was there, watching and like, reviewing or something."

She stops talking and the entire room is silent. Hector, Willow and Kristof are standing by the kitchen table, a tray of steaming, ignored brownies between them. Amelia's head is cocked, her arms now crossed like Ursula's, only she is standing, and Ursula is still talking, but quieter.

"I know I've gained weight, but trust me, I've done fine since you. And I've never been with anyone who behaved like that. Maybe it's not your fault. I don't know. I guess I'm angry because I don't understand how you can live that way. It frustrates me every time I think about it."

Amelia touches my shoulder.

"Santa?"

I nod, and she shivers.

"There's brownies," says someone from the kitchen.

14.

April 2nd, 2006, Julian Falls, Ohio

Her tibia snapped while I was still on the ridge I didn't realize was a ridge, even as she disappeared beneath its chin, and the pop of the shankbone splitting I assumed was just a forest noise, a crushed twig or settling tree. It hurt her a lot. I knew that. The first scream from below my foothold was a wet, hacking sound, almost like a consumptive cough. My erection began to fade in a cold wind issuing from deeper in the forest like the breath of a sylvan ghost. The second scream was a definitely a cry for help, but its grammar wasn't linguistic. I resettled my part and descended to her.

I don't know why I expected blood. She had not fallen far, but she had fallen awkwardly, and she landed not on rocks, but a bed of vegetation and twigs concealing rocks. There was nothing demure in her posture. She was sitting on the damaged leg, as it had folded beneath her during the fall, and her hands where touching the ground, the fingers like the legs of a white and blushing arctic spider. She said it hurt and I said I understood what that meant because it was truly difficult for me to look at the limb crooked beneath her bare buttocks. In the center of her right shin, a bend was apparent where one should not be, and the ankle was swollen and pink. Then came the third scream, which was more of a grunt not unlike that which passed from her mouth into the broad shape of the forest, when the ridge remained intact, and her back was to me, our pelvises locked and forming a sort of K shape on the hillside. We had come there to talk.

She wanted to stand up, but I said it was best if she didn't since she couldn't and that I had to leave her alone to make a phone call since we were too deep in the woods to get reception. And she said she didn't want to be left alone and I realized she no longer trusted me, or perhaps she never had, and whatever doubt remained with me regarding what to do (there was a little, who knows why) dissipated, and I knelt in the vegetation and twigs touched her face and hair and tried to keep the tenuous earth from shifting beneath us while I said I would be right back. I still imagine love as that moment.

I ran back to the trailhead, and made the call on my cellphone when I reached the road, explaining what had happened and where I was and after it had ended, I stood unsure of whether I should wait for the ambulance to arrive or return to her. I kept hearing a fourth scream, or it could have been a bird, perhaps a raven or crow like the one that had landed atop the tree neither of us realized was dead as I pushed into her and she pushed into it. A portion of the tree, a bit of bark she had used to steady herself, released from its mooring against the trunk with a mushy whisper, and her balance failed, and I slipped from her, before she disappeared below the bank, I felt within her not only the failure of gravity but the adrenal concave of her fear and the physical bite of the question she surely had time, in that single, unstuck second, to ask which was whether or not she was about to die.

Had I known this would be an outcome when I showed up at North Hall to fetch her after I finished at the Aurora and suggested we take a walk in Skinny Glen? Of course not. I intended to explain about the night before, about Ludmilla, and my shoes (earlier she asked, 'where are your shoes?'), and how I was certain it wouldn't matter much (best to suggest this, in case it did) but I wanted to make sure she heard something about it from me, rather than have it issue in a distorted form from the invasive rabble (our peers) on campus. Across the road, a student (one of them) waved to me beside Birch, and I waved back, not sure who it was, or if I should explain why I was shoeless and harried at the roadside, my checkered hunting shirt in disarray, my shit-colored dungarees muddy at the knees, and a bright orange stocking cap absent from my head. It must have been snagged from my skull as I ran from her, to here. Between breakfast at the Aurora, and my light knock on her door in Green Hall, had I changed my clothing? And if so, why had I not replaced my shoes?

It was Greer waving now, and leaving the campus, crossing the road toward me, her sloping shoulders, tundra bosom, and sallow, beer-leavened features, topped with an astringent bushel of hair burnt nearly white by a peroxide bath in a Woody Hall sink, my god, she was a vision of hatred searching for a vessel.

"If you're trying to peep in windows," she said, "farther down the line's a bit better."

She swept her twig-like arm toward the back of Birch facing us across the road.

"No. I'm waiting for something."

"What kind of something?"

And rather than answering, I heard the siren groaning down Corry Street, and I waved to them to pull over near me, and tried speaking to the EMT's emerging from the ambulance's rear but all I could really do was gesture toward Skinny Glen and begin walking, hoping they would follow me, and Greer, in the light from the siren, blue and red, pink when combined, looked undead. She followed us, me and my merry men, into the forest, keeping her distance, until we reached the place where El was still sitting, naked and in shock, her leg inescapably broken from the brutality of which I had become an inadvertent mechanism, and Greer, as her gaunt face absorbed the technicians retrieving El from the forest, and me, obviously responsible for it, and in something that passed from El to me, and onward to Greer, I suddenly knew that my first term at St. Margaret University would also be my last.

They wouldn't let me ride in the ambulance since I wasn't a relative and, for all they knew, could have been directly responsible for El's condition. Greer certainly thought so. She stood with me as they loaded El into the vehicle and watched it depart in smear of speed and sound toward Dayton, and I misread her (Greer) so badly, I still want to punish myself for this, I still do, because when it had all faded, when the ambulance was gone and the only sound was that screaming, problematic plague bird from Skinny Glen, and the middle distant well-bottom noise of students and drinking on campus across the road, I turned to her and realized I was unsteady and placed a hand on her shoulder which felt like the splintered joining of a park bench, and she jerked her body away from me and I fell, and didn't get up.

"Please can I borrow your car," I said, still grounded.

"Fuck you!"

Where did she go? Back to campus, to shout the news like a town crier, to announce to those who did not know me and those who did, that I had taken a lovely El to the woodland and snapped her ankle over my knee (like some bit of cannibal firewood), and left her while I dithered behind Birch, trying to catch a glimpse of nudity through a window. Maybe it was best to stay here, to remain in the forest, without shoes or food or anyone to ask me questions. But no one would, even then, I knew my side had been established, and with El gone to Dayton for god knows how long, I was on my own.

How could it all fall apart so quickly? I had barely yet adjusted to being a student. When El said I should apply after revealing her own acceptance, I didn't realize that she had submitted an application to MU in my name earlier that year along with her own, that she had gleaned all the necessary and vital information which she did not already know from cards pilfered from my wallet, and impersonated my mother over the phone in order to gain my high-school transcript, and even ghost wrote three letters of recommendation. I didn't know any of this, but when I returned home later that evening, my father was ecstatic after having received a phone message from the then dean of MU announcing my acceptance. My parents hadn't realized I'd applied, and were convinced that my saying it must be some mistake was related to pride rather than authentic confusion. El called shortly after and explained that there was no pressure. She just wanted to provide me with an option. And before leaving herself a few weeks earlier to visit relatives en route to Ohio, I still had not made my decision. I never thought it would all happen so easily, that this paper would pass from her hands into the toothless maw of mailbox, and that several months later my belongings would be packed in my mother's car, heading west.

And after orientation, after that first unsettling day, after Martin Bastarde had finished wincing through his ceremony, I wandered through the campus, through snow shoveled in four or five foot drifts against the wall of the student union and the sandstone flank of Main Building, past the trunks of huge bare trees hung with hoarfrost, and I was so obviously new, the look on my face was one of earnest misunderstanding, an expression of apology, and a bag full of plastic coat hangers clacked like the orphaned bones of a heron against my thigh, my mother's last gift to me before she dried her eyes, cranked up the satellite radio, and spun the rental car toward Dayton International. Yes, I am in Ohio, America, I thought, a college student in the hamlet of Julian Falls, there is so much to determine but for now, I must find her, because I know she is here, somewhere, and I am expected.

"I don't want to be a 'campus couple,' please."

When did El say that to me? It was after sex, after I entered North Hall (her dormitory) through a side entrance, the coat hangers clacking, and knocked on several of the wrong doors in the wrong hall on the wrong floor before I was directed by an abused-looking R.A. to the correct place, her doorstep. She opened the door as if she wasn't expecting me, and maybe this was the case. But she drew me in, and closed it, mentioning her roommate was living in the greenhouse attached to the science building. I said something unimportant, and then we were fucking without actually saying anything. I only discovered this muteness was a problem later that day, when I signed my name to the agreement ('Preventing Offenses…'), but at this point, with El squatting over me on the floor of her room, I was not aware of it. Our mouths met in a sort of salute to wordlessness, and someone may have knocked and said they were going to dinner, and asked if El would like to come along. She didn't respond, and they went away. It was only later that I discovered it was Greer who had knocked.

"I don't know what that means," I said. We were in bed, the sheet pulled to my chin and below her breasts, and outside the window snow winnowed and fell.

"I had sex with someone other than you," she said.

"That's fine."

"Don't be upset."

"I'm not upset."

"We should do what we want."

"We should."

"You should do what you want."

"I will."

"Please be honest with me. I'm being honest with you."

"Yes."

Maybe I lied. Maybe I was jealous. But only jealous enough to feel vindicated in my own desire to see what else occupied this new place. This was why I agreed (with her) to keep our knowledge of each other a secret, to not explain our friendship, or our history, or anything to anyone. Because it was such a small place (El explained), and it was best for me to be anonymous (if possible). I didn't ask who she had sex with in the small amount of space between her arrival and my own, because what would I have done with that knowledge? I knew no names, and only a minute gallery of faces, and I didn't even know where my dorm was in relation to hers. I accepted a cup of green tea from an electronic kettle atop a desk bolted to the painted brick wall and said I was glad I'd come.

*

June 14th–15th, 2006, Montpelier, Vermont

I realize the brownies are baked in marijuana butter after I've eaten two, and if I had to guess the time I would be unable, but everything in the apartment indicates that I have exhausted my welcome. And I still have to collect Lola from the bench on Langdon Street, a task that may as well be the slaying of a Minotaur after my brush with Kristof's baking. I stand up from where I've been sitting for I know not how long.

"I think I should go," I say, and no one says 'yes' or 'no', not even Hector and Willow who in all their distinction had been amicable until this point. They stand between the kitchen and living room examining the floor, as though waiting for the same bus, and rather than saying goodnight, I take another beer from the fridge embayed within the fireplace. No one meets my eyes, except Kristof, offering more confections as he sees me to the door, grinning with his mouth like a graveyard after a flood. And my own, like a clumsy compactor mashing his treat between jaws and watching Ursula watch Amelia distracting herself from meeting any look I might send her way. The stereo bleats a curious music like the sound of pages turning in a crawlspace (possibly something by John Adams). I tell Kristof I'll see myself out.

I don't realize he follows me to the porch, and down the steps, and to the end of the street until I turn right and he remains behind at the corner. And when I finally notice him, half-birthed in a cowl of night beside a monolithic hedge on the corner of Elm Street (indistinct, but alive in my periphery), it's as if some double has emerged from the house to see me home, and what Ursula saw ten years ago has now become an actual presence alive upon the earth. I extend a hand into the mantel of darkness at the corner, expecting a perfectly mirrored negative to grasp it, but the hand meeting my own is liquid with ink, tattoos swirling in their own gravity, a hyena in high heels galloping among them, and when Kristof releases me, he speaks slowly with his back to my face, walking away.

"Watch out for Lola."

And rather than asking Kristof how he knows her, or what he means, or what time it is, I say I will watch out for her, and turn on my heel toward town. The street is still as a painting as I wander through a velvet curtain of timeless night, past the dark windows of the housing complex from which Amelia and Ursula emerged, until I see the clock above the courthouse still reading 3PM, leaving the actual hour unconfirmed. What time is it?

But I appear to have a much larger dilemma, which arrives in the form of an empty bench up the street from the shuttered Taproom on Langdon Street. I have no idea how long I've been staring at the seat where Lola should be, or at which point I open the beer from the house, but the clock still reads 3PM in the cupola, which could mean no time has passed at all, but the bottle in my hand is half empty.

Though I can see the single blinking traffic light above the intersection of State and Main reflected in the window of the apothecary at the head of the street, it seems to take an entire geologic age to reach the corner and turn, ship-like, in the direction where I believe, somewhere, my car is parked. The town is pestilential in its emptiness and silence, and totally free of traffic, and when I look between my feet, I see two solid yellow lines running parallel to each other. How I arrived from the sidewalk to the center of Main Street is as big a mystery as Eleanor's disappearance, but since the demarcation seems to conduct my path in the proper direction, I hold the course, barely even pausing when a twelve point buck clops through the intersection ahead of me. He is many hands high, broad, powerful and without a master as the white fur beneath his gut and fringing his backside retreats down State Street. But in the highest reach of his rack, I could swear I see the outline of dark pinions, scaled black feet clutching a bony purchase, and an igneous beak like a falchion dipped in ink, this portrait swaying indefinitely with the buck's navigation. But it happens so fast, that it may not have happened at all, and when the line between my feet ends at his crossing, I become briefly lost in my own town, observing three of the four ways available to me, and nearly past hope of ever removing myself from where I'm planted, the red light above my head now blinking a caution to all those who might encounter me here, marooned beneath it.

I notice the cruiser only because it is stopped at the light beneath which I was standing a moment ago, and I am now on the sidewalk, shrouded in the darkness of a storefront, though I have no recollection of moving (How does this happen?). The vehicle pauses, barely braking, before proceeding toward City Hall, and against the passenger window, in the red light thrown from the traffic signal, there is a lovely face pressed grotesquely into the glass, the breath fogging it in a lopsided oval, the eyes closed in a restless sleep, and even in this abbreviated glimpse, I recognize Lola in repose, a criminal Olympia. The taillights turn left up the street, and I follow their path, imprinted on what feels like the inside of my eyelids, not sure of what I intend to do, but grateful, at the very least, for distinct direction in which to do it.

15.

April 2nd-3rd, 2006, Julian Falls, Ohio

When I was later accused of being out of control at the party above the student union, and when this was used as proof that I didn't care what had happened to El, or what happened to me, or anyone else, I was too surprised by the false equivalency to fight it. Because on the evening in question, I hadn't taken drugs, and only drank as much as everyone else, but how fast news spread from the parking/picnic area across the road to the clotted, angry space alive (in the technical sense), with music, conversation, and moving bodies. I walked between Mills and Birch Hall, possibly trailing Greer who had run ahead several minutes before, and turned in the direction of my room, but the prospect of that place filled me with a greater horror than attending the party where I could at least melt into the crowd, drink, and try to predict what might happen next.

I passed people strung like the remaining beads on a shattered necklace down a hallway hung heavy with graffiti (student artwork), through a fog of smoke to the darkened room to watch people dance which was something I liked to do, and a hush did not fall over the crowd, that was impossible, but eyes (many), fixed the assailant (me) where I'd stationed myself on a decrepit couch on the edge of the room, alone, but approached by Ludmilla who brought me a plastic cup with something in it, and who sat without saying anything until this became awkward, even with all the noise surrounding us.

"Is El all right? I didn't realize you two…"

I snorted some of the vague liquid onto my shirtfront, apologizing out loud to myself, and patting my pockets in search of cigarettes that I did not have.

"She fell in the Glen," I said. "I left her there, I did, but, wait, please, listen…"

I thought she was going to get up, and I touched her arm, which she pulled away from me with an oblique movement that was spotted by Greer and her cohort across the room. They must have been watching for just such a thing, because they crossed the floor rapidly, and one of them, Cloudfoot Banish (One eighth native, all woman! as she liked to say), had me by the throat while the others sheltered Ludmilla from my non-attack, and an ally of some sort knocked the arm holding my beer which was later said to be thrown, but was merely dropped at an angle that splashed the remaining contents on Greer and her coterie. I don't know when the music ('Right On Time,' by The Brothers Johnson) stopped, but suddenly there was only the sound of me denying, and them confirming as I was removed from the party. Cloudfoot was huge, over two hundred pounds of female that, even if I was prepared to deal with, was unlikely to stop, and she along with Greer dragged me down the stairs and to the exit by the loading dock. I was deposited on this, and rolled off the lip of the delivery platform, clunking the ground like a carpetbag stuffed with gelatin. I waited until the music started again from upstairs before walking back to my room and falling into a sort of sleep.

*

June 15th, 2006, Montpelier, Vermont
When I ask Arthur Stool whether the clock above the front desk is correct, he doesn't look in the direction I'm pointing (at the timepiece), instead fixing his rheumy eyes on my face.

"Is any of them?"

I don't know what to say, so I say nothing.

"Why your eyes all red like? And why you wearing that there queer hat?" he asks, closing the notebook into which he was conveying scribbles before I entered the station. The waiting area is of course empty, it being either very late or very early, and the light, bright and humming like a colony of insects installed in the ceiling, only serves to make the place feel like exactly what is: a newly rehabbed police station, sterile and without ornament.

"My eyes are red," I begin, addressing the pod of dullness that is Officer Stool across the desk. "Because I have been crying. You have a friend of mine here. And this makes me very sad."

"Your wife?"

"Yes," I say, trying to recall the particular details of the lie he is remembering. "Yes, her. My good wife. You have her here. I would like you to release her, please."

"She was dead drunk on a bench in front of folks. You can see her after arraignment."

"When will that be?"

"In a few hours."

"That won't do."

"It'll have to. You want I should put you in there with her? For to keep her company?"

I can't tell whether Arthur means this a threat or an accommodation. Briefly, I consider leaving Lola to be sentenced, because what difference would it make if she were free? Eleanor's parents are returning in a day, we have made no progress in locating her. I could simply file a report with Arthur right now, and just say that a friend of mine hasn't been returning my calls and I am worried. Lola will likely call me for a ride after court, and I can disabuse myself of her in Danville, and explain that since I have turned our problem over to the proper authorities, and there is no need for us to keep doing what we've been doing.

But I'm also now dependent on her silence. If I leave her here without making any effort to get her out, who knows what she'll say to the police? Once again, I picture the interior of the courthouse, and Eleanor's parents judging me from their seats, only, this time, Lola is there as well, tittering quietly as I explain why I left Eleanor naked and alone in the woods.

"Arthur, please, you're not listening to me. She wasn't drunk."

He is back to writing in his journal or whatever it is, which he slaps shut impatiently as I speak.

"She stank of beer."

"Arthur."

"Stop using my first name. It's Off…"

"Officer Stool, I am not denying that she had something to drink. I am merely stating that she was not drunk. Do you know why Lola, excuse me, my wife, has no hair?"

He shrugs.

"I assumed it was some sort of weirdo personal choice."

"No," I gasp. "Absolutely not! Who would do such a thing on purpose?"

The question is rhetorical, but he answers anyway.

"Big old lady lovers, I suppose."

"Perhaps, but that's not the point. My wife is a very sick woman. First the diagnosis, then the treatments, then great aunt Irma dying, and now we're just trying to get the medication right. But it's impossible. It really is hard."

Arthur blinks.

"And you, Officer Stool, are only making it harder."

"She looked drunk."

"And I'm telling you she wasn't!" I shout, slapping the desktop. "We had a glass or two of wine with our dinner, and I left the table to use the restroom, and when I returned, she was gone! We had this problem before, and Doctor Kristof said it would be fine, she could go ahead and relax and have a glass or two of wine with her husband, me…"

I point to myself.

"With me! Do you know how worried I've been? Do you have any idea?"

Arthur shakes his head.

"Is this really who you want to be? The guy who arrested a sick woman for trying to have a nice time? To escape her condition for a single evening? Do you know, Officer Stool, at first I thought that tonight, she and I might make love. It's been six months!"

"I understand. Been like eighteen for me…"

"But you're not married! Look here, do you want me to come into court tomorrow, and explain this to the judge? Do you know how cruel and foolish you'll look?"

And for a moment, I see, in Arthur's face, the age he has gained fade away and there he is at fifteen, the same irritating, unlikeable child desperate for the approval of his peers but completely incapable of securing it. I almost feel bad.

"And I know, Officer Stool, that she has a record, but…"

"She don't have no record."

"She…What?"

"Nope, no record. Clean enough to eat off it."

"Of course she doesn't, I…was talking about someone else," I declare, recovering. "It's been a terribly long, dreary night. I'm sorry."

"Well…No, look, I'm sorry. I didn't realize you folks was having such difficulties. I…"

He pauses, examining me.

"Wow. You married. I never thought that one'd happen."

He removes a ring of keys from a drawer, and makes as if to walk away.

"Why not, Arthur?" I ask his retreating backside. He pauses, appearing to consider his answer, before turning around.

"Well…I mean, don't take this the wrong way or nothing…You just… You always seemed like you would probably be alone. You know. Forever. But…I guess I was wrong, right?"

I don't say anything. He withdraws toward some annex of the station. Through a window embedded with chicken wire in waiting area, I can see an early, tenuous light creeping in between the buildings.

Lola doesn't thank me for getting her out of jail, which makes wish I had left her in there, to sober up on a stainless steel bench in an overlit cell, rather than in the passenger seat of my car which now reaches the top of Main Street as the sun rises over the town below. She squints, frowns, and twists the visor against the side window, and asks if we can get some coffee and if I have cigarettes.

"How do you know Kristof, and why didn't you tell me you know him? And why did you lie to me about having a criminal record?" I ask, handing her a rumpled packet from my rumpled pocket. The question surprises her minimally, if at all, and it could just be that I was hoping this new knowledge of mine, these facts, as it were, would be a sort of trump card proving something important. I haven't eaten anything since the brownies, and as a result am still a bit high from them. When I ask the question, it seems to echo, and I have the sensation as I drive of being enshrouded within a humming swarm of benevolent insects.

"Close your mouth," says Lola, and I think she is telling me to be quiet until I realize that my jaw is hanging wide open, practically unhinged, and my tongue is resting on my lower lip like a slab of cheese on stale bread. "And don't accuse me of anything."

"I wasn't accusing you."

"Can we please get coffee."

"You just asked that. I said yes."

"I did?"

"Yes. How do you know Kristof?"

"What did he say?"

"He said I should watch out. For you."

"Why?"

"He didn't say that."

"I need to throw up."

I hear her say this, but I keep driving.

"Stop the car," she says.

"Tell me what's happening."

"You know what's happening."

"Maybe I do. But I want you to tell me."

"I am going to vomit in your car."

"That's okay. I've done that too."

"Stop the car," she says, and she sounds weak, pitiful in fact, which is why I'm unprepared for her to grab the wheel and jerk once, sliding my Volvo onto the shoulder, and once more, which means when I break, the car skids sideways through a patch loose gravel, and onto a lawn beside the road, and I hear a smashing noise followed by a concussion beneath the car, but at least we're no longer moving. Lola is holding whatever she ate last night in her hand while she uses the other to fling the door open. I get out too and stand beside her as she kneels and vomits on the lawn. I examine the business end of a splintered wooden post extending from beneath the chassis of the car, and a milking can tipped over by the roadside, the missing portion still cemented in place.

"Do you still want coffee?" I ask Lola, who appears to be praying, her forehead resting in the grass beside a mound of sick. A door opens nearby, and I hear a male voice from the front steps of the house behind us.

"Now what in the…Marlowe? Marlowe!"

And when I turn, there he is, the man himself, or Mr. Shivers, as I know him. We're both surprised to see each other, he perhaps more than I, and in place of his normal deportment (Calvinist Undertaker), he wears a pair of heavily laundered running shorts, and magenta t-shirt advertising, of all things, Greatwood College.

"You," he says, stepping toward me, and pressing one of his bare feet into Lola's deposit. "Oh, my god! Well. Shit. Shit!"

"You don't live here," I say, because the one thing I know definitively about Abellard Shivers is that he occupies a haunted looking farmhouse a few miles down the road from PUS. Whenever Gustav and I pass it in my car, he holds his breath like you would with a graveyard. Gustav said it's something all the students do. But we are just outside Montpelier, and the house out of which Mr. Shivers appeared is a single level, bunker-like ranch, and through one of its ocular windows, I notice a curtain shift, and a face less familiar than the long, ginger braid attached to it, appearing momentarily and withdrawing. Mr. Shivers is watching me watch the window and he speaks before I can say anything about it.

"You're high as a kite!"

I lean down and tap Lola's shoulder, and she doesn't move, so I nudge her with my foot, one, twice, and on the third try, she stands up, and lurches back into the passenger seat. I close the door, and turn back to Mr. Shivers, who is scuffing the bottom of his foot on a patch of unfoul grass.

"If that's what you think, why don't you tell my father?"

He doesn't say anything, just glares, and even though he might not have known that I know where he lives, he does knows that I have met his wife, a mousy, nocturnal-looking woman who I've noticed toiling in the patch of dismal garden outside the house near PUS. She appeared with Mr. Shivers at several school functions, shrouded in a woolen smock of her own design, and bore her introduction mutely, but with a necrotic, yellow-eyed apprehension, as if meeting her husband's coworkers confirmed some suspicion on her part. And though her hair was muffled in a sort of homespun bag atop her head, a few strands of gray did appear from beneath it as the evening ground to a close, and I recall all this well enough to know that it was certainly neither long, nor red.

"I think you should go now," he says, tugging at the end of the mailbox beneath my car. "Yes. I think you should go."

"I thought you were against old wine in new bottles?" I say, walking around the car in case he decides it's not worth his time to negotiate and attacks me. There is a tearing sound as he looses the post and box, and then just stands, watching me, scowling.

"A clown," he announces, "is only as good as the circus with which he travels."

"Can I join yours?"

"Please. Go away."

"Sure I will. Enjoy your summer. God bless."

Mr. Shivers watches the car until it disappears around a bend, I watch him grow smaller in the rear view mirror, anticipating a certain peace between us in the future. I have no reason or wish to make his life any harder than it is.

16.

April 4th, 2006, Julian Falls, Ohio

I realized Doctor Dex didn't trust me when I called him to see how El was doing. I should have checked the time, but I was still flustered (not the right word) after being ejected from the party the night before.

"You're what?"

I heard the sucking sound of a refrigerator opening, the clink and rattle of a bottle, followed by a pop, and the cap landing on the granite counter in his kitchen. I was sitting in my room without any lights on.

"I'm flustered," I repeated, wishing I had not.

"My daughter's in the hospital," said Dex. "And you're calling at midnight to tell me you're 'flustered'?"

"You were up."

He ignores me.

"Well, to be honest, Marlowe, I'm a little 'flustered' myself, you know. It's not every day I get a call telling me my daughter broke her leg in two places out in the woods in gloomfuck Ohio. I'm going to go way out on a limb here and guess you were with her?"

"Yes. I was. I called the ambulance."

"Sure you did. They said she was, you know, kind of naked. When they got her. You have something to do with that?"

"Is that…important?"

"Not anymore."

I tried not to imagine what his response might mean. He seemed to be doing the same, because we both were quiet though oddly reluctant to hang up on the other since we both also wanted the company (despite ourselves).

"Look," I began. "I'm really only calling you to find out if she's all right."

There was a noise, but no actual words on the other end.

"Is she all right?"

"Well, the leg is fucked up, but you saw it so you know that. She might need pins or a plate or something, but they're still figuring that out. And the pain meds they gave her. She didn't respond so well to the morphine, but I guess they couldn't tell if she was in shock from the leg or the drugs, so…"

"It must be really hard. Not being here."

"You bet."

"Does she have a phone? Can I call her?"

"She does."

And I could tell by the silence following his confirmation that he wasn't going to share the number with me, so I didn't bother asking. But her father continued as though I had.

"I don't get to do too much. As a dad, I mean. As far as I can tell, you're fine. Not great, but fine. It's just, I know you're around the house, I know you sleep here. With her. I know about that. It's not really my business to police Eleanor's loins. It's just…"

"She has a bright future? And you don't want me to drag her down?"

"No. Shut up. Who do you think I am?" sputtered Dex. I thought he was going to continue speaking, but he didn't. So I did.

"Do you think I broke her leg on purpose?"

"I don't think anything. I just…I'm not there. I don't know you. Why should you be there? Who are you? I mean, who are you? I don't actually know anything about you, except what El tells me. And I tune most of that out. Because I don't care."

"So…you're punishing me for your not caring?"

"For now, yes. Maybe I'll change my mind tomorrow. But now, please, Marlowe. Don't see her."

And then we were both alone, Dex in the house in Northfield, and me, in my room in Ohio. I heard people returning from the party passing my room, dragging their shoulders drunkenly against the wall in the hallway, and decided that I had to see her before I left Ohio. El couldn't save me from what was coming, but visiting her would remind me that I was an idiot, rather than a criminal.

June 15th, 2006, Maple Corner, Vermont

On the way to a location I haven't been able to determine, because Lola won't tell me where she wants to go, I stop for coffee at the general store in Maple Corner. She refuses to get out of the car, and when I suggest we go somewhere to talk, she resists. When I return to the car with the coffee, I sit without starting the engine and tell her I won't drive anywhere else until she explains why she has no police record, and how she knows Kristof. In other words, I do to Lola what I did to Gustav several days earlier. And it works.

We're now sitting on a dock extending into Curtis Pond, just outside the village. The sun, which rose only a few hours previous, sits ensconced within a billow of clouds above the pond, providing the entire setting a moribund aspect, as our feet stir the tepid water. A convoy of ducks patrols nearby, and Lola casts a morose glance toward them.

"I wish I had some bread."

I don't see the ducks, and assume her request means she is hungry. From a brown paper sack beside me on the dock, I produce a cranberry muffin, which she inspects as though it's a piece of sporting equipment, before shredding it and tossing the pieces to the birds.

"I was hoping you would eat that," I say.

"They seem hungry."

"Please stop stalling. If you're not going to explain anything to me, than I would rather just get rid of you."

"Like you did with Eleanor?"

I don't expect her to say this. I remove a twin muffin from the bag and take a bite, chewing it without hunger or interest.

"I think if you thought I was responsible for any of this, you would have done something about it. You would have told Arthur, last night. I think you're just trying to not talk about what I want to talk about."

Silence between us now, abetted by the solitary, silk-like sound of a man across the inlet sliding a canoe into the water.

"Lola..."

"We went to high school together."

"Why didn't you tell me you knew him before I followed him last night?"

"It's all too embarrassing..." she says, without explaining why, and since the question seems to weigh heavily on her, and I want to find out as much as I can before she ends the conversation, I wait a moment before asking another. "I didn't know he would be there."

"I thought you were going to say you know each other from the Femammals."

"We did that together. You already know that. But we met at Octavian Academy in Pomfret."

"That sounds private."

"It is."

"I see," I say, even though I do not. Her confession illuminates nothing. "Was he your boyfriend?"

"No. Is that relevant? Why would you ask that? Just because he's a man?"

"No. I'm sorry. I meant...Was he...a...I'm not sure how to say this...a...slave...of some sort?"

"What?" she says authentically puzzled.

"Well...why did you and they, you Femammals, allow him to join? I mean...he's a...male person."

She snorts, becoming didactic.

"Anyone can be a Femammal as long as they have an awareness, and understanding of their..."

"Stop. I don't care. Please, spare me. You know what I'm asking."

"He was the only person we knew with a degree that wasn't in social sciences or visual art. We approached him. He edited The Report," she says, deflated. "He was our best Malely."

"Your best what?"

"Malely. Male plus ally, stupid."

"Don't call me stupid, you lying harridan."

The warm violence between us is like the woolen current of an approaching storm. We're both so tired of looking at each other, and when the end of her cigarette spins like a burning satellite past my glasses, I wonder whether it's actually worth it to push her further. But after everything I've done during the past week, and the little I've gained, I'm owed an explanation, and even if she's shouting now, I will get it.

"You!" she bellows, and the man in the canoe pauses in midcast to regard us. "You want to ruin everything! Everything, just like him, you selfish prick!"

"Who? Like who?" I say, edging away from her. She has rotated in her seat, squaring her shoulders as though about to charge. One small foot has withdrawn from the water, and is braced against the dock. "Please. Tell me."

"He kept everything," she moans. "He loved to keep things. Even his javelin trophies! His fucking javelin trophies! Who hangs on to that shit?"

"I...don't know..."

"I didn't understand what they meant at first. 'Powwow'. That's what they called me. Even Eleanor. I didn't understand, you know?"

I nod, unknowing.

"Powwow. Overnight, I had this nickname, and no one would tell me why. These people were supposed to be my friends. And always with that... that...disdain! Like they knew something about me that I didn't, like I had a secret but it was their secret. Those fucking photographs! Kristof should have gotten rid of them! But no, everything was framed, all of it, this little shrine to himself, and his fucking trophies! He didn't care what the girls thought! He always told them he wasn't going to apologize for his past because what he accomplished throwing his goddamn spear into a sandpit was real, and he was still proud! My god! I fucking hated him for that!"

The man in the canoe appears to be edging closer, dipping his paddle surreptitiously into the still water in order to hear the story. And oddly, though I'm sitting beside her, I have no better understanding of it than the nosy fisherman. I move to reclaim some of the ground I earlier surrendered, and as I draw close, I notice her trembling.

"Lola. What pictures? What did they see?"

She is not crying, but she sniffs, snatching the cigarettes from my pocket, lighting one, and blowing smoke toward the ducks, which appear to have grown bored.

"It was just something we did every year. The Academy Potlatch. Like a Thanksgiving thing. For students and their families. And they have a pageant. It's like a joke. And I didn't know. And Kristof didn't care. He just wanted to throw his fucking javelin, that bastard. I was always in it. We dressed up like the local people. And did a dance…and I was a dancer."

"Local…people?"

"The Algonquin, you turd! Or Pequot, or Mashantucket, I don't even remember! It was embarrassing, but I danced, so I had to do it while some asshole banged a drum, and they said, they said it would be a good extracurricular, and my father said if I didn't do it, I would disappoint him, and, and, and, I just did it! I participated! They held the games, and Kristof chucked his spear and everybody, all the parents brought a fucking covered dish, and we all ate corn and I had war paint on and feathers in my hair all day! Of course there were pictures! There may even be a video, I'm surprised he didn't have a copy in his apartment!"

"Sounds like a good ol' time, you ask me."

The angler has actually drawn within ten feet of our position, and, based on his contribution, is not even pretending to ignore our conversation.

"It was offensive, Sir!" Lola shouts at him, apparently unbothered by his participation.

"I like a good harvest festival," he announces, without looking at either of us.

"Sir," I plead. "This is a private conversation."

"But you're havin' it right here, ain't you?"

"Do you have any idea how hard it is to divest yourself of privilege? Do you?" asks Lola, but I can't tell whether she's asking me, or the fishermen.

"I knew an Indian once. Tall fellow. Sure liked his liquor!"

"All the time I spent, all the classes, the, the, the, work. It takes real work!"

"Sir. Will you please go?"

"Not just yet, thank you."

"I don't know when Eleanor and everyone saw the pictures. But... Powwow!"

"Ain't such a bad name. There's a fellow down Dog Pond Road named Shitheel Sam. A widower, but keeps a fine house."

"For weeks! Powwow! And I only found out on the train, when we were going home for the holidays. We took the Metro North and I started complaining about the name and he, that fucking bastard, he actually said he was sorry, that it might have been his fault, because some of the girls were over at his place to see the galleys on The Report and they saw his fucking trophies and then the pictures, his framed fucking pictures-"

"Wait. Lola. The Metro North? He...You..." I say, remembering Kristof's mouth, and his missing teeth, and suddenly it all makes incomplete sense. "You did that to him?"

"He deserved it!" she shouts.

"Hold on there, little lady. You're scarin' the fish."

"You...assaulted him...for having...memorabilia?" I ask.

"I didn't 'assault' him," she bleats, finally addressing herself directly to me. "I pushed him. He fell down and hit his face."

"But...you said you broke the guy's nose...and fucked up his eye or something..."

"Kristof fell. Hard."

"And the...the bruised testicles...?"

"Maybe," she says, leaning close to me, "I stepped on them. Accidentally. You know. Helping him up."

"Revoltin', " mutters our companion from his boat, which he has begun to paddle away from Lola, who looks oddly proud of herself.

"Why did you make all that up then?" I ask, surprised by my own anger. "Why did you say it was just some rapist, and that you had a record, and that we shouldn't go to the police, and that we should find Eleanor on our own? Why would you make all that up?"

Lola actually smiles at me with an unhidden bitterness.

"I couldn't tell you what actually happened. You wouldn't understand, you dropout. You're just another white male, taking up space."

"And how do you not have a record? After doing that to Kristof?"

"Because, stupid," she whispers, leaning close against my ear. "My father is the former D.A. Not Kristof's. His dad teaches American history at Skidmore."

She rolls her eyes, before locking them on mine.

"And daddy thinks I'm doing an internship in Soho, not out in Vermont, working with the T.C. He has a lot of friends. If my name appears on a missing persons report, my summer is over. Do you understand?"

"No, Powwow. Frankly, I don't," I say, turning away just as her foot collides with the side of my head, knocking my glasses from my face, and me, into the pond.

17.

April 4th, 2006, Julian Falls, Ohio

The decision to ban me from campus was rendered the Wednesday following my ejection from the party above the student union. There was nothing I could do to prevent it. The Community Standards Board worked tirelessly throughout the weekend building their case. Even when I attempted to proceed normally about my limited duties as a freshman college student, I could hear the sound of charges stacking against me like ordinance dropped into the mouth of a cannon.

A museum-like silence fell upon the masticating pods of students when I entered the cafeteria the morning after being ejected from the party by Cloudfoot Banish. The American Indian Alliance, Jew Crew, BAMN (By Any Means Necessary. The two black students and their associated White Allies), and the Society for Male Understanding and 'Trans'cendence (Greer's contingent) glowered like diverse livestock from their associated tables. Several respective members stood, including Cloudfoot, as I padded shamefully to the stainless trays at the opposite end of the room, watching the reflection of my peers in the sneeze guard to make certain none would sneak up while I was loading my plate with as much as possible in order not to return. Sitting was out of the question. Even among those groups not distinctly partisan, there was a contraction or closing, like the petals of an invidious blossom, the opposite of an invitation. I dropped a Belgian waffle on my way to the door, and was so flustered (that word, once more) that I did not bother reclaiming it.

The day was already hot (Ohio, America is stifling, even in April), the beginning of the tremendous heat which would dominate the town through most of the summer. By the time I returned to my room with the co-mestibles, I was soaked in perspiration, my heart was smacking the roof of my chest like laundry beaten against a rock. Since everyone was at brunch, I snuck upstairs to the dorm kitchen, and rifled the fridge until I found two bottles of Pisco an upper level student had smuggled back from an internship in Peru (Why was it in the fridge?), and smuggled these quietly back to my room, where I sat, sipping the drink which tasted close to the copper pot in which it was likely distilled, and imagining that I was Melville, a captive among savages on the Nukuheva, which, at this point, would have been preferable.

I've never understood people who knock upon a door they plan to open, and it seems as if the sound of Ludmilla's knuckles rapping on the portal continued after she was already standing in the room. Did she shut the door? Or did it close on its own? She was prettier in the absence of light which characterized my living space, though a small measure crept in through a space between the blinds (drawn) and the ceiling, illuminating her cleaver-like jaw as it rotated on her thin, Ostrich neck until the corresponding head found me, embayed in the corner and sweating into a plate of soggy breakfast food.

"Can I sit here?" she asked, gesturing at the bed, and then sitting there before I could say anything. "How's El?"

"I don't know. Her father wouldn't tell me."

"Are you okay?"

"No. Why are you here?"

She examined the bottle I was holding and I poured some Pisco into a cup holding pencils on the desktop, and, removing these to the floor, handed her the drink.

"I'm sorry. I know you were only trying to…talk…last night," she said.

"I just needed to explain to…to someone…but I…I think it's too late."

"That's why I came here. Actually. I had fun with you. And I feel bad that it has to end like this."

"Like what? Ludmilla, please…"

And before she could answer we heard, past the blinds, the sound of a bullhorn, and muffled, conversant voices outside the building.

"Whaddawewant?"

"Safety!"

"Whendawewantit?"

"Now!"

"Shit!" said Ludmilla. "They're here already?"

"Is that…?"

"Shut up!" she said, separating a pair of slats with her fingers and peering through them.

"They can't know I'm here."

I stood, swaying slightly, and bumped her aside to have a look. A group of between thirty and forty students, mostly woman interspersed here and there with an eager looking male, were gathered on the lawn outside the dormitory. There were a few hastily rendered signs, all bearing the same slogan 'El DIDN'T FELL (sic)! SHE WAS PUSHED!' and Greer, like a ghoul unhinged from its casket, at their forefront, megaphone in hand, leading the chant, her fist smothered in a black glove, and raised above her head.

"Wait," I said. "BAMN came out. For this?"

"Afraid so. They're in the back. Same with the Jew Crew. I think people are just bored. I mean, there's only how many of us here?"

"Less than a hundred."

"Right. Someone has to be the pariah."

"Does this happen often?"

"Every term."

I turned away from the window, settled myself on my bed with the Pisco, and Ludmilla joined me. She put an arm around my shoulders, and took the bottle from my hand, sipping it.

"How long will they be out there?" I asked.

"Until you're gone."

"Are you going to stay here?"

"I can't go out there. They'll know I was here."

"Thanks, Ludmilla."

"For what?"

"I don't know. Trying to…warn me, I guess."

"Well," she said, leaning her head on my shoulder. "I may have…explained a little too much…about our pool game. To Greer. I think it made her suspicious. And then this thing with El just…"

"It's all right."

"I honestly never thought they'd mobilize so quickly in this heat. I guess boredom is really the great motivator, right?"

I didn't say anything, because we both noticed a shadow outside the window, moving in awkward sloping gestures, each of which was accompanied by the hiss of an aerosol can. When I was summoned to the hearing the next morning, I noticed one of the picketers had painted the phrase 'WHITE MALE BONE BRAKER (sic)' on my window.

*

June 15th, 2006, Maple Corner, Vermont

I'm not hurt so much as startled by the sensation of being soaked in my clothes accompanied by blindness from the loss of my spectacles, which, despite their outlandish size, bob conveniently on the surface of the water. I return them to my face, in time to see the fisherman, still floating nearby in his canoe, make a gesture behind Lola's back that seems to ask whether I need help. I shake my head, answering him, and puzzling her as she stands on the dock with her hands on her hips while I slosh around in the shallow water.

"What? Do you have something to deny?"

Still hip deep in the shallows, I remove my shirt and wring it out.

"No, Powwow. I had water in my ears."

This enrages her further, but since I am in the pond, and Lola is on the dock, she does nothing.

"You're so fucking stupid, I could just kill you!" she shouts, and the fisherman repeats his should-I-make-a-phone-call gesture with a new urgency, but I ignore him.

"You kicked me in the face. And for that, I'm going to punish you, Lola"

"Really?" she asks, but the disbelief in her voice is perhaps tempered by the resolve in my own, and though she makes no move to escape, I can tell she is afraid of me. And rather than feeling pity, I'm glad, because at this moment I possess the sort of calm, resolute anger which can produce a crime both audacious and perfect. I sling the withered snakeskin of my shirt around my neck, and slosh to shore. Lola walks parallel to me, waiting to see what I will do next.

The narrow stretch of beach separating us is no more than fifteen feet, but I make no move to close the distance. In order to run from me, Lola will need to negotiate a thick grove of evergreens planted along a quarter mile of hillside sloping toward the pond. At the top of the acclivity, my station wagon is both parked and locked. There is nowhere for her to go.

"Run," I say, removing the coiled fabric from around my neck, and stretching it between my hands. My face has begun to ache from the blunt impact of her foot, which strengthens my decision. I turn toward her, and she takes several steps back.

"What?" she asks.

"Run."

"Where?"

"Away from me."

I don't move, but she begins walking backward toward the trees, her purple eyes dilating as she realizes what exactly I'm requesting, and what will happen if she does not do it. She starts to jog when she reaches the treeline, and this is when I begin to pursue her, my wet shoes squishing in the sand as I give chase. I break through a set of low branches, shivering beneath the cool breath of the foliage, and see her, not even twenty feet away, not heading toward the car, but following a narrow footpath along the shoreline. I jog after her, branches whipping my bare torso and shoulders as I close the distance between us, until I'm close enough to read the logo on the bottom of her shoes, and closer still, nearly, but not quite, within reach. We seem to have encountered a plateau in the chase, a place at which neither of us can run any faster, and thus, the distance between us remains roughly of a similar measure as we negotiate the twists and bends along the trail. Something must be done.

Still in mid-run, I twist the wet t-shirt between my hands until the fabric actually creaks, and then twist my upper body, and take aim. I flick my wrist, and there is a sound like a gunshot followed by a lupine howl as the tip of my shirt snaps Lola between her shoulder blades. She staggers, but keeps running, and I retract my lash, twisting it once more, but this time tracking a bit lower, and landing a direct hit on her right buttock. The shock actually causes her leg to freeze in mid-extension, yet the rest of her body continues running, which results in an ungainly toppling of her entire speeding figure as though her feet were suddenly immersed in quicksand. She bounces and rolls a bit down the trail, before skidding to halt, and I deliver a third snap to the back of the arm she uses to raise herself from the ground.

"What the fuck is wrong with you!" she says, rather than asking, as I straddle her back, with my face toward her kicking feet.

"You'll find out," I say, her hands slapping at my legs and sides, which hurt far less than the branches I ran through to arrive in this position. I put one finger from each hand beneath the waistband of her shorts, and tug them down just low enough to expose her behind, which I am pleased to see sports a wickedly purple bruise (the color not unlike her eyes) on the right cheek. A growl resonates through her body, and up into my own, as I squeeze her rumbling abdomen between my thighs.

"You fucking pussy!" she says, knocking the back of her head against my spine. "You aren't worth shit! You're so fucking stupid, and when you let me up, I'm going to tear your dick…"

The first slap I deliver to her rear as though closing a trunk, and she winces, and yips, but halts her threats. For the second, I come from the side, and the third, from above. I alternate this pattern seven more times, accompanied during each by odd little barks from Lola. And other than contempt, I feel nothing. Perhaps this state, with me pinning her to the ground, as she mutters impotent, savage remarks, resembles marriage in all its sexless formality. Her casual, entitled violence disgusts me, as I'm sure my careless, insensitive manner repulses her. And after I finish the spanking I sit for longer than I should, wishing for some way to remove myself without having to look at her ever again.

But of course, this is impossible. I rise quickly and escape to a safe-ish distance, which is smart, because as soon as she is free of my weight, the space formerly occupied with my head is cut in two by a wild haymaker, her small fist almost humming in the air. She spots me up the trail a bit, and stands, tugging her shorts up.

"Motherfucker," she whispers, taking a step in my direction.

"Lola," I warn. "If you hit me again, I will hit you back. In the face."

She steps closer, an unnatural ease overcoming her normally severe features, her mouth hung slightly ajar.

"Chicken shit limp dick…"

"Lola, I'm…"

But before I can complete my sentence her slack mouth meets my own in an equine kiss, her tongue licking my teeth and nose, while her hands prod and knead my bare chest, yanking one my nipples as though expecting it to produce milk, her arms pushing and pulling my body, forward and then away, as if she is trying to reconcile two contrary impulses, which, I suppose, is accurate. I stand shocked, absorbing this affectionate abuse without any distinct verdict, even as her hand clamps my genitals, tugging and twisted them in an odd semi-circular motion as if my body is a locked door, and these parts, the knob.

"Lola…" I squawk, removing my mouth from her own, just as she puts a hand in my chest and pushes herself away. She drops to her knees, tugging down the straps of her tank top and exposing her breasts.

"Pee on me."

I mishear her request as 'be on me,' and I think she is asking me to get on top of her, so I drop to my knees as well, and move toward her, but she shakes her head.

"No. Pee on me."

Her eyes close, anticipating my compliance, which is fortunate, because it means that she cannot see my face as it reflects a complete understanding of her request. I am so startled by it that rather than denying her outright, I say the wrong thing.

"I don't have to go."

She opens one eye, frowning.

"What?"

"I don't have to go. To the…bathroom."

"Can you try, at least?"

"I don't think so."

"Maybe drink some water?"

She waves toward the pond, and her inflection is so helpful, and oddly tender, such a profound break from her normal behavior, that I'm instantly immersed in guilt. And when I stand up, she bites her bottom lip, smiling and leaning forward slightly, expecting a torrent. But I feel sick.

"Lola," I say, "let's just…let's just go. Please."

She opens her eyes, looking at me, disbelieving.

"You…You don't want to…?"

I nod more to myself than her, glancing up the trail, toward the beach.

"No. No, I'm sorry. I'm not…into…pee pee," I say, hating myself for saying 'pee pee.' She stands silently, covering her breasts, and not meeting my eyes as she stomps past me. I turn to follow, but notice a peripheral splash of unnatural color, which is in fact the side of the intrusive angler's canoe, drifting through the shallows twenty yards away. He is just sitting in it and smiling (at me) and when we make eye contact, he winks.

When we're back in the car, traveling toward Danville, Lola says that tomorrow, I need to tell Eleanor's parents what happened.

"They're back from Massachusetts by now," she says. "Don't call them. You need to actually be there."

It makes sense. Our leads, weak as they were to begin with, are exhausted. Eleanor is still missing. And refusing to please Lola in the way she requested has left our dynamic a peaceful shambles, which is why I'm unloading her in Danville. It's hard to look at someone on whom you will not pee.

"Just me?"

"No," says Lola. "I'll come. I should be there. They know me a little. It might make it easier."

"Are you going to leave me hanging on this? Because that would be wildly shitty of you. This was our idea. We agreed to look together."

"I won't let them blame you for everything," she says, her bristle rasping my cheek as she leans her head against my shoulder, and even though she repulses me, I appreciate her proximate assurance. The weight of her head seems to indicate that perhaps it will be all right.

"You want to get it out of the way early?" I ask.

She presses her cheek into my shoulder instead of nodding.

"Meet me at guidance around ten. We'll head over there."

And then we don't say anything else. The car tips from dirt to pavement as we enter Pitkin, passing PUS, and the Greatwood College campus above all of which, a tumble of bloated rain clouds remain strung along the horizon like tattered laundry. And when we reach Danville, the rain begins falling in glass-like sheets, churning the dirt, washing down the windscreen, and Lola touches my face before exiting the car as though trying to reattach something, and is gone before I can ask her what it might be.

18.

April 5th, 2006, Julian Falls, Ohio

Rage and Douglas, when combined with the superfluous presence of Martin Bastarde, comprised the entirety of the Community Standards Board, which is exactly what it sounds like. An executive committee designed to deal with infractions that could potentially effect the safety, health, and generalized wellness of the MU community. Martin was the only member who seemed at all pleased to see me, though he did wrinkle his nose a bit at the scent of day-old Pisco blown into his open-mouthed grin by a gust of wind from the window which he would refuse to close two days later.

Ludmilla left at 5AM, an hour at which even the most dedicated identity politicians take their rest, and three hours later, I was awakened by a suspiciously respectful tapping on my door, the hand performing it attached to the arm of Security Mike, the campus safety officer, who arrived to escort me to the hearing in his golf cart.

"I'm sorry we have to do this," he said, and I couldn't tell if he meant the ride in the golf cart, or the route in particular.

"You have any cigarettes? I left mine."

"Sure, kid. I'm sorry it all happened for you. Like this."

He gestured toward the front of my dorm as we passed it on Corry Street. Several tents had sprouted during the night. A few of the signs ('EL DIDN'T FELL…') had been hammered into the ground facing the building. And of course, there was the graffiti scrawled over my window.

"Looks like you really pissed some people off," he said.

"This isn't the first time you've had to do this, is it, Mike?"

He shook his head.

"Nope."

He dropped me outside South Hall, and imparted the room where I was supposed to meet the CSB. Rage wrinkled her snout-like nose as I sat down.

"You smell like some kind of funky. You drunk?"

"Not yet," I said.

"What's that supposed to mean?" said Douglas.

"What do you think it's supposed to mean?"

"If we could," interrupted Martin, "get to it. So, it seems…"

He shuffled a few papers on the table in front of him.

"It seems you…oh my…Well, how about this, why don't you tell me what happened with Ludmilla?"

"When?" I asked.

"You mean there was more than one time?" shouts Douglas from her chair.

"I don't think it's really any of your business actually."

Rage's dewlap began to quiver with rage.

"I am the community manager! And you'll answer the question if you want to be part of this here community!"

"I'm sorry," apologized Martin. "I should have been more specific. What happened with Ludmilla at the party…two nights ago? Saturday night."

"Did she file a complaint?" I asked.

More shuffling of papers. I counted at least twenty documents.

"Well. No. I'm sorry. She did not."

"So, why does it matter what happened, if it's between Ludmilla and myself?" I asked.

"Well, oh my…" said Martin. "That is a good…question. I believe…"

The infernal shuffling once again, and I realized then that the documents I counted were grievance forms, and twenty of them meant a quarter of the campus population had a grievance with me.

"Yes, right here. Okay," said Martin, scanning a document. "Yes, it seems that your behavior was perceived as…threatening. I have here…'drunk and disorderly'…'out of control'…'abusive white male taking up space'…and in light of what happened earlier that evening with El…it seems…potentially dangerous."

"Did El file a complaint?"

"No," answers Rage. "You put her in the hospital before she could."

I tried to keep the outrageous anger bubbling somewhere between my brain and heart from spilling over into my response.

"Rage, her leg was broken. Should I have dragged her back here to fill out paperwork before calling an ambulance? Do you think making sure she got medical attention was part of my plan?"

"Don't speak that way to me. I am the community manager, and this is an official hearing! You will speak when spoken to!" she shouted, the precarious adipose of her bulk jiggling as she pounded the table.

"Well, that's not entirely true…" said Martin without completing his thought.

"If neither El nor Ludmilla filed anything, why am I here?" I asked him. Rage opened her mouth to respond, and I drew a finger against my lips. "Rage, whatever you say, I will ignore."

"How dare you!"

"Well…it…seems…" said Martin, his shoulders drawn up beside his ears as though he wished to withdraw inside himself until the hearing was concluded. "It seems…these events have made…those not necessarily privy to them…uncomfortable…I'm sorry, Marlowe."

"Why are you apologizing to him?" shouted Douglas at Martin. "He assaulted a student and tried to assault another like almost directly afterward, and had to be removed from a campus party and is not even complying with the process, and you're apologizing? He should be apologizing!"

We lapsed into a pregnant silence, each mulling this over. I was the first to speak.

"So? What happens now?"

Martin seemed to hate himself for the words he spoke in reply.

"We will…convene and…render a decision, after we have heard more …testimonies…"

"And there are plenty of them, let me tell you!" said Rage, pinching

Douglas's substantial flesh wing between two of her porcine fingers.

"Right. I know that. What happens to me?" I asked Martin, ignoring this display.

"If the committee finds these complaints have merit…we will…ask you to…please…leave campus for the term's remainder…"

"Readmission pending," said Rage.

"What?" I asked.

"You know. If you take some time over the summer and address your issues, you can apply for another hearing. And we'll decide whether you can come back."

"Bullshit," I said cheerfully, standing and extending my hand toward Martin, who took it as though I was his priest. Rage and Douglas' mouths were gibbering for the correct vitriol. "When do I return to receive my banishment?"

"Please be here at 11AM on Wednesday," said Martin. "We'll know by then."

"Fuck you two, very much!" I chortled in the direction of Rage and Douglas on my way out of the office. What I didn't realize that was one of them, I never discovered which (because it didn't matter) had placed a call to Greer after Security Mike had dropped me off at South Hall, and Greer had gotten a guilty male posing as me to call housing, and have the locks on my door changed. I never understood why they even bothered, considering that when I emerged from the building, her contingent, and their allies were there to meet me. As I bent to pick several partially smoked cigarette butts from an ashtray beside the door, I heard the sound of many feet, and a familiar shout.

"Cut him off! Cut! Him! Off!"

It was a strange thing to yell, since I had not even begun to run. But when I looked up, there they all were, the combined membership of the American Indian Alliance, Jew Crew, BAMN, and SMUT, bearing down on me from the direction of the student union. And I took off. I was not as overweight then, but I was certainly not in anything that might be called 'shape.' Still, I had a decent head start, and even as they spread out, trying anticipate and intercept my route, I managed to puzzle them by not heading back toward my dorm, but in the opposite direction, toward the abandoned golf course abutting, but not part of, the campus.

I didn't look back because that would mean slowing down. But as I ran, things began to land before and beside me. Stale fruit from the cafeteria. A Hackey Sack. A beer bottle passed my head in a threatening orbit, plunking against a tree. I had the prickling, animal sensation of them gaining on me, and I broke through the thick foliage of campus, onto the austere demarcation of the golf course, I stopped and turned around.

Greer broke through ahead of the rest, and was the only one who continued running. The others halted at the edge of campus as though the line was drawn with salt, and they comprised some insidious demonic parade.

"Greer, don't…"

But she ignored my warning, barreling onward with her hands extended maniacally before her, the fingers fanned but curled like talons, her mouth open in a predatory grimace, her eyes set in her hard, impossible face not burning with anger, but frozen in an arctic resolve more reptile than human. I knew that if I let her, she would kill me, but if I hit her, the crowd would kill me, so I compromised.

At the last second, I stepped aside, extending my leg where my body had been, and tangled it among her churning shins. She yelped before becoming airborne, and landed with a nauseating thump on the ground. She did not get up, and no one moved to join her.

"Listen," I said to them, making certain not to turn my back on Greer, who was tottering to her feet. "This is not the campus. This…"

I gestured at the bare, disused course.

"Is the actual world. You see the difference?"

Some of them blinked. No one nodded.

"Okay, look: If you assault me or do whatever it is you're planning to do, it's not just some shit that gets worked out internally. I don't fill out any forms. We don't have mediation. I got to the police. And you all get arrested. So you see the difference?"

I turned to Greer who was on her feet, and mopping blood from a gash beneath her absent chin.

"Greer. Do you understand? If you touch me or mess with me, I will get the JFPD."

She put a bloody finger in her mouth, and nodded wickedly.

"Now. Fuck off."

No one moved.

"Fuck off! Go away. Leave me alone."

As the thrill of the chase ebbed from the retinue, they began to peel off in groups of two and three, wandering back beneath the canopy of trees marking the beginning of campus. Greer went last, her pus-colored coiffure home now to a few blades of grass and an odd, green and white-banded caterpillar.

"You're never getting back in," she muttered without looking back at me.

"Believe it or not, I already made that decision."

"No. I mean to your room."

With that, she slid like a mamba back within the verdure, which served as her emplacement, and was gone. I wandered beneath a single, lopsided alder planted in the center of the bare field, taking shelter from the sun. She was right. I never got back into my room.

*

June 15th, 2006, North Calais, Vermont

After leaving Lola in Danville, I'm suddenly calm, so calm that when I breathe, I feel neither the effect of the thousands of cigarettes I've smoked, nor the dearth of exercise which has come to mark my life as an adult, and I have the sense that my eyes are seeing everything as I want to remember it, even as the rain falls, and the wind rolls against the body of the automobile. I notice the particular, jaunty swing of a sign advertising a sweet shop in Marshfield, the slant of a bumper suspending with twine from the rear of a pick-up streaked with mud outside the general store in East Calais, the winnowing tide of the lake as I drive parallel to it, passing a single lone person, sexless in rain gear, but walking with an eccentric cadence through the baleful residue of a summer storm. I raise two fingers from the wheel, and they do the same, and in this way, we hail the other as though in a tandem blessing. I wonder what it might feel like to be the other, watching my vehicle pass beneath an intractable raincloud from the shadow of a rubber hood.

For the first time since I was very young, I have the sense of the world ending the following day, or at least the shattering of my comfort into new, disparate pieces. It is the feeling of maintaining a huge, ghastly deception, that has grown too large to keep, and thus must be destroyed before it devours its creator. But how do I do this? I consider making a list of what I have done wrong and reading it instead of a narrative confession. Lola will be there to clarify. Yes, perhaps a prepared statement is the best way to go. Save myself the trouble of having to think on my feet, which easily grow tired. But immediately after I finish composing the document in my head, I realize how bad an idea it actually is, and that the only decorous way to address Eleanor's disappearance, and the mess I have made of it, is to just tell her parents what happened.

19.

June 16th, 2006, Middlesex, Vermont

The next morning, Lola doesn't speak to me during the ride to Eleanor's house. But when I turn into the precarious drive leading to it, she murmurs something.

"Be detailed."

"What?"

"Detailed. Worried people always want details."

I wait for her to touch my arm, or offer some sort of reassurance beyond this clinic. But even as we clomp up the bridge between the house and the lot from which I nearly fell to my doom several days before, the night of our first (formal) introduction, Lola seems tethered to me and this location by the sheerest filament. Whatever sentimental bone lying barely exposed will remain as such, since neither of us wishes to be the first to excavate it.

Eleanor's parents appear to have aged lightly, if at all. Lydia maintains her upset bowl of red, straight hair, stalk-like comportment and, most importantly, silent, green-eyed dislike of me, while Oliver, looking more ronin-like than ever before, continues to twine the opposing strands of his Fu Manchu between two chubby fingers as we, Lola, myself, and the two of them, sit glaring at one another beneath the atrium's skylight. The twining began at his first sight of me on the doorstep, at which he offered no traditional greeting, and instead stood aside as if he had been expecting us both. I took my seat and imagined how they might look from the inside of a jail cell.

The sun is directly overhead which casts the entire arrangement in an ethereal light. Lola is offered refreshment. I am not. We all sit with our hands wrestling in our laps, waiting for someone else to speak, and when someone does, it is Lola.

"We have something to tell you."

Oliver and Lydia blink like oxen. Since Lola does not supply this pronouncement with any other information, I realize that I'm supposed to speak.

"You're probably wondering where Eleanor is."

Lydia tilts her head to the side as though this might fix her impression of me. Her father yawns.

"I'm afraid I don't know. I realize that the two of you don't like me. I don't like you either. But I came here because your daughter, Eleanor, is missing. And I don't know if it's my fault. But I know that I can't find her. And I'm worried."

No response. Lola nods her head to indicate that I should keep going.

"The last time I saw her was Friday. We went into the woods. I took her…her clothes…and I…I left her there."

Oliver rolls his eyes. Lydia does nothing, which is normal for her.

"When I returned later to…to…to find her, she was gone."

The atrium is not only lit like a church, but silent as one.

"Are…neither of you concerned?" I ask, and Lola gives me a look meant to scold, but I'm rapidly losing patience with the uncredited effort this exposé is requiring of me. "No, Lola, this is weird. I'm just, I'm sitting here, explaining this, and they, you two…"

I point.

"You two act like I'm confessing that I stole your mail or something. Are you even listening to me? Your daughter is fucking missing! Does that not mean anything?"

"Why did you take her to the woods?" says Lydia in a voice like a necktie falling from a hanger.

"I…I…" I gibber.

"And you took her clothes…why would you do that?" asks Oliver, clasping his hands across his prodigious midsection as though this is some sort of negotiation in which he has the advantage (which I suppose he does). Lola raises her eyebrows, prompting me.

"It's just something I…like…to do."

Oliver claws at the armrest of his chair, while Lydia glares at my feet as if my shoes are coated in dogshit.

"You left her in the woods. Without any clothes. For how long?" she asks. I pause before replying, not because I am trying to recall the exact amount of time, but because I don't want to answer.

"Five hours. I was running errands for my mother. I was taking the recycling to the dump…"

Lola's somewhat overwarm hand touches my shoulder, silencing me.

"That's sociopathic," says Lydia primly. Oliver's head rocks on his plump shoulders. I wish I had either chosen my words more wisely, or not spoken at all. Lydia purses her lips and begins shaking her head as though she has just ingested something sour that she cannot spit out, and Oliver makes a strange noise, half wheeze, half whistle, which I later discover is a laugh.

"This is so…strange," he pronounces, and I, eager to agree with anything, begin rocking my head in time with his own.

"Yes. It certainly is a strange situation. And I take full…well, no, not full responsibility, because as I've explained, it was not my intention to harm her. Quite the opposite, as a matter of fact."

I realize I shouldn't have added the last sentence when Oliver stops nodding, and Lydia touches his arm with a reptilian speed in a forewarning of some kind, or to prevent him from doing I know not what. But an inclement ripple seems to generate from the place where her hand rests, and she glances at a clock affixed to the atrium's wall as if she is taking his pulse.

"Leave please," she says politely, watching her husband.

"But shouldn't we discuss what to do next?"

"We'll decide that, thank you. Please leave."

"I understand if you want to call the police, I can assure you that I will cooperate, but I would appreciate…"

"It's time for you to go."

"And I will in a moment, but I just want to finish explaining…"

"Leave! Now!" shouts Oliver, rising halfway from the horizon of his chair like a reluctant sun. "Go away. You're not welcome in this house, you pervert!"

Lola reenters the room, though at what point she left it I can't say, and quickly crosses the floor between us. She holds a backpack, which I assume contains the overnight items left in the house.

"Marlowe," she says. "You did it. We're done. Come on."

And I stand, trying to appear crisp and offended. But the word 'pervert' might as well be cast in stone and laid across my shoulders as I exit the living room, cringing and weasel-like (or mustelid-like, recall), with the four eyes of Eleanor's parents seeming to follow me (as they always did), down the hallway, and to the front door. But the difference now is that I've confirmed what they always suspected, and their satellite adjudication contains a verdict that I can't refute, thus the legend ('PERVERT') across my back. The tandem gaze lifts only as I turn out of the driveway, onto the main road toward Danville. I'm playing Lola's cabman for what I assume will be the last time.

"That went well," I say, because I want it to be true. "Do you think I'm a pervert?"

"Yes," she says, opening the backpack on the floor between her feet. "But you wear it well unless someone mentions it. You could pass for normal."

"What do you think will happen now?"

"I don't know, Marlowe."

"Do you think they'll call the police?"

"I really don't know. Shit!"

I glance at Lola and see that she has removed a clipboard with several sheets of paper affixed to it from her backpack.

"What? What is it?"

"This fucking petition. I forgot about it entirely. The girls at the bakery asked me to get signatures over the weekend. I was so busy with…with… everything. I forgot entirely. Shit!"

"What's it for?" I ask, not interested at all. As the categorical green forest, blue sky, and deep brown of Vermont in midsummer rush past the car, I'm seeing these familiar attributes caged, or with bars between myself and them as I try to imagine how my fairly easy life (until this point) will change now that all deception has been wrung from it. I expected to feel relieved after meeting with Oliver and Lydia, and relief may be present, but its stratigraphy is buried beneath a thick wedge of dread.

"The 'Shade a Somali Foundation,' " says Lola. " 'Help plant a tree in a country you are afraid of!' I think the Collective partnered with them recently. Anyway, this was my one assignment. And I fucked it up. Because of you."

I sense our dynamic reverting to its original pitch, that of tossing the blame for something unpleasant between us as if exchanging fire on a field of war, and, though I don't consider myself sentimental, I don't want the remainder of our final ride to elapse in an exegesis of how we've failed each other.

"Look, I'm sorry," I say. "Will it help if I sign your petition?"

"Not much, at this point."

"Well, give it to me. I'll sign it anyway."

"You're driving."

"Put the pen in my hand," I say, my own patience ebbing. "Hold the clipboard steady. If you need an email or a phone number, make them up. I don't want to get a message from Sudanese Tree Farm each day for the rest of my life."

"'Shade a Somali.'"

"Whatever. Pen?"

I scribble something like a signature on the clipboard, my eyes remaining locked on the jailed horizon, and this gesture seems to smother whatever antipathy remains between us.

"Thank you, Marlowe," she says, settling the clipboard in her lap. "Too little, too late, but at least you didn't embarrass yourself."

"Whatever that means," I reply as we enter Danville.

*

April 7th, 2006, Julian Falls, Ohio

When Martin dropped me in town after banning me from campus, I returned to the lone alder at the end of the fairway, and drank three beers beneath the broiling sun before deciding to spend the rest of his (Martin's) money on a taxi to Dayton. I wanted to see El because she was the only person I knew who would not attack me on sight. Except for Ludmilla, but I didn't expect we would meet again.

Since my current position was difficult to describe to the dispatcher, I asked him to send a car to the gas station from which I had just come. I packed my things, which were not many — three beers, a bag of chips, the keys to a door that would no longer open — in a plastic bag and withdrew from the shade.

It occurred to me on the ride between Julian Falls and Dayton that I had not actually seen the surrounding area in daylight since my mother and I had driven through it four months earlier. If anything had changed, I didn't notice. There were the expansive fields of corn burning in the toilsome earth beside asphalt meadows in which shoppers sheltered beneath the concrete arcades, perhaps weighing the distance between themselves and their automobiles cooking in the lot. This was all I knew of Ohio, America, a place without transition, no median between the functionally bucolic and tiresome pavement of this dreadful country, this place I might have stayed had my situation not become intractably fucked up. But I discovered the upshot as we, the driver and I, careened past a modernist chapel whose ample yard abutted the thruway, and in which was sunk a fabricated pool or duckless duck pond, containing a gargantuan rendering of Jesus Christ, the water lapping at his chest, one of his hands raised toward the sky, the other clutching his robes to himself, his stone eyes, each the size of a dinner plate, raised father-ward, or toward the sky, his mouth contorted in that horrible way that has become the standard among churchmen. It was unclear whether he was being boiled or drowning, but I realized upon viewing this grotesque diorama that, questions of equity and poetic justice aside, there was very little I would miss about Ohio, America.

After being entirely fleeced by the taxi driver, I was shown to El's room by a nurse as if I were expected. Her tawny head glowed in sunlight thrown wildly about the room by the reflective surface of the roof outside her window, her blue eyes found me in the doorway like two robin eggs set in a filigreed nest, and I realized, even before we spoke, that this would likely be the last time we saw each other.

"You look well," I said stiffly, placing my bag of booze and salty food beside the bed and leaning in to hug her. She reciprocated, barely. A sibling embrace.

"I'm fine now."

"Why are you still here?"

"I'm not much interested in returning to MU. At the moment."

She admitted that Ludmilla (Good, faithful Ludmilla!) had called her yesterday and explained everything. And she said she was sad for me, and that if she had been there, she would have done her best to prevent everything from happening the way it did.

"I will one day walk normally," she said, gesturing at her leg

"I'm sorry. About your leg. I didn't even ask."

"It's all right. We're okay. You and I are okay. Listen. Not that it matters. But, you might as well know."

"What?" I asked, dragging my chair close to her bedside.

"The person I slept with. Before you arrived. That was Greer."

"Really?" I said, aghast. "I didn't think you…liked girls! Or, girls like that."

"I don't," said El. "That was kind of the point. I was new. She was willing. Or I should say, very interested. I hadn't tried that. I tried it. Not for me."

She lowered her voice, and moved her mouth a bit closer to my ear.

"Her pussy tasted like wood glue!"

I made a sort of honking snort, spraying a bit of beer from my nose onto her bed sheets. I didn't realize I opened one.

"But," continued El, helping herself to a beer. "I'm glad it happened. I wouldn't do it again. At least with her. She had this…this…sick, no, I'm sorry, not sick, but almost elderly quality to her body. Like she wanted someone to take care of her. It was like she was asking with the way she looked. Does that make sense?"

"Yes," I said with finality, because, in remembering the time we spent together on campus, the monotony of each day passing morningless between barren classrooms in the afternoon and evenings measured in their

unwavering, military resemblance to one another, the same jawing, acceptable faces beneath buzzing florescent lighting and the underwater pounding
of semi-intelligible music through a dormitory wall, and the inconclusive, yet
omnipresent smell of pot smoke in unwashed clothing, and even amid the
clatter of chipped billiard balls, the feline noise of several lighters primed
nearby, and the concussive thump of a blown speaker in a low-ceilinged room
lit only with holiday bulbs and the lighters already mentioned, even there, in
all the mundane sanity of students acting their age, she was always there, like a
soiled sheet hung across each doorway, Greer, prowling, watching, waiting.
For El? Perhaps. But now, we would never know.

"Where are you staying?" asked El.

"The golf course. Beneath a tree of some kind."

"That sunburn looks bad."

"Well. I suppose I'm in the right place then."

"You're not coming back."

"Neither are you," I guessed (correctly), and oddly neither of us asked
where the other would go, but it seemed implicit that these locations would
be disparate.

"Don't leave," she said. "Stay here."

And since we now understood each other perfectly, I did not kiss or
touch her until the next morning, when we said goodbye. Even when nibbling off a segmented tray placed in her lap by a nurse, and making jokes
about how much better it was than eating on campus, and listening to the
description of the ghastly surgery required to make El herself once more,
and curling up like a dog between her bed the wall, even after all of this, I
never thought that just for the sake of our history I might ease myself over
the rail and onto the bed between her good, thick leg and the cast, tugging
the fuse of her gown, and settle myself one last time in the languid recollection of her at the house in Northfield, raising the sheet, presenting herself
like unto a profound heat, shuttering the lamp, and allowing the bowl of
night to tip all it contains into the room, our heads meeting like two horses
during a storm, my stomach and her own heaving like oppositional cur-
rents, and the sheet twining between our limbs like an Ouroboros until one

of us ended its (and our own) infinity with a final, untoward kick, and then only silence.

No, I never thought of anything like that, and none of it happened. Instead, I listened to El snore and woke with the nurse, who, rather than asking that I leave, said she would bring an extra muffin with the tray. We ate in silence with a sense of completion, chewing as though watching a television where there was only a wall. And when I stood, gathering the nothing I had brought with me, El took my hand and drew me into a matronly embrace.

"Take care of yourselves," she said, and I figured she must have misspoken. Perhaps whatever medication the hospital administered made her marble-mouthed. But I had a flight to catch. I kissed her cheek and the side of her lips and left the hospital.

20

June 16th–19th, 2006, North Calais, Vermont

I proceed somewhat dolefully through remainder of the week following my confession to Eleanor's parents, and consider fleeing the state only once before dropping the idea. Because where would I go? My last experience of life beyond Vermont ended poorly, and, though I wouldn't proceed past the North Calais county line with the express intention of remaking the mistakes of Ohio, the prospect of making new ones (of perhaps greater consequence) is not attractive. And there are many things I don't know how to do, an ignorance I can't imagine serving me without someone like Lola to cushion my bungling. In fact, on the first Tuesday following my confession, I compose a list of these on the flyleaf of her unclaimed copy of *'Beyond Coitus,'* while (apparently) supervising Gustav at Food Barn.

Things I, Marlowe, Do Not Understand:
1. How to pay for cell phone service. Ask parents?
2. Insurance. Automobile, or otherwise. Where does it come from, and how does it work?
3. Finding and maintaining a suitable rental property.
    a. What is done with garbage?
    b. Where is furniture bought?
    c. How is laundry done?
4. Proper composition of a resume.
    a. Include credits earned at St. Margaret University? Or list degree as 'In Progress'?
5. Requisite decorum and comportment following acceptance of

resume by potential employer.

    a.   Tying a necktie. Is this a necessary skill? Ask Hermes.

6. Cooking something that is not contained in either a can, or hermetically sealed package.
7. Both general and specific budgeting for items large and small.
8. Establishing 'good credit.' Why is this necessary? Ask parents.
9. What the fuck is a 401K?
10. Until what age is it appropriate to not have a career?

The list occupies the entire page, and leaves me sufficiently daunted by the prospect of leaving both my parent's house and purview for what was mostly certainly a gloomier horizon. A map of New England hangs on the wall beside me, with Vermont as the lush centerpiece. I consider the regions neighboring it, and what little I know of them. New York is entirely over-run with billboards and disheveled antique shops until it begins to resemble New Jersey at its southern extremity. Motorcycle gangs and disused water-parks comprise the entire remarkability of New Hampshire. I'd heard the woods in Maine are very pretty, and I'm certain the seacoast is nice, but would this natural beauty be able to obviate the fact that the remainder of the state is something between a stationary carnival, and a roadside flea market? Much of Massachusetts suffers from proximity to New York, and deteriorates completely upon reaching Springfield. I know nothing of Con-necticut, but it is similar to Pennsylvania in terms of being a barrier to nicer places (though more bourgeois). Of course, there is always Quebec, far be-yond the jurisdiction of Arthur Stool, beckoning northward beside New-port. But I assume my fugitive status would only augment the problems listed on the interior page of *'Beyond Coitus.'* No, it seems Vermont is the only place for me that makes any sense, which is just as well. Familiarity is the comfort of the unimaginative, and if I am to be jailed, I prefer it be here.

After establishing this immobile certainty, the week passes easily (if a bit sadly). I proceed through my work with Gustav, and spend the remainder of my time reading and smoking on the deck attached to my parent's house, the lake signaling its mystery (the occasional, gem-like twinkle of sunlight on the surface) through a fore-curtain of greenery beyond the yard, as it had the day I misplaced Eleanor beside it. Though I don't think the glacial body has betrayed me, I do my best not to invest it with an agency that it does not possess (the idea of an evil lake being absurd). Even so, I preserve the distance between myself, and the formerly welcoming water.

I assume any day, a cohort of law enforcement will wind its way up the driveway, and somehow Arthur Stool will be among them (though he is only a town cop), crowing his vindication as the other officers clap me in irons and lead me from the property to receive my punishment. But with this assumption comes peculiar tranquility that allows me to read my books and smoke my cigarettes in relative peace. The matter of Eleanor is no longer my responsibility, and whatever circumstances emerge are beyond my control. I worry about her safe return, but since doing so doesn't effect the outcome, I keep my attention mostly on my reading, though I do raise my goggle-like spectacles to the mouth of the driveway whenever the sound of a motor reaches me from the lower road.

The only interruption of this stasis arrives with my father, who is home each day (PUS having ended for the summer), and enjoys bracketing his free time with a walk by the lakeside in the morning, and another toward nightfall. I usually join him during one of these, most often in the evening, during which some form of the following question issues from his cuirass.

"So, what are you plans for the fall? Have you looked at any schools?"

"No, father."

"I thought not. And stop calling me 'father.' It's spooky."

"Sorry."

"You need to give it some serious thought. I got a book that I think you may like. 'Colleges for People Who Don't Want to Go to College.' Don't look at me like that. It's a real book and I didn't choose the title. But I think it might help you figure this out."

"All right, father. Dad! Sorry."

"Are you just saying 'all right' so that I'll leave you alone?"

"No."

"Because you can read on the deck for the rest of your life. But it's going to get pretty cold out there in a few months. Please take a look at the book."

And I do look at it, though I never open it. It is impossible not to. My father rotates the volume between the kitchen table, my bedside, and even the deck chair that I occupy during the time not spent with Gustav.

And today (Friday) when I return home from Food Barn, 'College for People Who Don't Want to Go to College' is clutched in my father's hand as he somewhat oddly meets me at the door, and beckons me inside. Though my father is neither cold, nor dispassionate, he is not the sort of person to rush to the door to greet anyone, especially without saying anything.

"Nice to see you as well," I say as I enter the living room behind him, but he can't hear me because the radio is turned up quite loud, so loud in fact that the thematic fanfare heralding a particular public radio program sounds as if it is being performed live inside my skull. I try to turn it either off or down, but my father makes a hissing sound, the sort of noise he uses to prevent Ignatz from scratching the couch. I withdraw my hand, angry with my father for being cryptic and treating me like a domestic nuisance, and myself for being so compliant. I open my mouth to say something to him, but as I do the voice issuing from it is similar to my own, but the modulation is duller, the familiarity lost, and I have absolutely no control over anything being said.

"Yes. It certainly is a strange situation. And I take full…well, no, not full responsibility, because as I've explained, it was not my intention to harm her. Quite the opposite, as a matter of fact."

I'm not speaking. My face is impassive, my lips frozen, and my tongue flat as the carpet beneath my feet. Yet I hear this, distinctly, because it is coming from the speaker. My father is watching me with something like pride, but appears to be searching my face for some congruity to explain why my voice is coming from the radio. And meanwhile, the conversation continues as it did when it was presumably recorded.

"I understand if you want to call the police, I can assure you that I will cooperate, but I would appreciate…"

My father has handed me the book about things I should do, and is leaning on the wall beside the radio completely absorbed, but jerks slightly at Oliver's concluding exclamation.

"Go away. You're not welcome in this house, you pervert!"

In the few seconds of silence following the recording, I try to speak to my father, but he raises a patient hand as the program's host begins to speak in sedate public radio voice.

"Welcome back. You're listening to 'The Creative Life' on Vermont Public Radio. I'm here with one of the young woman behind A.C.R.O.N.Y.M., a new experimental project that uses relational aesthetics to examine gendered heroism in young men. Is that a fair summation, Eleanor?"

"Yes, I think so. But I want to reemphasize the role of the Theodora Collective in the project. Without their support, the Femammals would still be selling t-shirts in Union Square."

The sound of her voice, which some part of me never expected to hear again, is like a small, yet powerful hand reaching upward through my perineum, and tugging at the base of my spine like the cord of a venetian blind. I lean against the wall opposite my father, the radio chattering between us as the interview continues.

"We were speaking earlier about the potential ethical issues involved in a project like this. How would you respond to charges of reverse-sexism, for example?"

"I won't deny that using young men as subjects for our work was a major selling point for the Collective. But that was our plan from the beginning. In general, women are encouraged to doubt themselves more frequently than men. It's not just a question of sex appeal. If we were to use women for the project, we would just be recapitulating heteronormative gender dynamics, and that work has been done."

"I agree," says the anchor. "But I suppose by 'ethics' I meant something more specific, like documenting the subjects without their knowledge. Or using yourself as the lynchpin, and your family as operatives. You said the raw footage we heard earlier was recorded only last week in your childhood home, and used your parents to…what was the phrase you used?"

"Broker a narrative conclusion. The project depends on the embedded archetype of the masculine savior. The knight-errant, so to speak. My mother and father admired the work, and were more than happy to participate."

"Of course. But are you concerned that your methodology might render the credibility of your conclusion as somewhat dubious?"

"Well, A.C.R.O.N.Y.M. is not a research project. It's art, which means that it is free to borrow from a discipline without adopting the prohibitive aspects of that particular field. That isn't to say the work has no archival potential, or that the documentary aspect is invalid. Our subjects are fully informed of the scope and intention of the project afterward, compensated, and asked to sign release forms, but the formal stricture ends there."

"Thank you, Eleanor. We're going to a quick break. More when we return, after this."

The program cuts to a fund-raising advertisement, and my father lowers the radio, a gentle smiling lurking like a stoat in the hedge of his cuirass.

"So," he says. "You've had an interesting week."

Rather than replying, I turn on my heel like a wooden soldier, and run out of the house.

I reach Danville in twenty minutes, but since it's already early evening, Guidance is shuttered. In fact, the entire town square is eerily dormant, the houses and shops girding it sit quiescently in the indolent sunlight spilling over the rim of the Worcester range to the west. I park the Volvo anyway, and leave the door open as I stomp onto the bakery's broad porch, a cigarette burning in my left hand as I use the other to rattle the door knob, and shade my face against the front window to see if there is anyone still inside. Well, not anyone. I'm looking for Lola, who may have already left town, gone back to Connecticut, thus completing the shortest internship ever in the annals of the Theodora Collective. No, she must be nearby, most likely at the compound outside of town.

Of course, I'm forbidden from visiting the property, but I'm so relieved and confused that the prohibition means nothing. And while the relief at Eleanor being both alive and apparently in control of everything (as usual) is welcome, it does nothing to mollify the confusion regarding how exactly the last two weeks of my life were spent, a confusion which reinvents itself as a wrathful anger as I pass the corn maze above town, heading for the compound.

What exactly do I know? Eleanor concealed herself in order to document my subsequent movement and action in searching for her. This concealment is part of something called 'A.C.R.O.N.Y.M.,' which is apparently artistic and relevant. Lola is obviously part of it, possibly as some kind of liaison. I remember her (strangely calm) insistence that we not call the police after I revealed that Eleanor was missing. Or her ridiculous gullibility when she found her friend's (and colleague's, it seems now) bloodstained clothing in my glovebox. And the way she manipulated me into needlessly breaking into the house of Hermes the Virile. Yes, she must be in on it, a bald (yet sexy) ambassador to the deception of Marlowe. Unbelievable!

As the corn maze retreats in my rear view, the reflection embarrassed only by a cloud of brown dust rising from beneath the car, a high wooden fence appears to the right of the roadside, indicating that I have entered the territory of the Theodora Collective. The fence is not impassable, but it's intimidating enough to dissuade any except the boldest from scaling it. At regular intervals, black signs lettered in orange remind those who might not understand the purpose of such a fence that the property it conceals is private, and trespassing is prohibited. But I don't intend to trespass. The past week has involved far too much of that.

I pull the station wagon off the road, into a small lot before a large gate, beside which sits a guardhouse. Before I've even turned off the car, a large (and bald) acolyte has emerged from the cottage set beside the entrance, and is watching me with her hands on her broad hips.

"Can I help you?" she shouts, as I exit the car, and start walking toward her.

"I'd like to speak with Lola," I say, stopping perhaps ten feet from her position, a position that becomes only more threatening as the distance between myself and it decreases. The woman is middle aged, and dull-eyed, with a face like an impatient baroness, and a build somewhere between a long haul trucker and an Olympic gymnast. In one of her huge hands, she holds a radio, which crackles unhelpfully, and in the other, I imagine my head being squeezed. Thus I preserve the buffer, and speak softly, without betraying the anger prompting my visit to the compound.

"Wait," she growls, raising the radio to her mouth and going inside the guardhouse. "Western gate. We have a man here who…"

I can't hear the rest of her broadcast, because she closes the door, only to emerge from it a moment later without the radio. I smile, and it is not returned.

"Okay. What's your name?"

"Marlowe. Should I wait here?"

"No. Please leave."

"But I need to speak with Lola…"

"That is not an option."

"Then why did you ask for my name?"

"In case you don't leave."

"I see. Is she gone, or will she just not come out?"

The women walks forward, and clamps her massive hands on my shoulders, rotating my body like the handle of a spigot, and shoving me in the direction of my car. I stumble a few steps and begin to turn around, but her voice stops me.

"Don't even turn around. Get in your car, Marlowe."

I have no doubt that if I do anything other than what the woman suggests, something bad will happen, yet the puzzlement, and anger remain. I am owed an explanation. As I start the car, and drive it out of the lot toward Danville, I watch the fence passing now on my left. For some reason, it appears lower, and more welcoming when driving away from the compound. Of course, this could be an illusion, a result of being barred from speaking with Lola who is undoubtedly inside. But either way, I'm climbing it.

The trunk of the Volvo doesn't contain anything interesting, but there are two plastic milk crates used to hold various automotive supplies (spare oil, anti-freeze, jumper cables, that sort of thing). I empty these, and carry them to the foot of the fence where I place one atop the other in order to give me a boost. It's about eight feet high, but with the makeshift stool, I can easily get a hand on top. Of course, hauling my carcass over the fence with the limited strength of my arms is a challenge, and I'm only able to do it by swinging my body sideways, and using the momentum to hook my foot over the other side, a maneuver that nearly unmans me (Like Eleanor's window sill, or the rain barrel of Hermes the Brash). But as I sit uncomfortably straddling the pinnacle of the fence, watching the sun fall over the mountains, I'm overcome by a sense of rectitude and peace. This is the final hurdle, and here I am, occupying its peak. From where I sit, I can see a cornfield on the other side of the fence, and past this, the main house, the roof of which peaks above the rows perhaps two hundred yards distant. Beside it is a larger roof, which must be the barn, and beside the barn, a narrow, whitewashed steeple that belongs to the chapel. This should be easy. I throw my leg over the foreign side of the fence, and lower myself down.

I only realize I'm trapped inside the compound after I touch the ground on the other side of the fence. Unless I manage to steal a ladder or step-stool after finding Lola, and extracting an explanation from her undetected, I have no apparent way to escape.

I take several steps backward, trying to judge if, by way of a running leap perhaps, I might be able to grab the top of the fence. In my reverse ambulation, I plant one of these steps in a shoal of mud and manure beside a duck pond. My foot slips from beneath me, and I tip backward into the murky water like a moatside turret hit by a cannon. I thrash about, gurgling in the shallow pool, displacing a mother duck and a procession of duck-lings, until I regain my footing. I smell like farm runoff. A feather is stuck to my upper lip. A grain of animal feces is lodged in my ear canal. I can't approach anyone, especially Lola, in this condition.

I remove my shirt, wringing it out and tossing it on the bank, and follow this with my pants and underwear. My shoes, which have sunk deep into the sludge on the bottom of the pond, are lost (I'm unwilling to retrieve them). I remain in the ankle-deep water waiting for my wardrobe to dry on shore, or at least become less wet, though this hope retreats as the last fan of sun leaves the sky. But a warm, salutary breeze blows from between the rows of corn behind me, and the soothing sensation of it on my bare skin relaxes me. Perhaps things like this fall in the duck pond prevent me from making larger mistakes. Aside from my ruined clothing and lost shoes, nothing has gone wrong. I haven't been spotted, and there is still plenty of time to find Lola. I'm calmed by this rehearsal of facts, so I remain standing like a heron in the small pond, as twilight descends on the farmyard.

There is a particular quality to swimming naked which transposes the shame of nudity with an overwise confidence in it. This may be why, when I'm suddenly caught in the beam of a flashlight, I use the hands that should conceal my private parts to shield my face instead.

"Oh! Oh my! What…are you doing?" shrieks a voice from the direction of the light. I say nothing. A duck honks.

"Natalie! The radio! We have an intruder."

I hear a static crackle, and the beam wavers slightly, possibly to accommodate the radio, and I slip into the corn.

"He went into the rows!" says someone behind me. "Call the others! We need to get someone on the other side!"

I run and trip through the field, ears of corn dropping at my feet, and the barren stalks swatting my face and nakedness as I follow the lights of the house. Since they made clear that there will be people waiting for me on the other side of the field, I turn left when I reach its center. I creep silently through the stalks, trying to avoid shaking them, until I reach the end of the row. Beyond it is an open lawn, with an orderly row of tractors and pickup trucks parked along one side, and several lower, utilitarian buildings arranged in a crescent. At first, I assume they are storage sheds, but there is light in the windows of each, and as several bald women emerge from one holding either rifles or beating sticks (too dark to tell) I realize they are dormitories. If Lola is anywhere, she'll probably be in one of those. The women get into one of the pickups, (three in the cab, four in bed) and drive off toward the field.

I leave the row, and run to the first dormitory, pressing my body to the side of the building, and craning my neck to see into the window. Aside from several bunks, and a few books and clothes left on them, the room is plain and empty. A dodge around the light cast from the window, performing the same action at the next dormitory. Several women sit at a folding table, playing a cheerless round of Scrabble. Lola is not among them. But in the next, I find her sitting cross-legged on the floor, and writing in a note-book, with her back to me. The bristle on her head is unmistakable, and I would know those sun-browned shoulders in the dark.

I walk around the side of the building to the door, which I open roughly and without hesitation. Why would I knock? It swings wildly on its hinge, hanging from the wall as I stomp naked and shouting into the dormitory.

"Lola!…"

Lola turns sharply at the noise, but the women journaling on the floor is not Lola. And neither are the other four women who I failed to notice from the window, reading and knitting in their bunks. I've acted impulsively. Anyone can grow stubble, and have a tan. It is a farm after all. In fact, the five faces now watching me with a manifold interest and disgust are all tanned, and each haircut is identical.

"I'm sorry," I announce to them. "I made a mistake."

"You're not supposed to be here," says the young woman I mistook for Lola.

"I realize that. I don't intend to stay."

"Call the main house," she says to one of the women. "Tell them we have an intruder in Hypatia Terrace, cabin three."

"Do any of you know where Lola might be?" I ask, covering my genitals with my hands as my former pride fades to shame.

"I think she had a meeting in the chapel," replies a younger and apparently dimmer denizen of Hypatia Terrace, cabin three.

"Quiet, Stephanie!" hisses the woman with the journal.

"The chapel?" I say over my shoulder as I walk back through the door. "Thank you!"

Outside, the sound of nervous activity peoples the normal emptiness of night on a working farm. Several engines rumble from the direction of the field, and as headlights appear over a low rise in the middle distance, I run around the side of the dormitory, searching the active darkness for the steeple I noticed at dusk. And there it is, rising between the house and the barn a hundred yards away.

Between the rumbling of engines approaching, and the sound of voices exchanging information that will inevitably lead to my capture, I need little to motivate my tired body as I sprint from the semi-circle of cabins to the chapel across the yard. As I reach the narthex, I glance back in the direction from which I ran, and see a truck idling before Hypatia Terrace cabin three. It won't be long now. If Lola is not inside, it's unlikely my body will ever be found. But what assurance do I have that she will protect me from the rest of the collective when they catch me (because they will)? I'd like to think that due to my refusal to make water upon her, we share an unlikely yet strong bond, strong enough that she will shield me from the mob massing in front of cabin three. But there's no way to be sure. I push through the door of the chapel, and step inside.

The interior is plain, and cruciform (an oddity for a New England church), with a delicate arcade on either side of the nave sheltering the pews beneath it. There is an unspecific alter under the domed apse at the head of the aisle between the pews, upon which burn dozens of candles, their wavering flame providing the only light in the entire space. Except for a line of illumination beneath a door to the left of the altar, in what would likely be the vestry, were this a proper church. If she is still here, that's where she will be (according to Stephanie). My bare feet slap up the aisle, and past the altar, and as I place an ear to the door, I hear what is most certainly Lola's prissy, somewhat pinched, voice on the other side. I place a hand on the knob, and throw the door wide open.

This time, Lola is actually in the room, sitting at long table with several people (all women, all bald) I do not know, and one I do. Lucia sits across from Lola, and seems to have been examining a set of photographs before I burst in. But as she notices me suddenly standing in the doorway, her child's educator and potential (formerly) mentor, naked and frenzied, she drops the print stack of prints, one of which drifts from the tabletop to the floor beside my feet. And in it, I see myself, in the woods beside the lake, hugging a stone.

"I took that," says one of the people I do not know, as I snatch the photograph from the floor, and use it to block the room's (but mostly Lucia's) view of me. I offer her a lopsided smile.

"Hello, Lucia. I didn't expect to find you here."

She shrugs. Lola turns in her seat to face me.

"Marlowe," says Lola, calmly. "Why are you naked?"

"I...I fell in the duck pond before some of your people found me," I reply, her question disarming me slightly. But I remember my purpose, narrowing my eyes in her direction. "I need to talk to you. Right now."

"Please, deal with this, Lola," says Lucia, returning to the photographs.

"Why is it," begins Lola. "That you, Marlowe, can't do anything covert without losing your clothes, or befouling yourself in some way?"

"I don't know how to answer that."

"Can we talk outside?"

I nod, returning the photograph to the table without thinking, and turning to the door. What I don't see is the Taser that Lola mentioned when we first met (under similar circumstances). But I hear it crackle once before it touches my side. My muscles spasm, my legs give way, and I fall to the floor facing Lucia, who is still examining photographs as my eyes close.

I wake up in a narrow bed, next to an open window through which early morning light falls across the coverlet, and a warm wind containing barnyard smells invades my nostrils. I'm no longer naked, but wearing a strange set of papery scrubs, and Lola is sitting in a chair at my bedside, reading what I assume is a new copy of *'Beyond Coitus.'* She notices that I'm awake, and sets the book on the bedside table.

"You're in the infirmary," she says. "I like the list of things you don't understand by the way. But I think it should be longer."

"Wait. You went through my car?" I say, sitting up, and snatching the book from the bedside. Yes, it is the same copy I've been muddling through during the past week.

"We moved your car. You parked it in an active driveway. And I have to say that finding your keys was an interesting problem. They were in your clothes, which you left all over the place."

"I have some questions. First of all...Wait, what the fuck is this?" I say pointing to a bandage on the interior of my forearm. I raise one adhesive edge, revealing a slightly swollen pinprick beneath.

"We had to sedate you while we calmed things down. You caused quite an uproar among the other women."

"Lola. I don't understand anything that's happening. I heard Eleanor on the radio. It seems the two of you used me for some sort of art project called A.C.R.O.N.Y.M."

"Sounds like you know everything. So why did you come here?"

"For revenge," I say limply. Lola laughs.

"Revenge. For what?"

"For everything you put me through. For lying to me, and making me appear foolish in front of strangers. And for making me worry about Eleanor."

"We only provide a framework," says Lola, still chuckling. "No one forced you to crawl through toilets, or expose yourself to old women, or stuff Eleanor's clothes in a glovebox where anyone could find them. No one told you to do any of that. And you worrying? About Eleanor? I've seen people more concerned over a set of car keys. However you might wish to portray yourself, you are the subject, not the hero, and this is why we picked you. Eleanor said that you have always been fascinated with yourself, which is why I think, after we have completed this project, it will please you."

A morose-looking woman enters the room holding a breakfast tray, which she drops on my pelvis with a clatter. Lola nods to her, and she leaves. I poke the food around the plate with a fork and take a sip of coffee before speaking.

"And I suppose you planted all the clues? The receipt and the condom wrapper?"

"The receipt came from the trash outside the general store. I found the wrapper on the floor of Eleanor's bedroom. I suppose you had something to do with that?"

"Probably," I remark absently, separating the bits of food that I can identify from those I cannot, and when this operation is complete, flinging the latter out the open window beside my bed. Lola makes a face. "I doubt she's replenished her supply since she was living at home. But how did you know I would break in on that particular evening?"

"I didn't. We were going to have someone make contact. But when you just showed up at the house, it made sense for me to help you so to speak. But the spontaneity is part of what makes A.C.R.O.N.Y.M. interesting. I'm surprised it worked out so well. I didn't know my clues would lead you to Hermes. Or Kristof."

"You didn't even know Kristof was in town, did you?"

"No. I was genuinely shocked when I saw him bartending on Langdon Street," she says. "I drank too fast. It was stressful."

"And my watch?"

"It was all arranged. Eleanor gave that to the T.C. people who picked her up after you left her in the woods. And they gave it to me. I was going to forward it to the liaison, but as I explained…"

"Of course," I say, no longer hungry, and unsure of where to move my tray, since the bedside table is occupied with a book and Lola's elbow, and the floor seems far away.

"Are you still angry?" she asks.

"No," I reply, dropping the remainder of my meal, the dishes, and the tray out of the window. "How is Lucia involved?"

"The fact that you even know that would be problematic," says Lola, watching the window out of which I defenestrated my breakfast. "But you've signed the contract, so unless you want to make a problem for yourself, you'll forget she was in the chapel."

"I'm not forgetting anything," I say, removing the sheet and standing up in my peculiar pajamas. "I work with her son. I can ask her anything I want. And I haven't signed anything. I'm leaving. Where is my car parked?"

I notice my clothes, washed and folded on a chair in a corner of the room, and I begin rifling them in search of my keys when I hear Lola's voice behind me.

"'Shade a Somali?'"

And then it all makes sense, or a kind of sense. She disguised her paperwork as a petition. Clever. At the very least, I understand why I'm being treated like a valuable nuisance. I turn to face Lola.

"You tricked me. You…You harridan!"

"Look," she begins. "It was really my mistake. We were running on a deadline for that radio interview, and I got the dates confused. I thought they were airing it in two weeks, not one. We wanted to use some new material, and there just wasn't time to make you fully aware of everything. It was my job to handle the paperwork. Oh, and speaking of fuckups…"

She reaches into a backpack beneath her chair, and withdraws a black folder with A.C.R.O.N.Y.M. stenciled in red across its face, and offers it to me. Inside is a large manila envelope, with my parent's address written on it, and postage affixed in the upper right corner.

"You want me to mail this to myself?" I ask stupidly. Lola looks shocked.

"No, you screaming fucktard. I don't want you to mail it to yourself. That envelope should have arrived earlier this week. But our intern, Stephanie, forgot, because she is a fucktard, as well. You two should be together."

"I thought you were the intern."

"That was a lie."

"I see. What's inside?"

"An outline of the project, and our expectations of you as a participant. But more importantly, your compensation."

The last part piques my interest. I rip open the envelope, and remove a sheaf of pages held at the corner with a paper clip, and a check with 'Theodora Enterprises, LLC' printed on it. I cross the room and toss the prospectus out the window, and sit down the bed, looking at the check.

"Please, stop doing that," says Lola, looking at the window once more.

"Is this correct?" I ask, holding up the check.

"Yes," she says, without looking at it. "And accepting that means the gag-order and everything else is in full effect, including forgetting everything you saw last night. Do you understand?"

"This seems generous," I say, ignoring her. "Until I consider the bullshit you and your Femammals Collective lesbian prison farm on a fucking hilltop put me through to get it. Lucia is your CEO. Is that correct?"

"Tear the check in half, and we'll have that conversation."

"No thanks. I'll keep it," I say, tucking it inside the front cover of *'Beyond*

Coitus.' "And this."

The morose woman enters the room again, apparently searching for the breakfast tray. She looks at Lola, then me.

"I threw it out the window," I say. She frowns, and leaves. I turn to Lola. "Where's Eleanor?"

"Not where you left her," she replies. Rather than trying to figure out what that might mean, I stand up with the book in my hand, and pat her head gently.

"I hope someday you find a nice young men to pee all over your pretty face."

I cross the room, gather my clothes, and leave the infirmary.

Like a rude steamboat, Hermes emits a plume of acrid smoke in my direction without offering to pass the joint he was smoking when I arrived home from my stay with Theodora Collective, and noticed his car parked in the driveway. Rather than mentioning it (the joint), I say nothing on the odd chance that he might require me to procure the substance in addition to the liquor.

"Wait," he says, and I wait. "The acronym for this…is it an art project?"

I nod.

"So the acronym for this art project is A.C.R.O.N.Y.M. Which means what?"

"Art of Crisis Response and Organized Negation in Young Men."

We pause. He puffs.

"That means nothing to me."

"Basically, they construct stressful scenarios for young men. They find a target, deceive them, and document their reaction."

"Why?"

I help myself to a glass of whiskey, before answering.

"Because," I say. "They believe it is art."

"Sounds like horseshit."

"Perhaps."

He appears to be reflecting, but it's hard to tell with Hermes the Oblique.

"I once knew a girl in college who kicked men in the groin at a student art show," he says, tapping ash onto my shoe.

"I assume she was removed."

"No. That was her installation."

"Oh. They volunteered? Or did she pay them?"

"That was never clear. Some may have enjoyed it," he says, extinguishing the joint in my glass. "Were you pleased that Elena was not actually lost?"

"Eleanor."

"What?"

"Nothing. I was at first. Now I'm…"

He interrupts me.

"I would like to be part of this project."

"I think us having this conversation means you are not the ideal candidate."

His massive head inclines toward the floor of the tree house.

"Are you and Elena no longer sleeping together?"

"Eleanor. And I hadn't thought to ask her."

"May I call her?"

I ask him for a pen, and scribble Lola's number on a label peeled from one of the bottles lining the wall. For good measure, I write and underline 'ELENA' above the digits, which he pockets with a miserly anticipation. Perhaps the two of them, Eleanor and Lola, will find a place for Hermes in the project. Or perhaps they'll exchange sex for his patronage. Or perhaps, he'll just embarrass himself, though he seems incapable of that. In either case, after the complete implosion of all I had come to regard as my reality since Eleanor's 'disappearance,' I am more than happy to make them his problem.

21.

July 21ˢᵗ–August 23ʳᵈ, 2006, Montpelier, Vermont

Varna actually reminds me very much of Ludmilla. They're both sort of adorably ugly, but beyond that, they each possess a helpful and assertive pragmatism that I do not. For Ludmilla, this meant knowing when to disappear. For Varna, this means renovating me. We've been seeing each other for several weeks now, but I believe that during out first meeting, when I offered myself to her in an effort to buy time rather than to forge any sort of lasting attachment, she was already creating an index of ways to improve me.

And I suppose an improvement (or two) is needed. Through a general lack of upkeep, my physiognomy resembles a bit of low-hanging, slightly putrid fruit, the nectar of which has collected somewhere between my knees and chest, leaving me shaped like a light bulb. This shape is most of the reason that squeezing through Hermes' hanging toilet was such a struggle.

Even the first morning after the first night we spent together in her condo, when she asked if I would like to come on her morning jog around Montpelier and I agreed and then made it two blocks up the acclivity that approaches College Street from Liberty before having to sit down on the curb, and put my head between my pale, sweaty knees with her, lithe, willowy and patient, bobbing from foot to foot above me, even then, I was glad to be doing this running thing with someone who cared about it, rather than someone who didn't, or alone, both options being, essentially, the same.

"It jesch getsh eshier," said Varna, slowing her pace in order that I might match it.

How odd that Gustav would have brought us together in his own sensualist way. Though the state of my physical being does not generally depress me, watching Gustav's resistance to the sloping plod of regular labor fade over the past several weeks has made me sad. When things change, they often take a turn for the dull, and since bagging groceries no longer bothers him, I have very little to do at Food Barn other than watch him and Varna do their jobs. My parents seem content to have me as long as I will stay, so I never needed the money. And after being compensated by the Theodora Collective (and Lucia herself, I suppose), I need it even lessĭ.

I only keep the job because Gustav has come to occupy the position of a platonic male friend in my life, and losing that would be emotionally complicated (on my part). I'm also afraid of his mother, who I see occasionally when I drop him off after work. Lucia remains pleasant and impassive, betraying nothing of our accidental meeting in the chapel, and the fact that she knows exactly how bad I look without clothing. My former impression of her as a trifling appropriator of various far eastern cultural traditions has been replaced with one of stolid, threatening professionalism.

Perhaps as a result of all these shifting impressions, I've begun paying more attention to Gustav. His observant quality, the one which noticed my agitation in Mr. Shivers' class the morning after Eleanor 'disappeared,' spotted something between Varna and me at Food Barn, and predicted our eventual union during the ride back to Pitkin.

"I saw you talking to Varna," he said from the passenger seat. "You looked happy."

"I am happy," I said without knowing if it was true, but hoping that it was enough to repeat it. "I am happy."

I could tell that Gustav was waiting for me to ask his advice. And I realized that, for some reason, I wanted it.

"Do you think I should ask her to eat with me?" I asked cautiously, the phrasing of the question making her, Varna, and I, Marlowe, sound like two hogs consigned to the same paddock.

"Yes. She is pretty, and you are alone," Gustav replied definitively, which broke a bottle across the prow of whatever tentative vessel I intended to launch into the Sea of Varna. And after delivering Gustav to Pitkin, I called her at work, and explained that I meant to ask her to do something with me when we spoke earlier, but that I was essentially a coward, and not much good at this type of thing (whatever 'this type of thing' might mean). But in any case, I was following up on my invitation of several weeks ago, when I asked her if she would like to get Indian food and talk about dogs. So, would she like to perhaps do one or both of those activities, or a completely different activity, with me, at some point, in the near, but not uncomfortably close, future? She said yes (or 'yesh') and asked me to call her the following day, which I did, after thanking Gustav.

"For what?" he asked, from the passenger seat, just like the day before.

"For being…" I began, wanting to say 'For being my friend,' but realizing this was entirely inappropriate considering our professional relationship. "For being a good…advice…giver."

That seemed to please him anyway. We continued driving in silence, while I ran the phrase 'My friend, Gustav' through my head again and again to see if it became any less awkward with repetition. It did not.

But there are few candidates to replace him, or none, actually, unless I count Hermes the Constant, though, like Ignatz, he comes and goes as he pleases, and in order to satisfy the role, he would need to be tethered to me in some way. My parents are now used to the sight of his Saab crookedly parked beside their home, and even though he gently (for him) refuses their invitations to dinner, they seem glad that I have made (or remade) what they believe is a friend.

Kristof, who I see occasionally wandering around town, is another possibility. His contract was finally approved, and he has been spending the bulk of his midsummer refurbishing the teen center beneath City Hall. He often greets me on the street, his clothing stained with paint, and sawdust in his hair, between errands, and is as friendly as one can be while remaining slightly disgusted. I suppose my association with the woman who knocked the teeth out of his head in a commuter train means we can never be best friends.

But toward the end of August, he invites Varna and me to a party at his house on Summer Street, which is surprising, though more surprising is his extension of the invitation to Eleanor and Lola, who arrive late with a cohort of strange men. I can't decide whether to hide or not, but where would I go? Varna is with me, and when Lola spots me across the living room by the miniature fridge shrouded in the fireplace, and tugs Eleanor's sleeve, sneaking away becomes impossible. They instantly detach themselves from the conversation in which they were engaged, and cross the room to start one with me. I find Varna's hand and squeeze it until she squeaks.

"Shtop! That hurtsh!"

Unfortunately, Eleanor remains beautiful, her red hair stylishly mangled atop her skull, the orbits of which contain two insidiously green eyes, not like emeralds, jade, or malachite, but the mercurial hue of the forest in which I saw her last. Apparently, she is also able to produce Anders at will. She introduces him again, and Lola introduces her own date, a dandy from New York calling himself Patience.

"I know you! Mr. Marlowe, right?" he says, using his other hand to point at my face. "Oh, yes. Yes, I do. I mean, we haven't met of course, but…I mean, let me tell you friend, I'm not the only one."

He is short, slick-looking, dressed in a black blazer and fashionably constrictive jeans, and while I absorb these superficial details in order to place him, I realize exactly how he knows me.

"Sorry," I say. "You don't know me."

"Patience is a curator," says Lola, as though trying to change my mind.

"Everyone, this is Varna," I say, ignoring her (Lola), and using Varna to change the subject. "She manages the Food Barn."

Eleanor blinks. Anders appears to be examining the ceiling. Patience and Lola look at each other and her (Varna), as she extends a hand.

"Nyesh to meet you…all," she says with a measure of trepidation.

Patience, who is apparently the most gracious among them, takes her hand as though trying to discern its weight.

"So, you're a…grocery manager? That must be interesting work, management. Did you study that in school?"

Though Patience is actually in complete earnest, Lola laughs, and Varna blushes, and suddenly I want to immolate them all (except Varna), but before I can speak, she replies.

"No. I shtudied archeology."

Patience nods sympathetically.

"Not a lot of digs these days."

"Ish all been dug up."

He chuckles.

"You're wise. A drink?" he says, and Varna shrugs. Patience offers his arm, and they depart toward the kitchen, leaving me alone with Eleanor and Lola. Anders doesn't count, as he remains occupied with some detail of the ceiling. We stand in the living room, none of us willing to speak first, until I can't stand it any longer.

"You find anyone to pee on you yet?" I ask Lola, loud enough for several other guests to hear. She flinches as though goosed, her purple eyes glistening.

"Are you going to bring that up whenever we see each other?"

"Yes. But I was hoping we wouldn't see each other again."

"Why not?" asks Eleanor, speaking for the first time.

And with this question, I imagine myself, as I have many times over the weeks since Eleanor reappeared, sharing every grievances against this pair, and explaining exactly how I felt about them, and the project, and the T.C., and the Femammals…but I say nothing (about that subject).

"You're both disgusting people."

And I leave it at that, because it isn't my job to educate them. I thread between other guests until I find Varna and Patience in the kitchen, laughing and drinking like longshoremen, and rather than tell her that I need to leave, I touch her shoulder in a passing salute, and go sit on the front porch where, several weeks earlier, I was cautioned to avoid scaring the other tenants. I can wait to leave until Varna is ready.

It is Sunday morning after the party, and I'm awake after Varna who is at the bedroom window throwing crumbs of bread to a raven or a crow dancing on the roof below the sill in the rain. We made love (I use the phrase to indicate growth) the night before, her taught athleticism twining around my receding folds and diminishing paunch, she drunk (a rare thing) and me oddly sober after the party, and when we finished, we realized the low, late-summer heat in each room of the condominium was unmitigated by the fans oscillating like pedestrians checking for traffic. She cast the sheet from the bed and climbed out the same window beyond which she now gluts the raven or crow on scraps, and I followed, tugging the invidious sheet to sit on, the both of us naked, myself huddled and smoking, a habit she disliked but could accept, given my other efforts. Yes, she stood in the moonlight, allowing the breeze to catch and toss her clownish hair like a tumbleweed, with her hands gently joined behind her lower back, and if it were not for all her limbs being intact she could have been some deserted masterpiece of Greece or Rome languishing beneath a skylight in an after-hours wing of antiquity.

What I wanted to say was how much I would like to see her exceptional form running through the forest by the lake, scratched by branches, knees caked with pine needles and loose earth, her scent caught in the breeze, now washing against me in bed as it did the night before, mixed with the fecund odor of the forest floor. I want to say all of that but I didn't say any of it, instead draping myself over her, even in the heat, as she came and sat on the blanket, the lax muscle of her buttocks pouting a bit (this is where I laid my hand), she took my cigarette, and puffed it dearly (the alcohol, to be certain).

"You like dogs," I said instead. "But you do not have one."

She exhaled.

"Ish a lot of reshponshibility and…"

"But you manage a grocery store."

"Yesh."

"Surely you can care for a dog?"

She leaned her thin face against my shoulder, not returning the cigarette, but tugging it thoughtfully with her lips.

"Keeping thingsh cooped up…Ish not good to to be alone all day…I'd feel show bad…"

"I can help."

"Ish thish you ashking me for keysh?"

"Well," I said, wondering if it was. "Yes, and no. I could always borrow yours, if you're uncomfortable with me having my own set. But the only work I do is with you at Food Barn. Otherwise, I do nothing all day. I could use a chore of some kind."

She didn't say anything, and I sensed her adding an item to her list of improvements.

"So, tomorrow, if any kennels are open on Sunday, let's see if they having anything you like. We like."

And she still didn't speak, but her lips touched my shoulder, not a kiss, but a taste, which made me wish that we, she and I, matched a bit more. But watching her now at the window, still naked, tossing bits of burnt toast to the bird outside, I see that we're beginning to (match, that is). Because when I sit up, and stand, not bothering to wrap the sheet around my waist, and settle beside her at the window, I catch a negative of myself in the mirror affixed to the interior of her closet door. And no, I'm not perfect, but I am perhaps becoming better and less repulsive. And in the closet mirror I see my reflection in another above Varna's dresser on the opposite side of the bedroom, and my face looking at my face watching my face watch me assess myself. I want to know if she sees what I do at this moment, or if she sees something that I don't during other moments, like last night, naked on the roof when she added something to her list, something to balance me between what I actually am and what she imagines I could be, and I try to ask.

"Do you…?"

But I can't complete the question because when she raises her head from the raven or crow, the sound of its feet pattering on the wet roof, one squawk, and then nothing, all I see are hands moving, tearing bread, her eyes not moving, watching me, and buried within them a diffuse contentment which I, right now, have the potential to end, or at least complicate. So instead I ask about the kennel.

Several weeks later, when I enter the condominium to take Eleanor (the name my suggestion), a white and brown bitch of indiscernible breed and modest temperament, for her afternoon walk, I find two things in the condominium which give me pause. The first is an application for MCC (Montpelier Community College) left on the coffee table in the living room, my name printed in Varna's handwriting at the top, the bits she doesn't know left unfinished, and beside this, a copy of Manhattan Bullsh*t, open to an article in the magazine's cultural section entitled 'Art Beyond Ethics: How A.C.R.O.N.Y.M. is Changing the Way New York Thinks About Gender.' I don't bother reading the rest of the spread, because it is long, and I know all I need to about Lola and Eleanor's project. But my eyes fall on a picture taken from the exhibit at Mountebank Gallery and Lounge: it is me, on my knees, kissing a stone in the woods by the lake. And rather than a caption, it is accompanied by a pulled quote from Patience, in response to a question about ethics.

"Over the summer, I had the pleasure of meeting Subject 13 at a party in his hometown of Montpelier, and though he hasn't taken the time to view the show, I believe his full support is behind us. He understands that for art to be moral, it cannot be polite. "

Do I understand that? Should I be angry? Is there something I should do? Eleanor climbs my leg, yipping for treats. I walk into the kitchen, and do what Varna has done, which is to say, I resolve not to mention what I just saw to her, or anyone else. If she brings it up, I'll pretend I've never heard of A.C.R.O.N.Y.M. or the Femammals or even New York City, if that's what it takes. I remove a biscuit from a drawer by the fridge and ask Eleanor to sit. She doesn't. And as for the college application, I am touched but not because it is evidence that Varna's list of improvements is dynamic and will change as we do, but that she selected a school within walking distance of the condominium because she wants me here, with her. I ask Eleanor to sit once again. She barks once and doesn't. Varna could have chosen any school, but she chose the most local because I am her project now. Why would I go anywhere else? I ask Eleanor to sit once more. She doesn't. I give her the treat.

Fomite
Burlington, Vermont

Fomite
Burlington, Vermont

Peter Nash — The Perfection of Things
George Ovitt — Stillpoint
George Ovitt — Tribunal
Gregory Papadoyiannis — The Baby Jazz
Pelham — The Walking Poor
Andy Potok — My Father's Keeper
Frederick Ramey — Comes A Time
Joseph Rathgeber — Mixedbloods
Kathryn Roberts — Companion Plants
Robert Rosenberg — Isles of the Blind
Fred Russell — Rafi's World
Ron Savage — Voyeur in Tangier
David Schein — The Adoption
Lynn Sloan — Principles of Navigation
L.E. Smith — The Consequence of Gesture
L.E. Smith — Travers' Inferno
L.E. Smith — Untimely RIPped
Bob Sommer — A Great Fullness
Tom Walker — A Day in the Life
Susan V. Weiss —My God, What Have We Done?
Peter M. Wheelwright — As It Is On Earth
Suzie Wizowaty — The Return of Jason Green

Poetry from Fomite...

Anna Blackmer — Hexagrams
L. Brown — Loopholes
Sue D. Burton — Little Steel
Christine Butterworth-McDermott — Evelyn As
David Cavanagh— Cycling in Plato's Cave
James Connolly — Picking Up the Bodies
Greg Delanty — Loosestrife
Mason Drukman — Drawing on Life
J. C. Ellefson — Foreign Tales of Exemplum and Woe
Anna Faktorovich — Improvisational Arguments
Barry Goldensohn — Snake in the Spine, Wolf in the Heart
Barry Goldensohn — The Hundred Yard Dash Man
Barry Goldensohn — The Listener Aspires to the Condition of Music
Barry Goldensohn — Visitors Entrance
R. L. Green — When You Remember Deir Yassin
KJ Hannah Greenberg — Beast There—Don't That
Gail Holst-Warhaft — Lucky Country
Judith Kerman — Definitions
Joseph Lamport — Enlightenment
Raymond Luczak — A Babble of Objects
Kate Magill — Roadworthy Creature, Roadworthy Craft
Tony Magistrale — Entanglements
Gary Mesick — General Discharge
Giorgio Mobili — Sunken Boulevards
Andreas Nolte — Mascha: The Poems of Mascha Kaléko
Sherry Olson — Four-Way Stop
Brett Ortler — Lessons of the Dead
David Polk — Drinking the River

Fomite
Burlington, Vermont

Janice Miller Potter — Meanwell
Janice Miller Potter — Thoreau's Umbrella
Philip Ramp — Arrivals and Departures
Philip Ramp — The Melancholy of a Life as the Joy of Living It Slowly Chills
Joseph D. Reich — A Case Study of Werewolves
Joseph D. Reich — Connecting the Dots to Shangrila
Joseph D. Reich — The Derivation of Cowboys and Indians
Joseph D. Reich — The Hole That Runs Through Utopia
Joseph D. Reich — The Housing Market
Kenneth Rosen and Richard Wilson — Gomorrah
Fred Rosenblum — Playing Chicken with an Iron Horse
Fred Rosenblum — Tramping Solo
Fred Rosenblum — Vietnumb
David Schein — My Murder and Other Local News
Harold Schweizer — Miriam's Book
Scott T. Starbuck — Carbonfish Blues
Scott T. Starbuck — Hawk on Wire
Scott T. Starbuck — Industrial Oz
Seth Steinzor — Among the Lost
Seth Steinzor — Once Was Lost
Seth Steinzor — To Join the Lost
Susan Thomas — In the Sadness Museum
Susan Thomas — Silent Acts of Public Indiscretion
Susan Thomas — The Empty Notebook Interrogates Itself
Sharon Webster — Everyone Lives Here
Tony Whedon — The Très Riches Heures
Tony Whedon — The Falkland Quartet
Claire Zoghb — Dispatches from Everest

Dual Language
vito m. bonito/Alison Grimaldi Donahue — Soffiati Via/Blown Away
Antonello Borra/Blossom Kirschenbaum — Alfabestiario
Antonello Borra/Blossom Kirschenbaum — AlphaBetaBestiario
Antonello Borra/Anis Memon — Fabbrica delle idee/The Factory of Ideas
Tina Escaja/Mark Eisner — Caída Libre/Free Fall
Luigi Fontanella/Giorgio Mobili — L'adolescenza e la notte/Adolescence and Night
Aristea Papalexandrou/Philip Ramp — Μας προσπερνά/It's Overtaking Us
Katerina Anghelaki-Rooke//Philip Ramp — Losing Appetite for Existence
Jeannette Clariond/Lawrence Schimel — Desert Memory
Mikis Theodoraksi/Gail Holst-Warhaft — The House with the Scorpions
Paolo Valesio/Todd Portnowitz — La Mezzanotte di Spoleto/Midnight in Spoleto

Story collections from Fomite...

MaryEllen Beveridge — After the Hunger
MaryEllen Beveridge — Permeable Boundaries
Jay Boyer — Flight
L. M Brown — Treading the Uneven Road
L. M Brown — Were We Awake
Michael Cocchiarale — Here Is Ware
Michael Cocchiarale — Still Time
Neil Connelly — In the Wake of Our Vows
Catherine Zobal Dent — Unfinished Stories of Girls

Fomite
Burlington, Vermont

Fomite
Burlington, Vermont

Peter Schumann — All, Nothing, Nothing at All
Peter Schumann — Bedsheet Mitigations
Peter Schumann — Belligerent & Not So Belligerent Slogans from the
Possibilitarian Arsenal
Peter Schumann — Bread & Sentences
Peter Schumann — Charlotte Salomon
Peter Schumann — Declaration of Light
Peter Schumann — Diagonal Man Theory + Praxis, Volumes One and Two
Peter Schumann — Faust 3
Peter Schumann — Handouts and Obligations
Peter Schumann — Planet Kasper, Volumes One and Two
Peter Schumann — We

Plays from Fomite...
Stephen Goldberg — Screwed and Other Plays
Michele Markarian — Unborn Children of America

Essays from Fomite...
William Benton — Eye Contact: Writing on Art
Robert Sommer — Losing Francis: Essays on the Wars at Home
George Ovitt & Peter Nash — Trotsky's Sink: Ninety-Eight Short Essays on Literature

Writing a review on social media sites for readers will help the progress of independent publishing. To submit a review, go to the book page on any of the sites and follow the links for reviews. Books from independent presses rely on reader-to-reader communications.

For more information or to order any of our books, visit:
http://www.fomitepress.com/our-books.html